RAIN
FALLING
on embers

Other books by Liana Gardner

7th Grade Revolution
The Journal of Angela Ashby
Speak No Evil

Forthcoming from Liana Gardner

South of Happy (Katie McCabe, Book 2)

Awards

Praise

7th Grade Revolution

"Combines treasure hunting, Revolutionary-era U.S. history, and teamwork. Reads like a National Treasure and Spy Kids movie combined." *~School Library Journal*

The Journal of Angela Ashby

"Hilarious, startling, and sometimes unexpected ... filled with achingly relatable tween moments and gentle lessons about the power of friendship, understanding other people's stories, and living with the consequences of one's actions." *~Publishers Weekly*

Speak No Evil

"[With] suspense and intrigue, Melody's story is grim, but hope is weaved in throughout. Highly emotional."
~School Library Journal

RAIN
FALLING
on embers

A Katie McCabe Novel

BRAM STOKER AWARDS® NOMINEE
LIANA GARDNER

VESUVIAN BOOKS

Rain Falling on Embers

Copyright © 2023 Liana Gardner
Edited by Christopher Brooks

Cover design by Michael J. Canales
www.MJCImageworks.com

Library of Congress Control Number: 2023937595

ISBN: 978-1-64548-089-1

VESUVIAN BOOKS

Published by Vesuvian Books
www.vesuvianbooks.com

Printed in China
10 9 8 7 6 5 4 3 2 1

This book is dedicated to all the kids who feel as if their world has been turned upside down, and to my sister, Dana, who is the reason the book was written.

"It is perfectly okay to admit you're not okay." ~Anonymous

Table of Contents

The Burning Shed

1

I drummed my heels against the bale of hay beneath me. "You know, I'll swear it was all my idea."

"But, Katie, it was." Tom reached behind his back and pulled out a flask. "Except for this."

"Are you getting sly on me, Tommy Wolff?" He never tried anything without checking with me first. "What's in it?" Other than something to get us both into trouble.

He shrugged and leaned back against the side of the shed. "Nothing much. Just a little rum to go with the sodas I brought." He cracked open a can and handed it to me. "Drink some out, so I can spice it up for you."

Tipping the can back, I swallowed as much as I could in a mouthful—no dainty sips for this girl—and gagged. The bubbles flew up my nose, triggering a coughing spasm.

Tommy slapped my back until I caught my breath again. "Are you okay, Katie?"

The urge to sneeze gripped me and I held up an index finger. When it came, the sneeze nearly blew me off the hay.

"Next time, give me more of a warning." Tommy stuck a finger in his ear and jiggled it. "I might be deaf."

I wrinkled my nose. "Sorry."

"You're so ladylike." He snickered. "NASA should hire you for testing sonic boom levels."

I smacked his shoulder, then passed the soda back to him. "If Daddy finds out, he's gonna blow a gasket."

Tom's grin faded. "You gotta admit, you make things tough for your dad. I can hear the news at eleven now." He rolled into his impression of a TV announcer. "Tonight's feature is on Sheriff Ron

McCabe. Honest and upright, Sheriff McCabe stands for truth, justice, and the American way, keeping our county safe."

I groaned. Trust Tommy to work in a comic book reference.

"But all superheroes have their kryptonite, so let's explore the secret he's hiding." He pulled the corners of his mouth as far down as he could. "While Ron McCabe upholds the law, his only daughter, Katie, is the biggest troublemaker this town has ever seen." Tom burst into laughter.

"Stop, already." I leaned back on the hay and studied the whorls in the ramshackle beam and board ceiling. If I had to hear one more time how I'd compromised Daddy's position as sheriff ... I turned my head toward Tommy and winked. "But you have more fun with me than anyone else."

He snatched up the rum and made his eyebrows dance. "Ready for some fun?"

Laughing, I sat up. "What made you think of this?"

He concentrated on pouring the rum into the can. "If we're going to start smoking, we should mark the occasion with a drink." He doctored his soda and set the flask on the pallet flooring. "Anyway, you're always saying I never come up with my own ideas. So, I did."

"I'll say. And what an idea." I gave him a high five.

A faint flush of pride colored Tom's cheeks. Although the afternoon sun shone bright, the inside of the shed remained dark. The only light filtered through the cracks in the walls. We kept the light off so we didn't attract any attention—not that we would, because a clump of trees screened the shed from the house. Even with the lights on and the door open, no one would see us. Besides, Mr. Pickford rarely ventured far from the house these days. And since I took care of his animals for him, he didn't have any reason to come out to his shed.

Tom held up his can. "Cheers."

I jumped off the hay bale to click cans and knocked the flask over. "Oh, Tommy, I'm sorry." I grabbed it and stood it upright. "I only spilled a little." I bit my lip. If his dad found out, Tommy would catch fire ... more for letting it spill than for taking it in the first place.

"Forget it. I should've put the cap back on." He raised his can. "To our adventure in smoking."

This time we clinked without mishap, and I took a big swig. My first alcohol at thirteen—I felt so worldly. Shivers scurried up and down my spine and heat warmed my cheeks.

Having watched other smokers do it, I smacked the pack of cigarettes on my palm and took two out. I stuck one in the corner of my mouth and handed the other to Tommy. "Light me."

Tom tore out a match. "I'll warn you, my dad smokes strong ones." He struck it and watched it flare. "Here you go." He dropped the matchbook and held the burning flame toward me.

Not wanting to gag, I didn't inhale all the way on my first puff. I had an image to preserve. Tommy struck another match and held it to the end of his cigarette. Though he tried not to, he coughed. I took another drag, a little deeper this time. I'd ease into smoking, one puff at a time. I snatched the packet Tom dropped.

"It's interesting how people get engrossed in watching a flame." I lit a match and stared at it while it flickered. Right before it could burn my fingers, I shook it out and dropped it. Lighting another, I held it in front of Tom's eyes. "What do you think about?"

He gazed at it without answering.

Over the summer, a new Tommy had emerged, and I didn't know exactly how to handle the changes. For instance, he wanted everyone to call him Tom instead of Tommy. Try as I might, the old, familiar name slipped off my tongue before I could stop it. He'd been my best friend since Daddy and I had moved here when I was two, but after he'd turned fourteen, he wanted more, and I wasn't sure I did. Neither of us understood what we were going through. Why couldn't things stay the same?

"Ouch." The flame burned me, so I shook it, and flung the match over my shoulder. I blew on my fingers then looked into Tommy's hazel eyes. "So? What do you think about when you stare at a flame?"

Tom stroked his jaw and gave a little half shrug. "I don't know, I kinda stop thinking. It mesmerizes me." He perched next to me on the hay bale. "Katie, are we still going to be friends once I start high school?"

"Are you kidding? Of course." I hated the thought of being left behind in middle school just because I was a year younger but couldn't fathom life without him. "You're my best friend, and nothing, not even you going to a different school, will change our friendship." I bumped my shoulder against his. "Don't be ridiculous."

Tommy slouched and stared at his sneakers. "But you might make all sorts of new friends and won't need me to hang out with anymore."

Was he nuts? "Hey, look at me."

He gave me a sideways glance.

"New friends? We already know everyone in this podunk place. Any new friends I have will want to be friends with you. You're a great guy, so don't let anyone tell you anything different."

Tom straightened, but then his eyes got big. A crackling noise came from behind us. Smoke overpowered the smell of the cigarettes.

I spun around. The dry hay had caught fire and the flames raged. It must've started from the match I thought had gone out. Grabbing Tommy's hand, I followed my instincts and ran.

I wanted to get as far away as possible, but Tom stopped and faced the shed.

What was he doing? "Tommy, come on."

He shook his head. "We gotta put it out."

"Are you crazy? We'll get caught." We didn't have anything to put it out with. But he had a point. If we let it go, it'd destroy more than the shed. Mr. Pickford's entire farm would be at risk, as well as the whole town if it got out of control. "How? It'll burn down before I can get water."

Tom threw his hands in the air. "How should I know?" He spun on his heel toward me and waved his arms around. "You're supposed to be the brainy one with all the bright ideas."

His words were a slap in the face, but I didn't blame him—his fear bled through the anger. My heart was racing, too. What if we couldn't put the fire out? "I'm thinking." Or trying to. "Call the fire department." *Brilliant.* "Say we were passing by." *Please, whatever you do, don't say I set the place on fire.* "Find a shovel and get back here."

I should've saved my breath. Tommy dashed off before I finished. Facing the burning shed, I took stock. What should I do?

At least the flames hadn't burned through the door. I ran to a young tree and broke off a long, leafy branch. I placed my hands on the outside of the shed door, and the weathered wood still felt cool to the touch. Stepping to the side, I balanced on one foot and kicked the door in, then jumped back. When no flames shot out, I peered inside. An inferno covered the floor. I beat the blaze closest to me.

Sweating from the intense heat, I smacked the flames in a losing battle. My eyes and throat stung, and I felt like help would never come. After the first branch broke, I grabbed another and continued flogging the flames.

Tommy thrust a shovel into my hands. "Someone should be here any minute."

I hurled the branch away and pitched dirt on the flames. Someone better get here soon. No matter how rapidly we shoveled, it burned faster than Tommy and I could keep up with. My muscles screamed for relief, and I drew an arm across my face to keep the sweat from running into my eyes.

The shed wall caught fire, so I whacked the shovel against it. My lungs burned from the smoke, and I coughed with each swing. My stinging eyes gave way to blurred vision from the combination of sweat and smoke. My head ached and I felt dizzy.

A siren sounded in the distance. *Thank God.* My knees buckled and I stumbled into the wall. In moments, the volunteer fire department surrounded us. They put the fire out in minutes. Thank goodness the whole shed hadn't burned to the ground.

I jammed the shovel into the topsoil and took a deep breath of the char-scented air.

"Katherine Elizabeth McCabe!"

Daddy. My heart seemed to stop, and I got a sick feeling in the pit of my stomach. Tommy and I should've made a run for it when the volunteers arrived.

I stiffened before turning around.

On the Run

2

People had followed the volunteer fire department and a crowd had gathered near the smoldering shed. Daddy stood, arms folded across his khaki uniform, on the outskirts. I inhaled deeply and trudged stiff-legged through the mob and stopped in front of him. "Little bit of a fire, wouldn't you say?"

Daddy frowned and the grooves in his forehead deepened as I approached. "What did you do?"

"I can't believe you automatically assume I had something to do with the fire." Maybe if I played enough of the injured innocent, he'd believe it. "What happened to giving someone the benefit of the doubt?" I cocked my head. "Or how about innocent until proven guilty?"

Placing his hands on his gun belt, he pierced me with a look. "Are you through?"

"All right." I shot my arms straight out in front of me. "Cuff me and take me away." Maybe I'd be better off in a jail cell. He'd be on the other side of the bars and wouldn't be staring at me with disappointment. And I could take a nap until he chilled.

He pulled me away from the townspeople. Struggling to maintain some dignity, I yanked my wrists from his grasp.

Sparks kindled in his blue eyes. "Keep a civil tongue in your head." His tight-leashed anger frayed. "Half the town is congregated, and you're flaunting how little you respect me and my position as sheriff. I've had enough."

Oops. I'd crossed the line. Avoiding his glare, I stared at the sharp creases down the front of his trousers. "I'm sorry." I mumbled the apology, then steeled myself for the questions that were sure to come.

He took a deep breath and set his square jaw. "How did the fire start?" He spoke almost gently, but then restrained anger came through. "And don't pad what happened to make yourself or anyone else look better."

He rubbed the area between his eyebrows with his middle two fingers, tipping his Stetson back. "And whatever happened, I know Tom was right there with you."

In other words, don't alter the facts. I'd say one thing for my dad—he knew me well. And he never gave me an inch. "It all started as a kind of experiment."

He raised an eyebrow. "Tell the story straight."

I glanced away. "I wanted to try smoking, and convinced Tommy we'd look cool if we learned how." Daddy'd blow sky high with this one. "So, we met in Mr. Pickford's shed, and when I goofed around with the matches one dropped and lit the hay on fire."

His silence became ominous. The quieter Daddy got, the more trouble I'd be in. I scuffed the toe of my shoe into the dry, weedy grass. "Then, I panicked. I should've put it out, but I ran instead."

If I mentioned the rum, he'd have a heart attack or something. "Everything in there was so dry the fire raged out of control in no time." Would a few tears soften him up?

Not a chance.

"Tommy and I tried to put the fire out." I swallowed hard. "I'm sorry."

Daddy's silence deepened as a light breeze ruffled the hair on his forehead. After a few moments, I squirmed.

He pressed his lips into a flat line. "You need to apologize to Mr. Pickford …"

My favorite thing to do in the world.

His eyes narrowed. "… and tell him you will pay for the damages."

There went my savings. I'd probably have to work off the balance until I graduated from high school.

He sighed. "I have to file the report. Then I'll be home."

And I'll be history.

Daddy grabbed his Stetson by the crown and took it off. His

blond hair, cut short on the sides and longer on top, was streaked with sweat. "Then we'll sit down and talk this whole thing out."

Translation, he'd talk, and I'd watch him pace and wave his arms around.

"Now get going." He gave me a swat and set the hat back on his head. "I want to get finished as soon as possible."

After I apologized to Mr. Pickford and promised to pay for the damages, I slogged across the field. I'd never been in more trouble in my life.

Running footsteps pounded behind me. "Katie, wait up."

I stopped to let Tom reach me.

"What's the verdict? I saw your dad with you."

Who hadn't? "I won't be able to do anything for a while." The biggest understatement of the summer. "I'm supposed to go straight home." Part of the punishment was the waiting in agony to find out how much trouble I'd be in.

I gave Tommy the once-over. He looked as grubby as I felt. "Why do we always get caught?"

He shrugged. "Our kind of luck, I guess. Is your dad going to file a report?"

I nodded. "He has to. Destruction of property is heavy duty, even for us."

Tommy slouched. "My old man's gonna love this one. He'll hit the roof, but the only thing he'll care about is who's paying for it."

"Don't worry. It's coming out of my pocket." I glanced around. "Look, I've got to get going or my dad will give me an extra ration for disobedience." One of his watchwords. "I'll give you a call when I can."

Before going into the house, I dusted off my pants and took off my shoes. My clothes were loaded with grime from the fire. I tiptoed across the threshold and into my room. With any luck, I hadn't spread any ash through the house as I moved. I grabbed a change of clothes and went into the bathroom. Not only was soot streaked across my face, but my blonde hair had been darkened a few shades.

The shower felt wonderful. As I scrubbed the ash off, the water at my feet turned black. The tension flowed out of me as I washed my hair. But my thoughts kept floating back to the fire, like I'd forgotten something. A nagging unease crept through my veins. I closed my eyes, tilted my head back, and rinsed the suds out of my hair.

"Oh, no." I snapped my head forward. "The flask." Neither of us had grabbed it before running out of the shed. Daddy wouldn't overlook it for a second. I was in more trouble than I'd bargained for.

My stomach churned. Daddy would either ground me until I turned eighteen or send me off to boarding school. I glanced at the clock. He'd be home any minute.

"*No, no, no, no, no, no, no.*" I threw on my clothes and raked a brush through my hair, ripping at the tangles.

A tiny voice at the back of my brain told me to take off. Not forever, just until his anger subsided a bit. No time to waste, I grabbed a knapsack from the hall closet, and ran to my room. If I stuck around too long, I wouldn't have a good enough head start. I'd made the mistake last time of not leaving soon enough, and I didn't want to repeat it.

After throwing a few clothes and some food in the bag, I took my money out of the shoebox in the closet and ran out the door.

The town was so small it didn't take long to come to the edge. Flat, open country surrounded the town for miles, and it contained no place to hide. If I stuck close to the road, he'd catch me for sure. I had to cross the whole territory before Daddy started searching.

My side ached after running for an hour and my lungs burned with every breath. Each step felt like it'd be my last, but I had to keep going. Still a long way from any hope of a hiding place, I couldn't afford to slow down. The sun sank in the sky, which happened to be the only thing in my favor.

Half an hour later, the sun dipped below the horizon and twilight deepened. The heat of the day cooled. I slowed to a walk, not able to run any longer. Marathons were never going to be my thing. I'd covered a lot of distance, though, but I needed to make it to another town—it didn't matter where.

An uneasy feeling made me turn around. The far-off beam of a flashlight swung across the field. Daddy. I fell to the ground and lay still. Would the tall grass be enough to hide me? If I ran, he'd see the movement and catch me in minutes. My heart raced and my breathing took on a raspy tone. The hay-like smell of the dry brush tickled my throat and my nose twitched. *Don't sneeze.* At the thought, the tickling sensation worsened.

A footstep sounded to my left. Holding my breath, I closed my eyes, willing Daddy to pass by.

The flashlight beam on my face shattered my hope.

"Get up, Katie." He put his hand out to help me. "Let's go home."

No yelling? No lecture? I must be in worse trouble than I'd imagined. If Daddy were talking, he'd at least be blowing off some steam. We walked back to where he'd parked the car and he drove us home in silence.

"Daddy?"

He held up his hand. "Wait until we get back to the house."

Great. Suffer in silence. He must be furious. When we pulled into the drive, the car barely stopped before I got out and ran straight into my bedroom. Plopping on my bed, I snatched up my teddy bear, Rupert, from his place on the pillow and hugged him tight. I'd never done anything this bad before in my life. I stroked his fur. "What am I gonna do, Rupert?"

The front door closed, and Daddy called me from the living room. "Katie, please come out here."

I stuck my hands in my pockets and shuffled toward Daddy. "I thought you'd want me in my room." Where punishment was usually given.

Daddy stood in the middle of the room in his I-mean-business stance. Back ramrod straight, feet apart, hands resting on his gun belt. "Sit down. We have a lot to talk about."

Dumbfounded, I sat on the couch. I might have pushed him too far. Guilt caused my chest to tighten.

He rubbed his temple as if to ward off a headache. "I've been thinking a lot about what's best for you."

Uh-oh. That didn't sound good.

"I've done my best, Katie." He sat in his leather armchair. "But I don't think it's enough anymore." Pain clouded his blue eyes.

A hard knot formed in my stomach as I stared at the floor.

He sagged against the chair and his shoulders slumped. "You must think so too, otherwise you wouldn't have run off."

"Daddy, it's not you." A heavy feeling blanketed me. "I don't know what's wrong with me." My emotions were all over the place lately.

He leaned forward, resting his elbows on his knees. "Why did you run off?"

To avoid some hassle. "I don't know."

Daddy waited for me to continue.

"You were angry." I bit my lower lip. "I'd have come home after you cooled off."

He bowed his head. "I always wanted us to be able to talk things out. But if you're afraid of me ..."

"I'm not afraid." The knot in my stomach burned. "I did something wrong." And didn't want to own up. "Sometimes I feel so restless I don't know what to do."

Daddy looked up. "In other words, you're not happy at home."

My body snapped against the couch back and I blinked. "What? No." I pressed a hand against my stomach. "It's this godforsaken hole of a place we live in."

Daddy's face turned into a thundercloud. "I don't like to hear you talk that way."

I hung my head and my cheeks burned. "I'm sorry, Daddy." When would I learn to keep my mouth shut? "I don't want to spend the rest of my life where the biggest news of the week is which way the wind is blowing the fumes from the Farleys' outhouse."

I stood and paced around the room. "I feel like I'm under a microscope. You're the sheriff, so everybody watches everything I do." My chest tightened as I felt the walls closing in. "And I can't breathe.

I want to see more of the world than what's right here."

My words were met with silence. They seemed to hover, vibrating, in the middle of the room.

Daddy stared at the rust and gold area rug beneath his feet. Then he sighed and straightened, and the lines from his nose to the corners of his mouth deepened as if they had been etched in stone. "Giving you a broader experience is one of the reasons I'm sending you to live with your uncle Charlie."

Sent Away

3

I stopped pacing and my mouth dropped open. Feeling like I'd had the wind knocked out of me, I struggled to catch my breath. Daddy couldn't be serious. He'd never send me to live with an uncle I'd never met. Would he? A scream built inside me, and I wanted to lash out. "Uncle Charlie? Which one is he?" I knew full well who Uncle Charlie was, despite my feigned ignorance. "I can't keep them straight."

The youngest of seven brothers, Daddy had told me stories about them over the years. McCabes stood tall, did the right thing, helped others in need before thinking of themselves, and were kind, gentle, moral, and spiritual leaders wherever they went. All the brothers except for Charlie had scattered from the town where they had grown up, spreading their reputation far and wide.

Daddy sighed. "Charlie's my eldest brother. I've talked about him before." He drummed his fingers on his knee. "You need to be looked after better."

I crossed my arms. "Don't tell me you've been listening to those idiots who think you don't take care of me." Some of the church ladies thought Daddy should resign as sheriff to look after me. But they kept voting him back into office, which made no sense.

He held his hands out in a *stop* gesture. "Simmer down." Daddy stared straight at me—no hint of a smile, not even a twinkle in his eye. "While you know I don't agree with them for the most part, lately I'm beginning to think they may have a point. Let's take this afternoon as a prime example. Accidentally burning down a shed because you're experimenting with cigarettes and alcohol might make some people argue you need a little firmer parental control."

He knows. My knees went weak, and I flopped on the couch

feeling as if I'd been hit in the stomach.

"Yes, I found the flask." He stood and rubbed the grooves in his forehead. "Katie, I don't know what to do with you anymore. I tried to raise you with a good, upright background, and you seem to be rejecting everything I ever taught you." He bit his lip. "Maybe a different atmosphere will be better for you."

I felt like crying. "I'll change. Don't send me away."

He shook his head. "There are things I can't give you. And I'm not talking about material things."

But I didn't need anything more. I stared through the living room window into the night, searching for a star to wish on. Anything to get Daddy off this track of wanting to send me away.

"My little girl is growing up, and you need a woman role model. If Marie were still alive, things would be different." His voice got kind of choky sounding, the way it did whenever he talked about Mama.

Perplexed, I pulled my gaze away from the window. "But I thought Aunt Liza died in the same accident as Mama."

Daddy's face went blank, and his eyes had a frozen look about them. "She did."

When I was a baby, another driver hit her and Aunt Liza during a storm and they crashed into a tree, killing them both. Daddy had moved us hundreds of miles away to this little town in the middle of nowhere after she died. "Did Uncle Charlie get remarried?"

"No. My brother Shane's girl, Sarah, lives there." A wistful smile crossed his face. "She's been living with Charlie for several years now."

I suppressed an eye roll. Good for her.

He hesitated for a moment and patted his breast pocket. "She'll be a good influence on you."

How did he know? He hadn't seen her since we'd moved eleven years ago. "Let me stay, Daddy. I'll behave. Honest."

"You sure changed your mind in a hurry. An hour ago, you were running away. You couldn't wait to get out of here."

I stood and walked over to the picture of us on the mantle. Daddy had been giving me a piggyback ride, my cheek laid next to his, both smiling and happy. "That's different." My voice had a harsh edge to it as I choked back tears. Crying meant weakness, and I didn't want to be weak in front of him. Not now.

I took a slow, deep breath and traced the wooden frame with my finger. "I only wanted to give you a chance to get over your anger." My control became firmer as I continued to rub the picture frame. I faced Daddy. "There wasn't anything to do, and I wanted to try something different."

Daddy frowned. "Boredom doesn't excuse your actions. You've got a good brain in that head of yours, and lately you haven't been using it."

"I never said boredom was an excuse." I hated when he put words into my mouth. "And I did use my brain."

"Really? Let's take a look at the results."

"I know what happened." My anger smoldered. "I didn't think I'd burn the shed down. It was an accident."

He threw up his hands. "Exactly what I'm telling you. You're not thinking through the consequences." He slapped the back of his hand on his outstretched palm. "You are a McCabe and you've got to start acting like one. For once, take responsibility. I can't do it for you."

Something in me snapped. "I never asked to be a McCabe and I wish to God I was never born one." Life certainly would've been easier. "It isn't fair I have to be a certain way because of my last name." I wanted to hurt Daddy, so I pointed at the ceiling. "Someone up there screwed up when they sent me to this family."

"Enough, Katherine." Daddy spoke softly, but his tone was anything but.

I slumped against the mantle. "You don't understand. I'm never allowed to just be Katie. On top of being a McCabe, you're the sheriff, so no matter what I do, I'm measured by a standard I can't live up to."

The overwhelming emotion of the moment choked me. I swallowed hard as I stared at the floor. "I don't want to leave you, Daddy." I loved him too much. "I'll even try to be like a McCabe if it will make you love me enough to keep me here."

Daddy's eyes softened and a tremor ran across his cheek. He reached out, took my hands gently in his, and pulled me closer to him. "Sweetheart, it's *because* I love you—more than I have words for—I want you to live with your uncle Charlie."

Tears welled in my eyes. "I can't believe you don't want me anymore."

He hugged me close and stroked my hair. "I do want you. This has been the hardest decision I've ever had to make."

When he released me, he took my hands again. The skin around his eyes bunched as if he were in pain.

"I need you to listen ..." He broke off and his mouth turned down. "This is so hard for me to say."

My knee rapidly bounced and try as I might, I couldn't keep still.

"Your behavior isn't the real reason I'm sending you to live with Charlie."

My heart stopped. I didn't want to hear anymore.

"I haven't been feeling well, so I went to the doctor last week, and he sent some blood tests for analysis. He gave me the results today and they aren't good." He took a deep breath. "The doc needs to put me through a bunch more tests, and I'll have to spend some time in the hospital. I need someone to look after you while I'm going through all of this, because I won't be able to." A single tear rolled down his cheek. "Please trust me. This is the best for you."

I pulled my hands from his grasp and took a step back. "But if you're sick, I should be with you. I can take care of you." *This couldn't be happening.*

His lips trembled as he pressed them tightly together.

Tears spilled over, and I grabbed him and buried my head in his chest. "Couldn't I go for a visit instead then, until you're better?"

"The tests are only the beginning, and it's going to take time. School starts soon, and I want you enrolled."

I pulled away from Daddy and plopped down on the couch.

"Sulking won't do you any good. Charlie suggested you go live with him over a month ago. He thought it'd be a good idea for you to get settled in before school started, but I didn't want to let go of you yet."

"You've known for over a month you were going to send me away, and you didn't tell me? How could you?" A lump formed in my throat and I bit my lower lip. The secrecy might be the worst hurt of all.

He knelt in front of me. "Let me explain. Your uncle suggested the move when I talked to him about how wild you've been getting, but I told him no. Charlie told me to think about it." He brushed the bangs away from my eyes. "As I felt worse and worse over the summer, Charlie told me the offer was still there to give me a chance to get back on my feet."

I can't handle this. Daddy can't be that sick. Can he?

Daddy stroked my cheek. "I couldn't face letting you go. But after the preliminary test results, I had to face it. I need to know you are being taken care of by someone who loves you, so I can concentrate on getting better for both of us."

We argued back and forth. Or I should say, I argued, and Daddy stayed calm, but didn't budge an inch.

"You'd better get packed. We have to get to the bus stop. And you're going, whether I put you on the bus kicking and screaming or not."

When Daddy got a certain tone in his voice, and his jaw looked like it'd been carved in granite, it was useless to put up a fight.

My packing consisted of throwing some clothes into an old, battered suitcase. *Do I need anything else?* In my room I had very few things, but an overabundance of one. Books. My bookcase bulged with them. I'd put shelves on the walls to hold them, and even then, they overflowed. I had to take some books with me, in case Uncle Charlie didn't have any I liked. I quickly pulled down five favorites, put them in the suitcase, and closed the lid.

I stomped into the next room dragging my suitcase behind. I wasn't sentimental but looking around the room brought a lump to my throat. My gaze slid over the worn, faded couch where Daddy and

I spent many hours together, the fireplace where we'd toasted bag after bag of marshmallows, and the plaques Daddy earned from the town. Everything looked worn, perhaps a little shabby, nothing new or shiny, but homey and loved.

I stopped scanning the room when my gaze landed on Daddy sitting in his chair with his eyes closed. His face was gray and wrinkled, and a shock ran through my body. Had I done that to him? Was it his illness? Why hadn't I noticed it sooner?

When younger, I used to think God must look exactly like my daddy; big, tall, blond, with a twinkle in his eyes, and a smile on his face. His very presence seemed to make trouble disappear. Daddy could do any and everything. Daddy was my hero, stronger than Hercules, mightier than Superman, yet more gentle and kind than all the superheroes put together. In my eyes, Greek mythological gods lacked sparkle next to him.

I wished I could turn back the clock to when I was young enough to climb into his lap. He'd hug me and suddenly whatever had been wrong would be washed away. He wouldn't be so worn and gray. But I couldn't alter time. Why had I spent so much time arguing with him instead of holding him tight and telling him how much I loved him?

The sky grew misty gray with the arrival of dawn, and it was time to leave. When Daddy drove me to the bus station, the silence between us hung as heavy as a steel anchor. Neither one of us said anything until the bus rolled in.

Daddy broke the silence first. "Do you have everything?"

I nodded.

"Here's your ticket." He held it out to me. "Have Charlie give me a call when you get there." The bus horn honked. "This is goodbye for now. Be good. I'll come to your uncle's as soon as all my tests are done, to check on how you're doing." He hugged me tight.

I twisted out of his grasp, grabbed my bag, and stalked on to the bus without a word. I wanted to run into his arms, cling to him, and never let go. I wanted him to tell me everything was going to be okay. If I waited any longer, it would've been too hard to leave. My throat constricted so tightly I couldn't speak. Besides, white-hot anger burned inside me and nearly drowned out the fear. How could I have so many emotions flooding through me at the same time?

As soon as I found my seat, the bus pulled out of the station. Miserable, I stared out the window until Daddy became a tiny speck on the horizon.

The bus rattled and bumped its way down the road, the seats creaked, and the sides seemed to groan more with every mile. The windows didn't stay shut, so my mouth felt as dry as cotton from the dust pouring in, and the heat of the day made the bus feel like the inside of an oven. My eyes felt gritty and burned from the dust and I was cranky from lack of sleep.

At least I had the seat to myself. No one would chatter away and interrupt my thoughts through the long ride. What a sight I must have been for the other passengers, my arms folded, a scowl for an expression, and my long, blonde hair hanging in my face. I crouched low and thrust my knees against the seat back in front of me. I didn't want to make this trip and didn't care what anyone else thought about me either.

How could Daddy send me away, especially when he was sick? What if he doesn't get better? I didn't even want to think about the possibility. He had to get better, he just had to.

The motion of the bus, along with my sleepless night, soon lulled me to sleep.

New Family

4

The bus hit a big rut in the road and bounced me into wakefulness. My head ached and the argument Daddy and I had played over and over. I needed to quit dwelling on the past and start thinking about what I'd face ahead. All I knew about Uncle Charlie, his two sons, Matthew and Mark, and cousin Sarah was from the stories Daddy told me. And they bore the name of McCabe, which meant they probably upheld the McCabe reputation.

With every bump in the road, I got closer to the home of the McCabe boys. I wanted to change my name so people would accept me for who I was, instead of forcing me into the McCabe mold.

The bus slowed as it approached a flat wooden bench in the dirt on the side of the road. My heart sank. If that was the *station* my hopes of living in a bigger town than the one I left evaporated. The most that could be said was it had a clear shelter surrounding it. Before the bus came to a complete stop, I stood, grabbed my bag from the overhead, and walked to the front. The door had barely opened when a man hopped on board.

"Katie McCabe?"

I nodded and brushed the hair out of my eyes. I stood at the top of the stairs frozen to the spot, speechless.

He grinned. "I'm your cousin Matthew."

He looked exactly like my daddy in some of the pictures I'd seen of him as a young man. I didn't know what I expected. From Daddy's stories I expected a kid, not someone so grown-up.

"Well, don't just stand there. We don't have all day. And I'm sure the driver wants to get on with his trip too." He reached up. "Here, let me help you."

As he lifted me off the bus, I noticed how wonderfully his muscles flexed. He definitely wasn't weak.

"Do you have everything? I'll take you out to the farm, then I've got to get back to work."

"Farm?" What else hadn't Daddy told me?

Matthew tossed my suitcase into the trunk and slammed the lid. "It's a small one, but Dad likes to work on it in his spare time. We all help out, too. Sarah's out there waiting for you. She'll help you get settled in. And in a couple hours, Mark, Dad, and I will be back."

We got into the car and Matthew guided it away from the open-air station and onto the road.

"The farm doesn't happen to be in the middle of town, does it?" I felt let down. Forced to come, I at least wanted to be where something might happen, not stuck out in the middle of fields.

"No, the farm isn't in town, thank goodness. We're not too far from it though." He glanced at me before turning at the crossroads. "Close enough, I'd say."

I stared out the window. Hills of deep green and contrasting gray green stood all around, covered with beautiful trees. The sunlight hit an occasional meandering brook, which sparkled like a river of jewels. The scenery belonged in a painting.

Matthew spoke after a moment, almost as if he read my thoughts. "It sure is beautiful, isn't it? It kind of makes you feel peaceful, at least it does me. It's why I like living out here, instead of around so many buildings." He turned the car off the road onto a little lane.

After we rounded a curve, I saw the house. A trickle of despair pooled in my stomach. We'd reached my unwanted destination.

Matthew glanced at me. "Welcome to the McCabe farm."

A nice, cheery place, white with blue trim and a long wooden porch, and a swing to go with it. As we came to a stop, a beautiful girl came out of the front door. She wore a simple peasant-style blouse and skirt and moved with grace and ease. She made me feel clumsy and not put together quite right.

I stepped out of the car and trudged toward the house. Matthew strode past with my bag. As I followed, reality hit me hard—my entire life had been turned upside down.

"The bus was a little late, so I grabbed Katie and we came straight here." Matthew turned his head toward me. "Sarah'll be able to show you where everything is."

I didn't want to know. I wanted to get back on the bus and go home.

After I climbed the stairs to the porch, Sarah gave me a big hug of welcome. "I'm so glad you're here, Katie."

The time for battle had come. I wrenched out of her embrace. If I didn't want to stay, I'd have to be as awful as possible. I strove to make my voice icy and rude. "Stop being so sickeningly sweet. I'm only here by force. I don't want to be here. I hate this place, and I wish to God I never laid eyes on you."

Then I brushed past her toward the house, but not before I caught the dismay she exchanged with Matthew. As I walked inside, I smiled, and a sense of triumph swelled in my heart. *Score one for me.*

Sarah followed me into the house. "Matthew went back to work. Grab your bag, and I'll show you to our room."

"*Our* room? Does this mean I have to share it with you?"

Sarah seemed determined to ignore the bite of my words. "Oh, don't worry. It's a good-sized room."

I glared straight into her big, green eyes. "The size of the room doesn't bother me. The roommate does."

Sarah pressed her lips tightly together and looked away. I'd scored again. By keeping up the rude comments, I'd get under her skin in no time.

We walked through the door and into the bedroom. I made a face like I had tasted something awful. "I can't live in this room."

Suspicion sprang into Sarah's eyes as she turned toward me. "Why not?"

"It's so prissy, I want to vomit." Actually, it was nice. Dainty flowered wallpaper and matching bedspreads, a vase of flowers on the chest of drawers, frilly white curtains at the window, and everything spic-and-span clean.

Sarah's jaw set. "Get used to it. You can't share a room with the boys, and besides Uncle Charlie's, this is the only other bedroom."

I scowled and drew out my words to give them punch. "I'd rather sleep in a barn."

She folded her arms and arched an eyebrow. "That can be arranged."

I'd forgotten when you lived on a farm you couldn't offer to sleep in the barn unless you were serious. Her tone said I skated on thin ice. Best not push my luck or I'd be sleeping on a bale of hay.

"The bed in the corner, the right half of the closet, and the middle two drawers of the dresser are yours." Sarah motioned to each item as she said it.

I put my suitcase on my bed and opened it. I didn't want to unpack and put my things in this strange bedroom. It was too sudden, too fast for me to be here with everything ready. Unpacking would make it real, and I'd have to face the unthinkable. Daddy being either too sick to take care of me or so fed up with my bad behavior he'd willingly give me up.

"How long have you known I'd be coming?" The small, vulnerable voice didn't even sound like mine.

"Uncle Charlie told us you might be coming over a month ago, but he wasn't sure of the exact date. Yesterday, he told us you'd arrive today. We've been anxiously waiting ever since." Sarah stood behind me and put a sympathetic hand on my shoulder.

A sense of inadequacy overwhelmed me as I glanced at the contents of my suitcase. I twitched my shoulder and faced her. "After all the anticipation, I must be a major disappointment."

Sarah opened her mouth as if to say something.

"If you say otherwise, you're either a hypocrite or a fool." I was getting good at being snotty.

She clamped her mouth shut, and her eyes narrowed.

"What did Uncle Charlie tell you about me? And what reasons did he give for me to come live here?" Part of me didn't want the answer. I didn't want to hear Daddy was too sick or didn't want me anymore.

Sarah hesitated and rubbed the rose-gold necklace she wore. "I don't think it's my place to say anything. You should ask Uncle Charlie if you want to know."

"What a cop-out. I hate people who play it safe." Why couldn't she tell me, anyway? "Let me guess. I'm always in trouble and Daddy sent me away. He decided I needed a motherly touch, and you're it." I raked my bangs out of my face. "What a laugh. I wouldn't listen to you if you were my grandmother, let alone a cousin."

Sarah pulled her head back and blinked as if I'd tried to hit her. "Enough." Her lips tightened, and anger sparked in her eyes, making them look like flashing emeralds. "You need to get a grip and shape up if you want to live here."

I turned back to the bed and dumped the contents of my suitcase out. "My point exactly. You've known for over a month? I found out last night." I slammed the suitcase closed and slid it under the bed, then faced her. "Forced to leave with no say in the matter—I don't want to be here."

"Since you are here, I suggest you make the best of it. If you have any questions, I'll be fixing supper. When you finish unpacking, I'll expect your help." She spun on her heel and strode out of the room.

The small pile of clothes looked pathetic heaped on the bed. Opening my side of the closet, I noticed Sarah had stocked it with padded hangers. I'd never had those before. I hung up the one dress I brought with me. I had more dresses, but at home, there seemed to be no reason to wear them except to church. Surely Daddy would come to his senses and call for me to come home before too many Sundays passed.

The dress looked silly hanging alone. I grabbed my shirts and hung them in the closet too. After putting everything away, I went to the kitchen, as commanded.

Dinnertime Dustup

5

Sarah stood against the sunny yellow background of the kitchen, prettier than ever, if possible. Her long, wavy, auburn locks were tied into a loose ponytail with a cream-colored scarf. Intent on stirring something in a pan, she bent her head forward, her long, thick, dark lashes almost resting on her steam-flushed cheeks. The light from the window made the purple heart-shaped stone in the center of her rose-gold pendant sparkle.

The aroma of cooking steak wafted toward me, and my mouth watered. I could almost taste it. My stomach grumbled in protest.

At the sound, Sarah gave me a big friendly smile. When someone showed they had true sweetness in them, like Sarah, it was harder to be rotten to them. True sweetness was something no one would ever accuse me of having.

"You're in time to help me out. Everything is almost ready, and Uncle Charlie and the boys should be home any minute." A quick frown crossed her face as she gazed at me. "We need to get your hair out of the way before you start. I've got another scarf. Come here, and I'll tie your hair back like mine."

After tying the scarf in my hair, she turned me around to take another look, and smiled. "Much better. Now, there's lettuce, red onions, cucumbers, celery, and carrots in the vegetable drawer. If you'll make a salad, I'd sure appreciate it. Then the table needs to be set, and we should be able to eat."

Hallelujah. *Starving* didn't capture how hungry I felt, and the smells from the cooking food nearly drove me crazy. I hadn't eaten since early yesterday, because I'd been running through a field at dinnertime last night, too angry to eat breakfast, and too forgetful to remember to pack a lunch for the trip. My insides were hollow.

Sarah opened the refrigerator door. "Hurry now. I got started a little late, so I'm behind."

At least she didn't say she blamed me for the lateness. She probably thought it, though.

I hunted through the drawers and took out the vegetables. "What happens if it goes on the table a couple of minutes late? Does Uncle Charlie turn into a beast and throw you out of the house?"

"No." Sarah chuckled. "Uncle Charlie would never say a word if supper were late."

I pulled the lettuce apart.

She pointed the spatula at me. "Don't forget to wash the vegetables first."

My lip curled at the words. What did she think I'd do, roll them on the ground? Oh well, I shrugged and turned on the faucet.

Sarah rattled on about Uncle Charlie. "He's a good, sweet man. The best kind there is. So, I like everything to be the way he likes it."

How sickening. I tore apart the lettuce and tossed it into a bowl. I grabbed the carrots, cucumbers, and celery and cut them. When I finished, I sighed as I looked at the carrots. They were chunks instead of slices and I'd have to take the time to cut them again.

She glanced out the window. "Will you please set the table? Uncle Charlie and the boys just turned off the main road. I'll finish the salad."

She said it nicely enough, but it felt like a put-down. After opening a few cupboards, I managed to find the plates and glasses. When I reached the table, the plates slipped, and the stoneware banged with so much force it sounded like they might break.

Her head whipped toward me. "Take it easy."

"I didn't mean to put them down so hard." I couldn't do anything without her saying something about it.

She peered past the breakfast counter to the stack of plates. "All right. Just be more careful."

We worked in silence as I put the plates around the table. Boots shuffling on the porch broke the stillness.

The door opened, and in walked a tall, lean man. He had dark brown hair, almost black, with a touch of gray at the sides. Even in blue jeans and a plaid shirt, he looked like a man of importance. Daddy had told me Uncle Charlie owned a construction company and Matthew and Mark worked for him.

"You must be Katie." His voice sounded deep and strong, like Daddy's. A comforting voice because it was solid and couldn't be shaken.

I wanted to shatter his calm, so I tried a smart answer. "Good guess."

He hung his keys on a peg before entering the dining area. "Sarah got you settled in all right?"

My first attempt at being obnoxious had fallen flatter than a pancake. Uncle Charlie held the power to send me home, so I'd have to do better. "Yeah. I'm all unpacked. My question is when do I pack again?"

A trace of confusion crossed Uncle Charlie's face. "Pack? Why?"

"I'm going back home. You don't think I'm going to stay here, do you?" I swiped at my bangs to get them out of my eyes, and my voice got louder as I continued. "This is temporary. You'll see. Daddy'll call and ask for me to come home when his tests are all done. He'll be too lonely without me."

I spoke with more confidence than I felt. Daddy didn't often change his mind about things, and he wanted me to stay at least through the school year.

A troubled expression replaced the confusion on Uncle Charlie's face, and it gave me a sense of satisfaction. He drew his brows together. "We'll talk about this later. Right now, I need to wash for supper."

Drat. I'd wanted more of a reaction.

Boots stomped outside on the porch. Matthew opened the door and crossed the threshold. Right behind him another big, tall, hunk of a guy followed. Only Mark had dark hair and eyes, and dimples in his cheeks. Where Matthew looked like my daddy, Mark looked like his. Maybe I shouldn't be so hasty about wanting to leave. If all the guys around here were like my cousins, I'd be in hog heaven. The only guy I hung around with at home was Tommy Wolff. He didn't care about Daddy being sheriff, or my last name. Besides, he was about the only guy around even close to my age and was my closest friend.

Mark leaned against the doorframe to the kitchen. "Is supper ready? I'm so hungry I'm ready to eat the hide off a horse."

Sarah rolled her eyes and shook her head. "Get yourself washed up, and it'll be on the table. Katie, will you please help me carry things over?"

I stood there, fork in hand, not moving. Mark strode out of the room, and my eyes followed his every move until he disappeared. He hadn't even noticed me, and I felt strangely let down. I wished he would've at least said hello.

I went into the kitchen in somewhat of a daze. "Sarah? Are all the guys around here as cute as those cousins of ours?"

Sarah gave a short laugh and her eyes crinkled at the edges. "No, Matthew and Mark are kind of special, although we do have some nice-looking guys in the area." Her smile widened and her right eyebrow rose as she teased me. "Changing your mind about wanting to leave?"

My cheeks warmed. "Well, I might think about sticking around for a while, with the right type of bait, of course."

"Oh, of course. Nothing but the best." Sarah carried the last dish to the table, then patted my shoulder and gave me a quick squeeze.

Footsteps sounded as Uncle Charlie came into the room. "Are we ready to sit down?"

Sarah nodded, then called toward the hall. "Come on, Mark. It'll be cold if you wait much longer."

He came in and sat directly across from me. Mark had to notice me now. Matthew followed him and smiled at me as he sat, and my heart did a cartwheel. After a few moments, I tore my thoughts away from my cousins. I needed a plan so they'd send me back home as soon as Daddy got better.

Time to go back to being as unpleasant as possible, so I'd quickly become the unwanted guest. If Uncle Charlie were anything like Daddy, he'd flip if I ate before the meal was blessed, so I deliberately dished food on my plate and took a bite.

Uncle Charlie's nostrils flared. "Hold on there, little miss. We haven't given our thanks to the Lord yet. At this table, you don't touch the food until grace has been said. Understood?"

I stared at my plate and felt the back of my neck flush. "Yes, sir."

While Uncle Charlie said grace, I brooded over having reacted like a child caught with her hand in the cookie jar. After all, I'd done it on purpose. But I didn't want Matthew and Mark to think poorly of me. Why did I want their approval? Those feelings had to be set aside if I wanted to go home.

As soon as the prayer ended, Mark grabbed the bowl in front of him and smirked. "Hey, is this some sort of new-fangled salad? We've never had carrot chunks with greens before."

My face grew so hot it must have been beet red.

"Is it all right to eat now?" I intentionally made my tone as snotty as possible to cover my embarrassment.

Mark's eyes twinkled, and he looked like he might laugh.

Uncle Charlie answered me in a dry sounding voice. "Yes. I'm frankly surprised Ron didn't teach you better table manners. He knows what's expected at the table, and I thought he would've taught you the same."

A spurt of anger ignited, and I glared at him. "Yeah? How do you know Daddy didn't raise me in the holier-than-thou McCabe tradition?"

His jaw set. "By your actions."

Fury rose and threatened to overwhelm me. Why attack Daddy for something I'd done? "You're wrong." Anger burned my throat. "Daddy taught me a lot of things, including how to behave. He'd have tanned my hide for the way I've acted today, but you wouldn't know about that, would you?"

The lack of sleep and food hit me, and I felt my control slipping away. My voice had risen, and I took a deep breath, trying to calm down. "I decided on my own not to do things the McCabe way anymore. It has nothing to do with Daddy. So don't you ..." My control snapped. "... don't any of you ever say anything against my daddy again!"

Uncle Charlie grimaced and lowered his fork. "Katie, there is no need to shout. Settle down and apologize for your behavior, or you may leave the table."

He spoke calmly, but his voice had the same rock-solid tone Daddy's had when he wasn't going to stand for any more.

"I don't allow shouting at supper, or any other time." He pressed his lips into a flat line.

I stood abruptly, knocking my chair over, but took a moment before I answered. I wanted to be in control. Or at least seem to be. "I won't apologize, and I don't care what you don't allow at your table, or in your house."

Anger flitted across Uncle Charlie's face. "Then you're excused to go to your room."

Should I make a dash for the front door? Matthew or Mark would probably catch me before I got off the porch. I'd be mortified if they hauled me back inside, and I'd already been embarrassed enough for one meal. Besides, once outside, I had nowhere to go.

"At least in my room I'll have better company." I ran out of the dining room.

Mark hooted with laughter. "It looks like Uncle Ron raised a little hellcat."

Down on the Farm

6

I rushed into my room and slammed the door to drown out their conversation. After pacing back and forth, venting under my breath, I flopped on my bed and punched the pillow. How could I have left without packing Rupert? I needed my teddy bear to squeeze. Without Rupert, I felt like all my ties to home had been cut. He was the last present Mama had given me before her accident.

Worse than not having Rupert was not having Tommy. When things like this happened at home, I always ran to find Tommy Wolff. We'd go down by the riverbank and talk for hours. He listened and understood what I was going through. Then he'd say something to make me feel better.

The town biddies labeled Tommy an outcast, and told Daddy he shouldn't allow me to *associate*, as they put it, with Tommy. His father wasn't the right type, and therefore a bad influence on both of us. What burned me was the self-righteous hypocrites acted like it was their duty.

It was none of their business.

In the town's eyes, Tommy had led me astray. If they'd turned it around, they would've been more accurate. Daddy never paid any attention and told me if they didn't bother to get to know Tommy before saying anything about him or his father, then what they said had no value anyway.

Tommy and I had so much fun getting into trouble. Like the time we terrorized our teacher, Mrs. Simpson, by making everyone think she couldn't stop farting. We taped a remote-controlled fart machine under her desk. Then we rigged a mechanism to squirt stink-bomb fart spray activated by a second remote. It smelled nasty. Tommy fired off the fart machine using the loudest settings, and then I triggered the stink bomb. The entire class was in hysterics while plugging their noses. Mrs. Simpson turned fire engine red. First from embarrassment, but then she became irritated and demanded to know who was pulling the prank. Tommy had slipped the remote into his pocket, which turned out to be a mistake. He had to keep one hand in his lap to set the machine off. When he got caught, I confessed—we were in it together and I couldn't leave him hanging.

We got immediate passes to the principal's office, but our science teacher gave us an A for the stink-bomb mechanism. Daddy picked me up and took away all my privileges for two weeks and piled on the chores. Tommy had to talk to the principal, and didn't get in trouble at home, but I think he suffered more than I did. He didn't like having a bad reputation, and I thrived on making one.

We got caught a lot. Even when we didn't get caught, Daddy'd ask me about something, and I couldn't lie. He always knew when I was involved somehow.

I wished Tommy were here with me. I missed him. Daddy understood me, too. He never backed down an inch from his expectations, but he'd take me in his arms and my troubles would disappear because he loved me, and nothing else mattered.

Thinking about them, and knowing I was so far from Tommy and Daddy, made me feel scared and alone. I wanted to be at home with Daddy hugging me tight and telling me tomorrow would be a better day.

As the bus had pulled away from the station, Daddy had looked smaller, almost shrunken, with tears streaming down his face. He'd miss me as much as I missed him. I'd ask Uncle Charlie to call him, except I didn't think he'd let me tonight after the way I'd behaved.

Brooding about home wouldn't help matters any. Daddy wanted me to give this a try. Maybe I should try to do well and fit in for his sake.

He always wanted me to have the best. Didn't he know the best for me was being with him?

Sarah tapped on the door, then came in and sat beside me. "I tried to bring you some supper since you didn't have a chance to eat any, but Uncle Charlie said you missed out for tonight." She handed me a paper towel with something warm wrapped in it. "I brought you a biscuit anyway, knowing you haven't eaten since early this morning."

My stomach gurgled as I smelled the biscuit. I quickly unwrapped it and brought it to my mouth, but then stopped. I wanted to eat it, but couldn't, so lowered it to my lap.

I was the one who'd blown it. And I'd done it on purpose. I didn't deserve for someone to be kind to me. After one last sniff, I handed it back to Sarah. "Thanks, but I don't want it." My stomach gave a loud grumble.

Concern passed across her face. "But you're hungry."

I bit my lip. "Yeah, but I don't feel right about eating it."

A little respect crept into Sarah's eyes. Respect because I had some principles.

"Thanks for bringing it, though." I hung my head. "I feel kinda bad about the way I acted earlier, and about the things I said to you."

"I understand." She smiled. "You're hurting inside. Otherwise, you wouldn't have lashed out. It's hard when you have to leave home."

Sarah stroked my hair, and it gave me a sense of comfort. Things might not be as bad as I thought.

"Uncle Charlie wants you to help me clear the dishes. Then he wants you to go straight to bed and get a good night's sleep."

I heaved a big sigh. "I need it. I'm exhausted."

After finishing the dishes, my head barely touched the pillow before I fell into oblivion.

When I opened my eyes in the morning, Sarah was buzzing around the room, dustcloth in hand, humming as she worked. I didn't see how anyone could be so bright and cheerful so early.

She smiled at me when she saw I was awake. "It's about time you woke up. The way you were sleeping, I thought you might be out until noon."

I pushed up to a sitting position. "What time is it anyway?"

She glanced at the clock next to her bed. "A couple of minutes before six. You'd better get up. We have a lot to do today."

I flopped back on the pillow and pulled the covers over my face. "Six in the morning isn't a time for any decent person to be getting up." I peeked out from under the blanket. "My brain doesn't even start until ten or eleven at the earliest."

She laughed. "Get used to it. You need to get moving now. There are eggs to be collected, breakfast to be made and cleared, then we have to go into town."

When I didn't move, Sarah threw the dustcloth at me.

I sat up and tossed it back. "When's breakfast?" The hollow area formerly called my stomach vaguely remembered food.

"You'll need to collect the eggs first." She smirked. "I think Mark is over at the barn right now. He'll be able to help you out."

My heart gave a leap at the thought of spending some time alone with Mark. It might be crazy, but I had a ridiculous crush on both my male cousins. Ridiculous because nothing could ever happen because we were related and, though I hated to admit it, they'd never feel the same way about me. To them, I was just a kid. I slowly got out from beneath the covers and got dressed.

When I returned from the bathroom, I stopped in the doorway and stiffened. Sarah had made my bed. "I'd've made it. You didn't need to." I couldn't keep the accusatory tone out of my voice. I didn't want any favors.

She waved a hand. "It was no big deal. I saved you a little time this morning."

I didn't want to owe anyone anything. Not even something so small and insignificant.

Sarah tilted her head. "Don't expect it to happen every day because it won't. Go meet the hens and then see if Mark needs a hand."

I stepped out into the bright sunlight. The air had the sweet, musty smell of morning, and it felt cool against my skin. The barn looked like a picture, with its cracked and peeling red paint, and warped and weathered boards against the blue summer sky. Beyond it, the hens clucked in their coop. I'd better check with Mark to see if he needed my help first.

My eyes took a moment to adjust to the dark as the big door closed. I barely made out Mark's outline as he squatted and leaned forward to milk the cow. As I took another step forward, a huge German shepherd rose to its feet with a growl, and I stopped in my tracks and raised a hand in greeting.

Mark peered at me through the dim light. "It's all right, Günter. It's our little spitfire, Kit-Kat."

Kit-Kat? As I remembered his comment last night when I'd stormed away from the table, my face got hot. It could've been worse. At least he hadn't told Günter to attack instead of giving me a nickname.

Mark pointed toward the wall. "Why don't you grab the stool over there, and I'll teach you how to milk ol' Bossy here."

It seemed too nice of a morning to be spoiled by a know-it-all, so I didn't tell Mark I already knew how. The strength of his hands over mine reminded me of when Daddy had taught me. Daddy believed in helping your neighbors, so he used to send me over to help Mr. Pickford with the milking and feeding of his animals.

Mr. Pickford kept a cow, a goat, and some hens, as well as a horse at his place, and he was getting too old to take care of them. He told me if I did a good job, one day he'd give me the horse. Bella was a beauty, and I wanted my own horse, so I always made sure the animals were doing well. Setting fire to the shed had probably ruined my chances, though.

After we finished milking Bossy, Mark took me to the chicken coop, introduced me to the hens, and insisted on showing me how to collect the eggs. Afterward, he gave me a short tour of the barn and promised to show me more tomorrow. The whole time we were out there, Günter never left Mark's side.

Venturing Out

7

I went back to the house and helped Sarah fix breakfast. The moment I got a whiff of cooking food, my stomach let out a loud grumble. It wouldn't surprise me if people heard it in the middle of town.

Startled, Sarah looked up from the range. "My goodness. You must be ready to eat."

No kidding. The beast of hunger was on the loose. Maybe it had something to do with the fact I hadn't eaten in about two days. Fortunately, the food was ready in a few minutes.

Matthew sat across from me. He reminded me so much of Daddy, I missed him more than ever. But at the same time, the likeness comforted me in a weird way. And Matthew seemed super sweet, so he'd won my heart already.

Uncle Charlie folded his paper and drank his coffee before pushing back from the table. "Katie, I want you to mind Sarah while I'm gone. As far as I'm concerned, she's in charge when I'm not here."

Great, all I needed. One more person to boss me around.

"I'll see you when I get home." He placed his hand on the doorknob. "Maybe after we finish this part of the job, we can spend some time together and get to know each other better."

As I helped Sarah clear the breakfast things, I wondered why she lived with Uncle Charlie instead of her own family. I'd never find out if I didn't ask. "Sarah? How long have you lived here?"

"Let me see, thirteen years I think." Her forehead wrinkled as she concentrated. "I moved in when I was ten." She paused as if to say more, then pursed her lips and gave a slight shake of her head. "Why do you want to know?"

I'm nosy. She didn't seem upset by the question, but I turned away and shrugged. "No reason."

Sarah pulled a black apron over her head. "Be a sweetie and vacuum for me. It's in the entry closet."

While I vacuumed, Sarah dusted the cabinets and scrubbed the counters.

After a while, she motioned for me to turn it off. "Go ahead and put the vacuum away. It's almost time for me to leave for work."

She stopped for a moment and gazed at me.

I checked to see whether I'd spilled anything on my pants or blouse but didn't find any spots.

She tapped a finger against her upper lip. "Before we go, I want to fix your hair."

I let my hair hang wild and free all day. "What're you gonna do?" I couldn't keep the suspicious tone out of my voice.

Sarah narrowed her eyes as she studied me. "Braid it."

That shouldn't be too bad. "Okay, but I don't want anything prissy."

She braided it straight down the middle of my head. I'd've pulled it into a ponytail and then braided it. Bits of hair might stick out every which way, but it would've been tied back.

When she finished, she frowned, then grabbed a barstool from under the sideboard and brought it over. "Sit there. I'll be right back."

Not wanting to sit, I wandered over to the fireplace. Framed pictures filled the mantle. Several of the photos were old. Some of the uncles I'd never met, grandparents who died before I was born, Matthew and Mark as little boys. All kinds. In the middle, tucked behind some others, stood a picture of Daddy and his brothers outside of their house. He must have been about six, the shortest of the bunch with his front tooth missing.

Sarah strode back in. "Come and sit down."

I turned around and stopped. She carried a pair of scissors. "What are those for?"

She held them up, blades open. "Your bangs are too long."

Oh no. "They are not." Daddy and I had argued more times than there were stars in the sky about my bangs being too long. Except he hadn't said a word about them all summer.

She snipped the air with the scissors. "I can't see your eyes, so I'm going to give them a trim."

I brushed them back. "They just fell in my face for a minute."

Sarah arched an eyebrow. "And they stay there most of the time. You need to sit on the stool so I can cut them."

Ugh. How could I get out of this? I hated the feel of cold scissors against my forehead. And the sound of them sent shivers up my spine. Plus, little hairs got into my eyes afterward, fell down my top, and made me itch. "I don't want them cut. I'm growing them out." *How lame.* But in that moment, my mind had gone blank.

Sarah put the scissors on the table and gazed at me in an unruffled manner. "All right. Let's get a barrette and clip them back so they won't fall in your face anymore."

"Barrette?" I practically squeaked. How awful. Barrettes caused my hair to stick out from the side of my head. I'd look like I was about four years old. But she was right. They were completely out of control, and they were starting to bug me. Maybe I could let her trim them a teeny tiny bit. I shuffled over and sat. "Only trim them as far as my eyebrows. I don't want them any higher."

Sarah giggled. "You looked like you were walking the plank." She combed the hair forward over my eyes and made the first cut.

I jumped to my feet.

Sarah put her hand on my shoulder. "Sit down or they'll end up crooked."

"But you're cutting them too high." I sounded like a whiny brat. I'd never been a whiner before.

She pushed me onto the stool. "Since I've started, I have to finish. They'll be fine."

She had a point. Walking around with one chunk cut out would be disastrous. "You did that on purpose. If I don't let you cut the rest short, I'll look stupid."

She adjusted the angle of my head. "I can't finish until you settle down, so quit grumbling."

The damage was done so it was useless to argue.

"As soon as I'm finished, we'll go into town. I work at the gift shop next to the post office this morning from nine to one." As she talked, the scissors mercilessly continued across my forehead. "It'll be all right for you to come with me, and it'll give you a chance to meet some new people. Then we'll run some errands before we come back here."

Sarah stood back and gave me a critical once over. She smiled. "You sure are a pretty thing."

"Me? You're the one who's pretty." I wasn't ugly, but certainly not beautiful like Sarah. When she smiled, the whole room lit up. I felt like ground hamburger next to her.

"See for yourself." She nodded toward the mirror over the mantle.

When I peeked, I couldn't believe the difference, but made a face at the mirror. "Oh no." I put as much agony in the two words as possible. I wanted to get Sarah back for cutting my bangs shorter than I wanted. "I hope they grow back soon."

With my hair pulled back from my face instead of hiding it, I was almost pretty. As I sneaked another look in the mirror, my blue eyes sparkled. There might be a chance I had inherited some of the family's good looks after all.

Sarah smirked. "I can see I'm going to have to keep an eye on you with the boys. They'll be falling right and left over you." She didn't seem at all upset I didn't like what she'd done. "If you can pull yourself away from the mirror, we have to go, or I'll be late."

I'd let her see right through me. So much for pretending I looked awful.

It took less than ten minutes to get to town. Good. If I had a bicycle, I'd be able to get to and from town easily. I didn't want to rely on anyone for anything.

When we arrived at the shop, Sarah introduced me to her friend and boss, Mrs. Dunn. Tall and lean, she had gray hair, grayish skin, and everything about her seemed drab and faded. I felt uncomfortable being introduced. I didn't know what to say, or what was expected of me. So, after an awkward pause, I turned away and pretended to be interested in decorative spoons.

Mrs. Dunn soon went back to her office, and Sarah took out some books and marked items with a pricing gun. It didn't take long to pore over everything in the small shop. It had all sorts of knickknacks, cups, stationery, and little gift items. I wanted to get out and see the town, not stay cooped up inside.

I walked over to the counter. "Is it all right if I go out and look around town?"

Sarah shook her head. "No. I don't want you to go out alone." She kept her eyes on the three-ring binder in front of her.

I shoved my hands in my pockets. "Why not? I'm old enough to take care of myself." I wanted to see what there was around this place. "And I won't get lost."

She switched her attention from the book to a figurine, then flipped through some pages. "I'm sure you're old enough, but you don't know your way around. And I want to know where you are. Please don't argue. We'll be out of here soon enough."

I spun around and stomped off. "All I wanted was to go outside, but noooo ..." I said the words under my breath.

"What did you say?" Her voice had an edge to it.

"Nothing." I had no problem making my voice sullen and bad tempered. She treated me like a baby, and it made me mad. After all, she said I'd be able to meet people. At home, I could have gone out instead of being held captive for half the day. If I'd known I'd be a prisoner, I'd have brought one of my books. I plodded toward the back of the shop.

"Stop right there and turn around." There was a new demanding tone in her voice.

I stopped and kicked my foot against the hardwood floor. Who was she to be ordering me around anyway?

"I said, turn around. Now." Her angry tone blistered the air.

I slowly turned but couldn't make my eyes meet hers.

Sarah drummed a pencil against the counter. "I want to know what you said, and I expect an answer."

Snapping my head up, I glared straight into her green eyes. "I answered you."

Her jaw set, and her chin jutted out. "*Nothing* is not an answer. You said something and I want to know what."

I hadn't said anything I couldn't repeat, but she couldn't make me talk.

Sarah crossed her arms. "I'm waiting."

I pressed my lips tighter together. She'd be waiting for a long time.

Mrs. Dunn came down the hall. "Sarah, I've had the most wonderful idea." She bustled into the room. "I called Denton Junior, and he's on his way here to show Katie around town. I thought it'd be a shame to keep her inside on a day like today."

Hallelujah. I never thought I'd be so thankful to a woman who looked like an old gray sheep for butting into my business. Since she'd already called Denton Junior, I didn't see how Sarah could turn down the offer without seeming rude.

Sarah swallowed her anger and forced a smile before answering. "Thank you, Harriet. It was so nice of you to think of Katie, and she'll enjoy it. Won't you, Katie?"

"Yes. Thanks ... I appreciate it, Mrs. Dunn." I shifted my weight from one foot to the other. *What else could I say?* "It's a great idea."

Sarah kept looking at me like she wanted more.

Mrs. Dunn clasped her hands together and smiled. "I'm so glad. Junior should be here in a few minutes." She bustled back to her office.

Now I had to get back on Sarah's good side and not make her angry before I left. If I did anything to upset her, she'd keep me from going. "Thanks, Sarah."

She flung me a sharp look. "I only agreed to make Harriet happy."

She was going to make it difficult. Maybe I should apologize for my earlier attitude, but she'd made me so mad. "I know. I'm still glad you said yes." I glanced at the counter. "I'm sorry about earlier."

She still wasn't happy. Well, I'd done my part. If she wanted to be a grouch, that was her business. At least she'd forgotten about grilling me.

Sarah's eyebrows drew together, and she gazed at me intently. "Katie, I want you to be on your best behavior with Denton Junior." She fingered her infinity heart pendant.

There she went, treating me like a baby again. What did she think I'd do?

"Do you understand?" She flipped a lock of her dark auburn hair over her shoulder.

"Yes." Why couldn't she trust me? I stared at the floor.

"Katie, look at me." She kept her voice low, but there was an urgency to her tone.

I gave a sideways glance in her direction.

She looked straight into my eyes. "My reason for asking you to be on your best behavior isn't because I don't trust you, but who you're going with."

Propping my elbows on the counter, I waited for Sarah to continue. This sounded interesting.

She leaned forward. "Denton Junior isn't someone I'd normally like you to spend time with—especially alone."

A little nugget to tuck away for the future if I needed to come up with a way to upset Sarah. "Why not?"

She rapidly wiggled the pencil between her thumb and forefinger before piercing me with a stare. "He's liable to say some mean things to you or play some kind of a trick. Despite what he says or does, I want you to be nice in return. Remember, you are a McCabe."

Remember? No one ever let me forget.

She put a hand on her hip. "And no smoking or drinking while you're gone, either."

"You know about that?" I was sunk. They'd never trust me if they'd heard about the shed and the flask. I stuffed my hands in my pockets and stomped over to the jewelry-box display. Why had Daddy said anything? It'd be like being in prison for a year.

I pretended to be interested in a carved wooden box, while staring out the window trying to catch a glimpse of Denton before he arrived.

I spotted a person down the street coming toward the shop. As he drew near, the figure became a short, pudgy boy about my age. It must be Denton. He wore rumpled dark blue slacks, a half untucked white shirt, and dirty tennis shoes with untied laces flopping on the ground. As he turned to come in the door, a lock of frizzy brown hair fell into his eyes, and I noticed beads of sweat across his freckled nose and upper lip.

I hoped his personality turned out to be better than his looks.

The Banker's Son

8

Denton swung the door open and stepped into the shop. "Hey, Sarah. Where's this girl I'm supposed to show around?" His voice had the skittery sound of being between a boy's and a man's.

Sarah motioned toward the door. "Katie, come on over."

I set the jewelry box back on the shelf and gave a weak smile as I walked toward them. After all, it might be fun.

"This is Denton Dunn, Junior." She clasped her elbow and gazed at me through anxious eyes. "You have a good time looking around but be back before one."

Once outside, I spun back to wave and give Sarah a smile. She stood at the window as if to watch us out of sight. Though still morning, the heat made nearly invisible waves rise from the street. As soon as we walked outside, some sweat beads on Denton's face merged and trickled down his cheek.

"Where are we going?" Just being outside made my heart skip a beat in anticipation of new experiences.

He smoothed back his hair, which had fallen into his eyes. "I thought I'd take you to see my old man first." His wide, flat lips made him look like a smug toad wearing a frizzy, brown wig. "He owns the bank, and everything else in town."

Was I supposed to be impressed? Like his father owning things made *him* important. Maybe Denton was, but he sounded like a weasel to me.

As we stepped off the curb, I marveled at how big and wide the streets were compared to back home.

"Well, Katie McCabe, how do you like it here so far?" Denton wiped an arm across his forehead.

The question startled me. I didn't care about the town. "I guess it's all right. I haven't given it much thought." More than anything, I wanted to go home. "And I go by Katie. You don't have to tack on the last name."

A weird expression passed over his face, like he meant to get under my skin and succeeded. "Sure."

We'd arrived at the bank. When Denton opened the door, a blast of cold air gushed out. Denton walked coolly past the front desk and straight back to the executive office. Even there he went in without knocking, almost as if he owned the bank instead of his father.

Denton strode across the plush carpet toward the huge desk at the rear of the room. "Dad, I brought Katie McCabe to meet you." He plopped into a chair and sat with his legs splayed in front of him. Then propped his head on a fist, as if bored.

Mr. Dunn had grisly, graying hair, and he wore a suit with wide lapels and a string tie. Not exactly the male fashion statement of the century.

"How do you do?" He stood and held out his hand.

He wasn't tall, but thin and wiry. He had a strong, aggressive handshake, which hurt a bit. "Fine, thank you, Mr. Dunn." In my mind, I couldn't put him and Mrs. Dunn together. She reminded me of an old-fashioned schoolmarm, and he had all the qualities of a shady used-car salesman. How did people trust him with their money?

"Call me DL. Everybody around here does." He smiled, but it never reached his eyes. "Now which of the McCabe boys is your daddy?" He leaned back in his chair as if getting ready for a long chat.

"Ron McCabe."

His eyebrows rose. "Little Ron? What's he up to now?"

Little? Daddy was a big man. A lot bigger than Mr. Dunn, anyway. "He's a sheriff."

He picked up a pen and tapped it against his hand. "An upholder of the law. Exactly what you'd expect a McCabe boy to be."

I didn't know how to respond. Denton didn't help matters either. I felt him staring at the back of my head, and it made me uncomfortable. My shoulders twitched.

"An elected official. There's something to think about. I didn't know he had those aspirations." DL pursed his lips, and his mustache wiggled like a caterpillar crawling across his face. "Come to think of it, I do remember Ron going into law enforcement. I was surprised he didn't go into the force here."

Something didn't make sense. Daddy *had* worked on the force here until Mama died when I was a baby. Mr. Dunn had to know.

DL smoothed his mustache. "He left a long time ago and hasn't been back since."

He must know why Daddy left. Why was he pretending he didn't know about it? He'd better not say anything about Mama. I wasn't sure how I'd handle hearing about her from a total stranger.

"I'd like to see him again." He narrowed his eyes. "I've known your daddy since he was born. Did he come with you?"

I shook my head. At least that explained why he called Daddy *little Ron.*

"I expect he told you he grew up in these parts." DL opened a drawer and pulled out a polished wooden box and set it on his desk. "Your uncle and I were boys together."

I could imagine a younger Uncle Charlie, but not this man. He had the look of being born old, wearing an ugly suit.

"I remember Ron always tagging along after Charlie, trying to be like him." DL popped his chair upright. "Enough talk of the past. I hear Junior is giving you a tour of the town, and I'm sure you want to get on with it." He chuckled. "And I'm sure Junior is eager to be seen taking a pretty girl like you around town."

His nose wrinkled in distaste, Denton rolled out of the chair. My stomach twisted. The things grown-ups thought and had the nerve to say.

"Get along now and have fun." DL opened the box and took out a cigar.

I backed toward the door, happy to leave before he lit the stinky thing up. "Nice to have met you, Mr. Dunn—I mean DL. Bye, now."

I tripped on the doorjamb.

As we walked out of the bank, Denton smirked. "Where do you wanna go now?"

"You're asking me? I'm the new one here." Hanging out with Denton was like pulling teeth.

He shrugged. "Well, there's not much to see."

Terrific. We'd waste my precious freedom standing on the curb waiting for Denton to decide where to go.

"I don't feel like going on a tour of my old man's grocery store or his barbershop and his movie house isn't open yet." He paused to wipe more sweat off his forehead.

Trying to impress me with what his father owned? Again? It was getting old.

Lowering his eyelids to half-mast, Denton scuffed his toe against the ground. "I guess we could go to the park and see who's around. Afterward, we'll go by Dad's malt shop and ask Max to fix us something."

I gave Denton a hard stare. "Is there anything your dad doesn't own?"

His face went blank for a moment. "He doesn't own your uncle's construction company or his farm." The smug expression returned. "But that's about it."

As we approached the park, the sun glinted off a lake in the distance. The shade from the trees at the edge enticed me ... anything to get out of the heat. Going for a swim would be heaven, but not without a bathing suit.

Three guys played football on a flat patch of grass near the shore. The game looked friendly, and I wanted to go closer and ask whether I could catch a pass or two, since I couldn't go in the water.

Denton should introduce me. After all, meeting new people was one of the things we were supposed to be doing. And since his dad owned everything, according to Denton, then he must know everyone in town.

Instead, he stopped beneath a big shade tree near the lakefront.

"Your uncle is the only one of the McCabe brothers my dad hasn't been able to run out of town so far." Denton slouched against the trunk, and shoved his hands in his pockets, making him look more like a toad than ever. "And your uncle is such a coward, he hides out at his old farm most of the time."

Why would Denton say such bad things about my uncle? I didn't know Uncle Charlie well, but he seemed like a fighter. And from the way Daddy talked about him, he wouldn't run away from things like a coward.

A glint appeared in Denton's mud-colored eyes. "My old man ran your daddy out of town and didn't break a sweat."

What on earth was he talking about? Daddy left after he'd applied for a deputy position working for a small county hundreds of miles away—he hadn't wanted to live in a place with constant reminders of Mama.

"My dad has said over and over how Ron was the weakest of the McCabe brothers." He simpered as he waited for my reaction.

"You can stop right there, Denton Dunn, Junior. I don't have to listen to you say bad things about my family." I tromped toward the football players. No one could say anything against Daddy. To me, anyway. I had to get away from him.

"Katie. Wait." His feet pounded on the grass as he ran after me.

I didn't stop but slowed my steps. Maybe he wanted to apologize.

He caught up and walked beside me, puffing from lack of breath. "Where are you going in such a hurry?"

Anywhere away from him. I stopped and faced him. We'd almost reached the guys playing football, so I tried to keep my voice low and under control. I wanted to scream at him but didn't want to make a fool of myself in front of total strangers. "You've got no right to be saying things about my daddy or my uncle. They're both good men." I glared straight into his eyes. "From now on, if you have something bad to say about my family, don't say it around me."

"Oh yeah?" Denton put his hands on his hips and sneered at me. "What'll you do?"

"Probably punch you." My hand itched. I wanted to hit him so bad it hurt.

Denton laughed. "I'd like to see you try. You'll be sorry for even thinking about it."

My hand formed into a fist, but I remembered what Sarah had said about being nice to Denton. How could she honestly expect me to be nice to such a creep? But I think she'd meant it.

"Don't push me to it." My anger had reached a boiling point, so I concentrated on the guys playing ball. The football arced through the air in a perfect spiral while one of the guys ran full-out to catch it.

Denton's lip curled. "Such tough words."

The jeering tone of his voice made me grit my teeth.

"But then you're weak like your daddy." He put his pudgy, sweaty arm around my shoulder and hissed in my ear. "Only cowards run away. He's such a wuss."

My skin crawled at his touch and the warmth of his breath oozed into my ear. Gross. I suppressed a shudder. "How would you know? You hadn't even given up your pacifier when we left town."

Denton ignored me. "He stopped working and spent every night crying into his beer." He paused and put his mouth so close to my ear his slimy, toad lips brushed it. "Sounds pretty weak to me."

I shrugged his arm off, gave him a light shove, and stepped away. Then my anger got the better of me. I spun quickly back around and hit him—hard.

He walked right into it and went down flat.

I hit him so hard I had to shake my hand out to loosen it. The guys who'd been playing football cheered.

My heart sank. I'd made a big mistake.

I reached down to give Denton a hand. He slapped it away.

I thrust my hand toward him again. "Come on, Denton, get up."

He pulled himself to a sitting position and rubbed his jaw.

"Hey, slugger. Why don't you hit him again?"

If I'd had to do something stupid, why had I done it in front of an audience? I tried to act like it didn't bother me. "Show's over for today, guys."

Denton crawled to a nearby tree, then stood.

One of the guys walked over and motioned for his friends to stop jeering. "I'd like to shake the hand of the person who finally put Denton Dunn in his place."

How embarrassing. I didn't want to be known as a tomboy or a slugger. "I didn't mean to. He made me mad, and I lost my temper." To make matters worse, the guy was cute. Tall with dark brown hair and gorgeous brown eyes, muscular arms, and he had a kind face.

"I know. You've done what we've all been itching to do for a long time." He smiled a nice, almost shy smile. "My name's Logan Cruz. What's yours?"

"Katie."

Denton stamped back and forth nearby, glaring at me when he caught my eye.

Logan took a step closer. "Katie what?"

Here we went again. I'd say my last name and he'd expect me to fit into the McCabe mold. "Katie McCabe."

His smile broadened, and amusement put a sparkle in his eyes. "Well, Katie, if you're going to stick around town for a while, I'll have to watch out for that McCabe right hook of yours. I hope we'll be seeing a lot of each other."

A warm feeling welled up inside me. "Really?" Maybe I hadn't blown things after all. "I'll be going to school here when it starts."

"Really." Logan moved even closer. "I'd like to show you the town, the school, and a few other places, then we'll finish by going to Max's for a shake."

Denton shoved his way between us. "I'm taking her, Cruz."

I took a step back and fought to keep my lip from curling. Denton had made a bad first impression and things had gone downhill from there—fast. He disgusted me.

Logan scowled. "She doesn't have to stay with you, and I don't think she wants to."

Denton's cold eyes narrowed. "Fine. I'll go back to the shop and explain to Sarah where Katie is." He lowered his brows and wrinkled his nose as he gave Logan a mean frown. Junkyard-dog mean—the only thing missing were fangs.

He wouldn't hesitate to run back to the shop and tattle on me. I had a vision of Sarah tracking me down at Max's and dragging me out the door in front of everyone. I wouldn't live through the embarrassment. If Denton talked to Sarah alone, who knew what he'd say?

He trudged away from us toward the street. My heart raced and a vein throbbed in my neck. I'd have to swallow my pride and call him back. "Denton, don't go yet." I hoped Logan would understand.

He turned, his grin distorted from the swelling of his jaw. A sick feeling twisted the pit of my stomach. Had I hurt him that badly? My hand throbbed and I looked down.

It was swollen. Perfect. Denton's face beat up and the evidence I'd done it marked my hand. "Let's get some ice for your face. It looks terrible."

Denton's mean grin faded, and he shook his head. "I don' wan' anything for it." He spoke slowly, and his words were slurred.

I barely understood what he said. My stomach roiled. "Logan, shouldn't we help him?" I needed backup. I felt like I ought to do *something*, even if I wasn't sorry I'd hit him.

Logan shook his head. "We can't make him do something he doesn't want to do."

But ... the swelling ... the bruising ... I sighed. Logan was right. But how would I keep Denton from rushing back to the store and Logan from leaving at the same time?

Logan put his hand on my shoulder. "Why don't you let him go?"

"I can't. He'll make things worse." I kept my voice low so Denton wouldn't overhear. "My cousin Sarah wouldn't understand."

Logan's buddies tossed the ball back and forth while they waited for him. He gave my shoulder a squeeze. "I know Sarah. She seems like an understanding sort."

I shook my head and bit my lip. "Not with me, she isn't."

Logan cleared his throat. "All right. What do you want to do, then? We can't stand here doing nothing for the rest of the day."

Exactly what I had been trying to figure out. "Why don't you and your friends practice somewhere close by, and I'll get Denton to join me at the edge of the lake. Maybe I can get him to soften up when it's just the two of us."

"Aren't you worried you'll be tempted to push him in?" A smile lit his face. "Don't talk to Denton for too long."

"Don't worry." Who was he kidding? The sooner I got away from the creep, the better.

Friends and Enemies

9

Denton gloated when Logan ran off. "I thought he'd never leave. You don't want to spend too much time with him."

I had to control my temper. Slowly, I took a deep breath. "Can't we try to get along?"

"With that guy?" Denton gave a derisive laugh. "You've got to be crazy. I don't hang around with people like him."

Logan would probably say the same thing about Denton—with more reason. I picked up a stone and skipped it across the lake.

"Denton, I'm sorry I hit you." I practically gagged on the apology.

Denton shrugged and ran a hand over his jaw.

I shuddered to think what would happen when Sarah found out, so I wanted to stay away from the store for as long as possible. "Do you want to go to the malt shop now? An ice-cold drink would do you good."

He shook his head. "Let's wait."

Why did he want to wait? He wasn't going to take me anywhere else, and with his jaw so swollen, he wasn't saying much.

Denton picked up a stone, aimed, and hurled it toward the lake.

Ker-plunk.

Not even one bounce. He snatched up another rock, took more time aiming, then flung it as hard as he could.

Bounce. Splash.

Except the bounce was before it got to the water. The force he put into it changed the angle and even put a divot in the mud at the water's edge. I bit back a laugh.

To my left, the perfect skipping stone lay half hidden in the grass. Round, smooth, and enough weight to carry while spinning. It even had a small, slightly flattened section on one side, which would give it more torque.

Denton grabbed another rock, too big and bulky this time. I waited for him to go through his wind-up process, and as soon as he tossed it, I flicked mine.

His landed with a big splash and sank immediately, while mine skimmed the lake surface, bouncing and sending ripples out with each skip. A perfect throw. I held my breath and counted the skips. Fifteen. A record high for me.

Denton turned his back and made it plain he didn't want to talk to me.

I walked over to a big tree and sat underneath it. I turned my head to watch Logan throw a pass to one of his friends. Logan glanced at me and held his palms toward the sky as if to ask *well?* I shrugged. I had no idea when Denton would talk to me, let alone when he'd want to leave the park.

The sun filtered through the leaves of the tree, and the rays danced gently on my face. I closed my eyes and the tension drained from me. I'd been so keyed up, I wanted nothing more than to sit back and relax for the rest of the day.

After several minutes, a shadow blocked the sun, and I opened my eyes.

Denton stood over me. "Do you want to go out in a boat?"

Going out on the water might be fun, but I didn't want to go with him. I shook my head. "I'd have to check with Sarah first." If Denton had his way, I'd wind up at the bottom of the lake.

"Let's go then." He walked off without waiting for me.

I looked around for Logan, but he and his friends weren't there anymore. As we walked down the street, Denton stayed a few steps ahead of me and as far over to the side as possible. He didn't want to be near me. The feeling was mutual. He didn't like me and made it clear from almost the moment we met. I understood part of it. No guy wants to be knocked down by a girl. He'd deserved it for the things he said about my family. But why had he started the fight to begin with? *Did he think I'd sit back and take it?*

As we passed the bank, Denton picked up his pace. When we got to Max's, he went straight through the door and over to the counter to talk to the man behind it. He kept his voice low, so I couldn't hear what he said.

Someone walked up behind me. I spun on my heels. "Logan." I smiled.

He shoved his hands in his back pockets. "Hey, slugger."

I couldn't get over how good he looked with his T-shirt stretched tight over his chest. "Where did you go? I looked for you and your friends, but you disappeared."

"You weren't having any luck with Denton, so I thought it'd be better if we left and caught up to you here." He stopped speaking and glared over my shoulder.

Denton stood right behind me. "Whaddya wanna eat?"

His breath hit the back of my neck in little puffs. I suppressed a shiver. "Nothing, thanks. I don't have any money with me." It made me self-conscious to admit I didn't have any money, but he might make a big deal out of it if I only ordered water, and I'd be even more embarrassed.

He flicked his head back to get the hair out of his eyes. "I already fixed it with Max, so go ahead and order what you want."

Wow. "Thanks, Denton." Maybe he did have a good side to him. How surprising.

We walked to the counter and sat on the high stools lining it. Logan's friends came in a couple of minutes later and joined us.

Logan touched my arm. "Katie, I'd like you to meet my friends, Mike and Pete."

Mike reminded me of a big huggable teddy bear with sandy-brown, shaggy hair, and a crooked smile. Pete gave me a shy grin. He was the shortest of the three, but even he stood taller than Denton. His glasses magnified his brown eyes, and he had short dark hair parted neatly on the side.

Mike leaned against the counter. "Are you here for a visit, or are you moving here?"

I avoided looking him in the eye. *I'd rather walk naked down Main Street than spend another minute in this town.* But I had to say something. "I guess I'm moving here. I'll be living with my uncle during the school year."

"Great. We'll all be at the same school then." Mike raised his soda as if in a toast.

My insides squirmed. They must have thought I was in high school. Max brought my chocolate malt over, and I took a sip, so I didn't have to say anything.

Mike slapped Logan's shoulder. "I'm a junior, and Logan and Pete are sophomores."

I'd guessed they were older than me.

"What class will you be?" Mike did a drumroll with his fingers on the counter, waiting for my response.

"I'll be at the middle school." I cringed inside, waiting for them to decide I was too young to hang out with.

"The campuses are right next to each other." Logan winked. "So don't worry, we'll see you during breaks and lunch."

I took a deep breath and braced myself. "What class are you in, Denton?"

He turned his head and refused to answer.

Logan grinned. "Ol' Dent'll be a freshman."

At least we wouldn't have any classes together. "Do you have good teachers?"

All three of the guys shrugged. Mike stopped drinking his soda. "Some are better than others. The same as any other school, I guess."

Max brought over their burgers and fries. Logan picked up his meal and cocked his head toward the tables. "Let's move to a booth."

"Okay." I stood.

Denton stayed on his stool and played with a fry, ignoring the rest of us.

Stuffing down my irritation, I took a deep breath. "Are you coming, Denton?"

He shook his head.

What more could I do? I'd apologized to the weasel, even though he didn't deserve it. I'd tried talking to him and asked him to join us. If he'd rather sit alone and play with his food, then it was up to him.

I slid into the booth. "I'm a little worried about classes starting. This will be the first time I've ever gone to a new school, and I'm sure it's a lot bigger than my old one. Plus, I don't know anyone."

Logan sat next to me. "Hey, you know us. We'll take care of you."

Mike laughed. "Anyone who has a right jab like her doesn't need to be taken care of. She can do it herself." He stopped laughing and a serious expression crossed his face. "Maybe I should get you to be my bodyguard."

Heat spread to my cheeks. I'd blown it with that punch.

Logan reached across the table and lightly slapped the back of Mike's head. "Come on, Mike, give the girl a break." Lowering his voice, he leaned forward. "All of us have wanted to do the same to Denton at one time or another. She beat us to it."

Pete offered me some of his fries. "We'll be glad to be your protectors, Katie." He gave me a self-conscious smile.

I raised my glass. "You'll be my Musketeers."

After I finished my malt, I checked my watch. I had ten minutes to get back to the shop. But where was Denton? "I'll see you later. Gotta find my way back."

Logan got up when I did and walked to the door.

When we reached the doorsill, a plate banged on the counter, making me jump. I whipped my head around.

"Hey. Where do you think you're going?" Max, his face contorted in a frown, leaned forward, fists bunched on the countertop. "You can't leave until you pay for the food."

I swallowed hard. "Pay for it?" Logan had paid when he'd ordered, so this must be Denton's petty way of getting back at me for having hit him. "Denton told me he'd take care of it."

His frown deepened. "He told me you'd be paying the bill for both of you."

He'd stuck me for both bills? *The snake.*

Logan reached for his wallet. "How much is it?"

Max tilted his head. "Gimme five bucks and we'll call it even."

I couldn't get over how sweet Logan was. I'd even the score with Denton for this stunt. "Thanks, Logan. I'll pay you back as soon as I can." I'd no idea when. Every cent I owned had gone to Mr. Pickford to pay for burning down his shed and I didn't have a job.

He held the door open for me. "It's my treat."

My cheeks heated and I curled my toes as I tried to hide my embarrassment. "Looks like you get to be a Musketeer for me already. Still, you shouldn't have to pay for Denton too."

Logan waved his hand. "Don't worry about it."

I curled my lip and gave a short laugh. "If you won't let me pay you back, I'll have to tell you how I extract my revenge."

Logan grinned. "I'm sure it'll be an entertaining story." He cleared his throat. "We're having football practice tomorrow morning. Will you come and cheer us on?"

I didn't know if I'd be in town. "If I can, I'll be there."

"Great." He beamed.

I had a feeling Sarah would be keeping tabs on me, so I wanted her to like Logan. Hopefully then I'd be able to see him as often as I wanted. "Would you like to walk me back to the shop?" Tilting my head, I grinned at him. "Then you can explain how Denton stranded me and you showed me the way back." He'd make a good impression on Sarah.

The perfect plan, except before we got to the shop, Denton walked out from a side street two blocks ahead.

He glared at Logan. "Come on, Katie, you'll be late if we don't hurry."

I frowned. "Forget it."

Denton shrugged and turned away. "It's your funeral."

I kept forgetting he could say anything once he walked through the door. I couldn't let him have a head start. "Denton, wait." I had to yell for him to hear me.

"Let him go." Logan put his hand on my shoulder.

"I can't." This was so hard. I wanted to stay with Logan. "Denton can't get the jump on me. Especially since I hit him, I can't trust anything he might say."

Disappointment covered Logan's face. "I'm sorry. I forgot about the fight." He shook his head. "Besides, you can trust Denton about as far as you can throw him while he carried a bag of wet cement. Even before you knocked him flat."

"Are you coming or what?" Denton hadn't budged an inch from where he'd stopped.

I grimaced. "I gotta go. Thanks for everything, Logan. I'll see you around."

He smiled. "You can count on it."

I jogged down the street until I reached Denton. "What a mean, rotten, low-down, jerk of a trick you played on me back there." I paused to catch my breath.

He gave me a fake innocent look. "Me? You were the one talking to those other guys, and I figured if they had your attention, they could pay for your food."

"Liar." My anger rose. "You told Max I'd pick up the tab for both of us after you made sure I didn't have any money." I swallowed hard so I wouldn't lose my temper. "You're not only cheap, you're disgusting."

He smirked and shrugged. "So? What're you gonna do about it?"

I knew what I'd like to do. Pound him into the pavement until he was nothing more than a greasy spot.

He curled his lip into a sneer. "We'd better go in or you'll be late."

I'd already be in trouble for hitting Denton—what difference would it make if I got in a little more for walking in the door late?

Sarah had her back to us as we entered the shop. "It's about time, you two. I'll be with you in a minute." When she turned around, the smile of greeting quickly faded from her face and her hand flew to her mouth. "My goodness, Denton, what happened to your face?"

Now I'd get it. Denton pulled himself as tall as he could, which was a losing battle, to bluster his way through the story of what had happened. "Some guys down by the lake started picking on Katie, and I tried to stop them."

What? I couldn't believe my ears.

He tilted his chin up. "There were three of them, and they started by making rude remarks. Then things got worse."

Worse? My eyebrows rose.

Denton stared unwaveringly into Sarah's eyes. "One stroked her hair, even though she told him to stop and tried to walk away. Then another of the guys caught her and forced her to hug him. She struggled to get away, so I grabbed one of their arms and then they all got mad."

I stumbled back a step. How could he lie so convincingly? He didn't even blink.

Denton screwed his face up like he was in pain and let his lower lip quiver. "One of them held my arms behind my back while the other two hit me."

Aghast, I stared at Denton. Sarah looked horrified.

He put a hitch in his voice. "Katie screamed, so they let go of me and ran off."

I still couldn't believe it. I'd expected him to say right out I hit him, then sit back and watch me squirm.

"How awful." Sarah inspected his jaw. "Go on back to the office and let your mother take care of you. If she needs me to, I'll stay until she's had a chance to ice it to get the swelling down."

He looked away and gave a shake of his head. "No, you go ahead. I'll be all right."

Sarah pressed a hand to her throat and laid the other on my shoulder. "Katie, are you okay?"

She believed Denton? Even though she'd warned me against him? "Yeah. I'm fine." Maybe I was off the hook after all.

She searched my face. "Did you get the names of the boys who did this?"

Shocked by Denton's performance and outlandish lies, I couldn't speak.

But Denton stuck the knife in and twisted it. "I'm not sure, but I think it was Logan Cruz and his buddies."

My jaw dropped. What a filthy, rotten, lying scumbag. No word I could think of was bad enough for Denton.

"Logan?" Sarah's hand slipped off my shoulder. "That doesn't sound like him at all. He's always been a nice, polite boy. I taught him in Sunday School, for goodness' sake."

Denton tried to give her a world-wise expression, but the swelling caused his face to twist into a grimace. "You'd be surprised how much he's changed now he's on the football squad. He thinks he can do anything he wants because he might be the starting JV quarterback this year."

Sarah put her arm across my shoulders and gave me a quick squeeze. "I'm so sorry something like this had to happen on your first day in town. Uncle Charlie will be so upset. I wouldn't be surprised if he talks to Logan's parents."

Things kept getting worse and worse. "I'm fine. Really." I barely stammered the words out.

She patted my back. "We'll talk about it later. I can't thank you enough, Denton, for looking after Katie for us."

I was at a complete and total loss of how to start fixing this whole mess. If I'd called Denton out on his lie right at the beginning, it would've been better, but I couldn't get the words out. I didn't even know what to say. And then the little creep had thrown Logan and his friends—who had been perfect gentlemen, unlike the slimy Denton—into the mix, and the whole thing spiraled out of control.

For once in my life, I wasn't getting into trouble for something I'd done wrong, but this was even worse. Daddy would've taken one look at Denton's swollen lip and known I'd hit him.

Confession

10

After doing some errands in town and a little grocery shopping, Sarah and I returned to the farm. I helped put the groceries away, and Sarah planned to study, so I had a bit of free time. Maybe I'd be able to come up with a solution to undo the mess Denton had created. Preferably one that didn't involve a full confession on my part. Logan shouldn't get into trouble because Denton told such a despicable lie. I wouldn't be able to live with myself if I allowed it to happen.

Sarah pulled a textbook out of her book bag and put it on the table.

I gathered my courage and sat across from her. "Is it okay if I call Daddy?" If I talked to him, he'd help me straighten things out. He'd be upset, but he'd at least listen.

Her eyes grew sad. "I wish you could, honey, but he's in the hospital having tests done and won't be able to talk to you until later. He promised to call when he's done."

Oh, yeah. I'd forgotten he'd be having tests. I felt so cut off from him. Elbow on the table, I plopped my head on my fist and my hair fell across my face.

Sarah reached out and tucked a lock behind my ear. "We'll try giving him a call after supper. His tests should be over by then."

"Okay." The few hours' wait would seem like forever and I shouldn't bother Daddy with this while he was in the hospital. I wanted to explain the situation, but as Sarah scribbled notes on her pad, I didn't know how to start.

Maybe I should talk to Uncle Charlie instead. He hadn't heard Denton's lies, so it might be a little easier to explain. Or not. "Do you mind if I go for a walk around the farm?"

She shook her head. "Be back in time for supper."

Uncle Charlie had a lot of land attached to the farm, quite a few animals, a pasture for grazing, and a garden where the family grew their own food ... most of it, anyway. I walked past the pasture gates and into the woods surrounding the property. Stepping onto a path through the trees, a sense of peace settled over me. Here I could be myself without anyone to pester or bother me.

After hiking through the woods a ways, I came to a little clearing. The stream running through the property bordered the clearing on one side and reminded me of my special place at home. Tommy and I went there when we had things to discuss or trouble to run from. It was a good place to think.

I sat and leaned up against a tree trunk. Why had Denton told such a twisted and evil lie? It didn't make sense. If he wanted to see me squirm, why hadn't he told Sarah I'd punched him?

I don't know what I'd have done if he'd said straight-out I'd hit him. Maybe tried to explain and make excuses. But when he lied ... it shocked me so much, I didn't know what to say. He made himself sound like some kind of mini hero, and in reality, he was the complete opposite.

Why blame Logan? If they had a bad history, it'd be Denton's fault. Logan wouldn't start anything.

I closed my eyes for a moment and brought his face to mind. I liked Logan. It'd been sweet of him to pick up the tab on the spur of the moment. Not everyone would've been so nice, especially when it wasn't only for me, but for the wormlike Denton too.

It made me sick to think Logan had been accused of assaulting me. I'd die if he ever found out I stayed silent after Denton lied. I had to get Denton back using some sort of painful method of revenge. The little rat deserved it.

I'd think of something. I always did.

My name floated to me from a distance, breaking through my musings. I gave a start and sat upright. How long had I been away from the house? Brushing the dirt and tree leaves off my pants, I hurried back. As I jogged along, my name was called out again.

I'd better answer. "Coming."

Sarah stood by the kitchen garden with her hands on her hips, waiting for me to get closer. "Where did you disappear to?"

I shrugged. "I went exploring."

She put her arm across my shoulder. "Rambling around the property is fine, but I need your help in the kitchen now, so go in and get washed up."

I pretended to grumble. "Work, work, work, that's all you want me to do."

She laughed and gave me a slight swat. "Just get washed."

As we were getting supper ready, Sarah kept talking about Denton. "I can't get over the way he stood up for you today. He's finally beginning to grow up." She pressed her lips together and gave her head a shake. "I'm still surprised about Logan though. Never in a million years would I think he'd do something so terrible."

I felt queasy. Over and over, she went on about how wonderful Denton had been and how disturbed she was about Logan. The butterflies in my stomach put on boxing gloves and each flutter packed a punch.

What would Sarah say if she knew the truth?

After supper had been cleared, we settled into chairs to talk about the day—a McCabe family tradition, apparently. I wanted to call Daddy, but Uncle Charlie told me we'd call him later and they'd give me a little privacy.

Uncle Charlie, being the head of the family, began. "We got behind schedule because the concrete didn't set."

Mark jumped up and paced through the middle of the room. "I still think it's the stuff we bought from DL's hardware store." His eyes smoldered. "He must monkey around with it before he sells it. Kind of like watering it down, so he can sell more for less cost to him."

Uncle Charlie frowned. "Mark, I've told you before about making accusations you can't prove. I agree the concrete we bought this last time isn't what it should've been, but we don't know where it got tampered with or who did it."

Mark fumed. "You know he's doing it. He's a crook."

Could Denton be the apple fallen not far from the tree?

Matthew opened his mouth, but Uncle Charlie continued before he got the chance to say anything. "When you can prove it, then we can talk."

Mark scowled and flopped in his chair.

Matthew turned toward Sarah. "How did you and Katie get along today?"

Oh, no. In trying to smooth things between Mark and Uncle Charlie, Matthew had put me in the hot seat. He hadn't meant to, but ...

"Things were quiet at the shop, but Katie had some excitement." Sarah tilted her head. "Why don't you tell them about it?"

I bit the inside of my lip. If I had to say anything about the heroism of Denton I might gag, but if I let Sarah start, she'd go on and on about it. "It was really nothing."

"Nothing?" She leaned forward and gazed directly into my eyes. "You can't pretend nothing happened. The best way to deal with it is to meet it head-on." She settled back in her chair. "Harriet called Denton Junior and asked him to take Katie on a tour of the town, so she wouldn't have to sit in the shop all day."

Mark sat a little straighter. "You actually let her go with the little weasel?"

My ears perked up—too funny he'd called Denton the same thing I did. It made me feel better knowing Mark didn't like him either.

"I was a little wary at first, but then decided not much could happen in a few hours." Sarah took a sip of tea. "Besides, I didn't want to disappoint Harriet. And Denton showed himself to be a different boy than I thought."

"What do you mean?" Mark sharply rapped out the question.

Sarah pursed her lips. "Believe it or not, Denton came to Katie's rescue today. Some boys were picking on Katie, and from Denton's description, they were getting close to assault, and he stopped them. He even took a blow to the jaw that made it swell horribly. He's going to be sore for quite a few days from it."

Everyone started talking at once.

Matthew raised one eyebrow while the other lowered. "The story sounds a little fishy to me. I didn't think Denton had it in him."

"Who are these boys?" Mark folded his arms and stood. "I'll need to go have a word with them."

Uncle Charlie quietly took part in the conversation, almost as if he were talking to himself. "It goes to show, good can be found in everyone."

Overwhelmed, I couldn't stand it. "Not in him there can't." The words slipped out a little louder than I intended, and everyone stopped talking to stare at me.

Sarah's eyes opened wide. "What do you mean, there isn't any good in him? He defended you."

I took a deep breath. "Things didn't happen exactly the way Denton said they did." I had to do the right thing and it was now or never.

Matthew smirked. "Junior can't be as good as Sarah's painting him."

Sarah continued to press me. "Do you mean he stretched the facts a bit? It's understandable under the circumstances to do a little exaggerating."

Stretched the facts? He never even touched one of them. "Not exactly." I rubbed my forehead. "No one picked on me." Except Denton.

Disbelief covered her face. "Denton got into a fight?"

"Kinda." He definitely started it.

Uncle Charlie set his coffee down. "Katie, I think we'd better have the whole story."

Where do I start? "Denton did get in a fight." The only part of the story he'd told with any truth to it. "Things didn't exactly happen the way he said, though." I raised my eyes toward the ceiling and sighed. "He started the fight, and I finished it."

Total silence ensued while they all stared at me like they couldn't believe their ears.

My shoulders twitched. "While we were down by the lake, Denton insulted Daddy, Uncle Charlie, and the whole family. I tried to ignore it, but when he said things about Mama, it got to be too much." I pressed my lips into a flat line. I couldn't turn back now. "So, I hit him."

Each face was etched in shock.

"You?" Sarah faltered. "You did the damage to Denton's face?" She shook her head. "I don't believe it."

Terrific, tell the truth and no one believes you. "Why would I lie?" Why did I even try to explain? "Do you want me to get some witnesses?"

She closed her eyes for a moment and seemed to be in pain. "How many times did you hit him?"

"Once. I hit him hard, though." I'd made it count.

She gazed intensely into my face. "So, the story of those boys attacking you ...?" Her voice trailed off.

"Never happened." I rapped the words out to hammer them home.

Sarah rubbed her temples. Had I given her a headache?

"I'm having a hard time understanding why Denton would've invented a fake attack on you." She paused. "If you were attacked, you might've felt helpless. And telling us it never happened and you were the aggressor in the situation might give you a sense of control you need right now."

What kind of psychological mumbo jumbo was this? Had she pulled it straight out of her textbook? I jumped up and thrust my fist in front of her. "Look at my hand. How did my knuckles get so swollen?" I marched to the mantle and gripped the edge and tried to regain some control. "Denton is a twisted creep, and he lied."

Inspiration struck me. "He's the one who felt helpless and wanted to make it seem like he wasn't. Who wants to get knocked flat in front of the football team?" Some of them, anyway. "By a girl." Another thought flashed through my mind. "It might be why he invented the attack on me. He saw me making friends with people he's never been able to be friends with, so he put me in a position where I'd have to let him blame my new friends or rat myself out." I turned around to face the family. "I can't stand by and let someone be falsely accused."

Uncle Charlie's jaw tensed. "Katie, on the one hand, I don't like you being involved in a fight." He held up his hand when I opened my mouth. "Violence isn't something I condone, and I don't want it happening again." He leaned forward in his chair. "On the other hand, I'm proud of you for standing up for your friends and telling the truth." He took a sip of coffee. "Sarah, you need to tell Katie what her punishment is for hitting Denton."

"Me?" Her voice rose to a squeak.

Uncle Charlie set the cup down. "You were responsible for Katie when this incident occurred, and she needs to know you have the authority to discipline unacceptable behavior."

Sarah gaped at Uncle Charlie in disbelief.

He raised his shoulders. "If you don't, nothing you say will carry any weight."

Sarah closed her mouth and blinked twice, then took a deep breath and faced me.

Now I'd get it.

"Since you had enough excess energy to hit Denton so hard, we'll have to work on getting rid of it." She raised her eyes to the ceiling while she thought for a moment. "Tomorrow, instead of going into town with me, you'll stay here and clean out the pigsty, then scrub the trough and reslop it."

Disgusting.

She touched her middle finger to her thumb as if ticking things off a list. "Give Günter a bath." Her thumb tapped her ring finger. "Muck out the floor of the chicken coop and put fresh straw down."

How much more could she give me to do?

Sarah gave a short nod. "And scrub the bathroom from floor to ceiling, to my satisfaction."

She made it sound like satisfying her would be about as easy as climbing Mount Kilimanjaro. At least she had come to the end of her list. "Is that all?"

She clenched her jaw. "Yes."

Matthew frowned. "Doesn't Katie have the entrance exam for school in the morning?"

"You're right, I forgot." Sarah tapped her fingers on the chair arm and pinched her lips together. "It's before work, so we'll go in, Katie can take her test, and I'll bring her back here before going in. I scheduled it early so there'd be time to spare."

Great, exactly what I wanted to do. Take a test and then come back and work all day long. Well, not all day. Sarah would expect me to be finished by the time she got back, or close to it.

Uncle Charlie stood. "I'm going to give Ron a call now, so we'll give Katie some privacy."

My heart leaped into my throat. I missed Daddy so much; it was almost more than I could stand.

As Mark passed, he ruffled my hair and the corner of his mouth quirked up. "You're a little firebrand, Kit-Kat." He leaned over and whispered in my ear. "I know something about Junior, and I'm sure he deserved what you dished out, so don't worry too much about it."

Hard Conversation

11

Uncle Charlie held out the phone. "I have your daddy on the line." I took the receiver from Uncle Charlie, and he left the room. "Daddy?"

"How are you doing, Katie?" His voice sounded scratchy and weak. "These tests they're doing are giving me cotton mouth." He sounded a little stronger, but not much.

"I'm doing okay." My stomach dropped and it hit me. He was extremely sick. I couldn't tell him how much I wanted to come home. I had to focus on positive things, so he wouldn't worry about me.

"I've already made some friends." I didn't need to tell him I'd made an enemy as well. "And tomorrow I take the entrance exam for school." What else? My mind raced for positive things to share. "I let Sarah cut my bangs, so they're not in my face anymore." Not willingly, but he didn't need to know that either.

"Tell Sarah my hat's off to her. She got you to do something I couldn't without a fight." His laugh turned into a wracking cough. He took a sip of water to calm the spasm. "I'm glad you called, because we need to talk."

My stomach churned. The last time Daddy had said we needed to talk, he'd sent me away and gone into the hospital. Whatever he had to say—it wasn't good news. "Why don't we wait until your tests are finished and you're feeling better?"

Silence grew from the other end of the phone. The longer it stretched, the more frightened I became. The phone shook against my ear and my fingers hurt from gripping it so hard. *Tick. Tick.* The clock on the mantlepiece measured the passing seconds and set my teeth on edge.

Daddy cleared his throat. "Sometimes we have to face things we don't want to. This is one of those times."

Tears pricked my eyes.

Rustling sounds came through the phone as Daddy shifted. "I wanted us to talk about this face-to-face, but it's best to tell you now." He took another sip of water. "The test results aren't good. The doctors still need to run a few more to determine how far things have spread."

Hot tears ran down my face. I couldn't stop them.

"There's no easy way to say this, Katie." Daddy's voice cracked. "It's cancer."

He waited a moment, but my tears had a stranglehold on my throat.

After a deep breath, he continued. "And it's widespread and terminal."

Noooooo. I opened my mouth, but only a whimper escaped.

Daddy made comforting noises. "I'm going to fight this as hard as I can, so I need you to be strong."

Strong? I felt like I'd been run over by a semi. Completely flattened. My breath hitched in my chest.

A machine beeped in the background, but Daddy ignored it. "As soon as they release me, I'll spend time with you at the farm."

A chill ran through me, and I shivered. I needed him here now. More than anything, I wanted his arms around me, hugging me tight. His hugs had fixed the biggest problems in my life.

Until now.

A door closed and the beeping machine was silenced. Daddy covered the receiver and said something to the person who had entered before continuing. "I'll see you in a few days. I love you very much, Katie."

"I love you too, Daddy. I miss you so much." The words came out in a whisper.

After I hung up, I felt numb. My mind refused to accept that Daddy was dying.

Uncle Charlie came into the room and sat next to me. He didn't say anything but patted my hand and let me cry. I'm glad he didn't try to tell me everything would be okay. I felt like nothing was ever going to be okay again. The silent stream of tears continued to fall.

"He told you?" My voice croaked like a frog.

Uncle Charlie nodded. "I told the others as well." His strong arms encircled me in a tight hug. It wasn't the same as Daddy's. He took a deep breath. "I don't know what to say, other than I'm here if you need me."

I buried my wet face in the front of his shirt, and he held me and patted my back until I stopped crying. Daddy wanted me to be strong for him, so I'd better pull it together and at least try. "Tomorrow's going to be a long day, so I'd better get some sleep." I stood and turned to leave the room.

"Katie."

I stopped and looked back through bleary eyes.

Uncle Charlie swallowed hard, as if he bit back some words. "I know it might be difficult, but try to get some rest."

Somehow, I didn't believe that was what he meant to say when he called me back.

As I entered our room, Sarah looked up from the textbook she pretended to study. She'd been crying, too. I was wrung out emotionally and didn't want to talk … about anything. She seemed to understand without my having to say a word. I grabbed a book. After a day like this one, I needed to escape into a fantasy world, where all the problems weren't mine, and I didn't have to think.

Morning came a little bit easier as I fell into the household routine. Sarah and I had to leave around seven for the entrance exam. Taking a test would give me a reason not to think about anything else. Like Daddy. As if I could forget Daddy for even two seconds.

Mr. Conway, the middle school principal, dressed like an old grandpa, with a cardigan sweater over pants belted two inches too high and a collared shirt complete with bow tie. He wasn't old enough to be one, even though he wore half-glasses on a chain around his neck.

Fussing about a lot of nothing, Mr. Conway checked whether the pencil he'd given me *met the criteria*—his words—for the test. And whether I understood the directions and time limits, what to do when I'd completed the test—the list was endless. I wished he'd leave so I could take the test in peace and get it over with.

I finished early, but Sarah wanted to talk to Mr. Conway about my past school record and what classes would be best for me. I wandered outside to check out the campus. The football field lay in the distance and players were milling around on the grass. Maybe Logan would be there. The coach yelled at the team as I strolled closer.

With helmets masking their faces, it was hard to tell who was gathered at the scrimmage line, but then Mike took his off, shook his hair out, and ran down the line punching shoulder pads to pump up his teammates. They formed a huddle and I finally recognized Logan—the quarterback giving directions.

After executing a pass play, Logan looked at the sidelines where I stood and waved. I grinned and waved madly back. At least I'd been able to make it for part of the practice.

With a whistle blast and the sweep of his arm, the coach called the guys off the field. With a little bit of luck, they'd be taking a break and I might get to talk with Logan.

"Katie." The name floated on the breeze from the administration building.

Darn it. Did Sarah have to call me now? With one last glance at Logan, I broke into a run. Time to go back to the house and pay the price for hitting Denton.

After reminding me of my jobs, Sarah left. It shouldn't be too bad, and if I worked quickly enough, I might gain some time to read or wander the farm. Anything to keep from thinking about Daddy. Why couldn't it all be a bad dream?

Drudgery

12

First, I had to figure out which awful job of the never-ending chore list to do first. I'd deal with the pigs last—after scrubbing the trough, I'd need to shower for self-preservation. And after my shower, I wanted to be done. So going from cleanest to dirtiest job, start with the bathroom, next give Günter a bath, then clean the chicken coop, and finally ... the pigs.

Wiping the sweat from my brow, toilet brush in hand, I paused to blow a strand of hair off my face. Why did cleaning always make you feel gross and sweaty? No one would ever call scrubbing toilets or scouring showers glamorous work. But once I cleaned the mirror and mopped the floor, I'd move on to bigger and better things ... or dirtier and grungier. Whatever.

I pulled the big metal tub Sarah'd shown me from its peg, took it outside the barn and filled it. I grabbed the shampoo from the shelf and set it beside the tub. Now all I needed was the dog to bathe. I didn't know anything about Günter, so I didn't have the slightest clue where to find him. Hopefully, he'd come when I called.

"Günter."

He barked in the distance but didn't come.

I yelled a little louder. "Günter. Come on, boy." *Please come.* I didn't want to chase him.

He crashed through the woods, his paws pounding against the ground. When he got close, I grabbed his collar. He sat and dug his feet into the ground, jerking my arm as I walked toward the tub. "Come on. Get up."

It was like dragging a hundred-pound sack of flour, but that would've been easier. On top of that, he wouldn't stay in the tub. No one told me I'd be in a wrestling match with the dog. He was so big I couldn't stop him from doing anything he wanted.

"Günter, sit." I forced his back end down in the water, then grabbed the shampoo, and lathered him up. But before I rinsed him, he stood, shook the water off, and jumped out of the tub. He stopped long enough to shake himself again, flinging a glob of soap into my eye, and ran toward the woods.

It burned like crazy. My eyes watered so much I felt like I was crying. I turned the hose on my face and forced my eyes open. The water felt good, but my vision was still blurry. Once I could see, I'd find Günter and finish the job.

He came quickly when I called this time. I sprayed Günter with the hose instead of trying to get him back into the tub, then towel-dried him and combed out the tangles. It'd taken longer to bathe him than expected, and I wanted to get all my extra jobs done. If I worked fast, I still might finish early. The chicken coop shouldn't take too long.

Raking out the floor then putting down fresh straw seemed like the best way to get started. As I raked, I imagined all the things I'd like to do to Denton. Thinking about revenge was way better than thinking about what was happening with Daddy.

Hitting Denton again would only get me into more trouble. Besides, slow torture would be the best. Too bad I couldn't trap him in a box and fill it with big, hairy spiders until he begged to be let out. I closed my eyes and visualized him in a glass box while the spiders crawled through a hole in the top. His eyes bugging out ... *bugging out—ha* ... while he avoided the spiders dropping on his head. I snickered. Then the spiders would work together to build a massive web with Denton bound and captive in the center. Sweet.

I opened my eyes and my shoulders drooped. Great daydream, but not practical. I quit leaning on the rake and cleared more straw. Maybe I should find a way to embarrass him in front of his friends— give him a huge dose of his own medicine.

My heart had nearly stopped when Max asked me to pay for the food. If Logan hadn't paid for it, I don't know what I would've done.

Since I was new in town, Max wouldn't have accepted an IOU. And where would I get the money? Sarah? Uncle Charlie? Yeah, *that* would've gone over well.

I raked under the nesting boxes with a vengeance ... all my concentration focused on what I'd do to Denton.

Crack.

The rake hit an old egg and a horrendous smell filled the coop. My eyes watered and my stomach heaved. I rushed outside to get a breath of fresh air.

Great. One more thing to slow me down. It'd been my own carelessness, but still ...

The morning was half over and the worst job still remained. What would happen if I refused to do anything else? What could they do to me?

Oh well, the day had to end sometime. I snatched the rake and went back inside. The smell wasn't quite as bad as earlier, so I finished the raking quickly, mingling the old straw with the gooey sludge of the egg. As I put the fresh straw down, my thoughts went back to Denton. I didn't know enough about him to get him back good. There had to be some way.

The big town picnic was tomorrow. It might be a good place to embarrass Denton. The whole town would be there, so if opportunity knocked, I'd be ready. I'd have to be careful, though. I didn't want to get in trouble this time.

Done with the chicken coop, I moved on to the pigsty. Uncle Charlie kept three pigs. Amazing how much mess so few pigs made. The muddy ground around the trough had become slimy from the food the pigs spilled. The pigs squealed when I climbed into the sty. One ran over and tried to rub against me like it was a puppy. Somehow, I didn't think this was how every girl wanted to spend one of the last days of summer vacation. It sure wasn't my idea of a fun time. But it had to be done.

My plan of attack—scrub the trough first, then pick up the surrounding area. As I approached, the smell nauseated me. Curdled, sour milk á la potato peels, a delicacy fit for pigs. Yuck. After getting up close and personal to the pigs' feast, I wouldn't want to eat supper, let alone touch any lunch.

Curling my lip, I pulled on gloves, held my breath, and emptied the trough into slop buckets. A hungry pig pushed against me trying to get to the trough, making me drop the bucket and slop spilled everywhere, including on me. Disgusting. As I bent to grab the handle, I caught a whiff of my own odor—*peeee yew*, I stunk. Hot water and soap better get rid of the smell, or I might have to stay in the shower forever.

Cleaning out a pigsty should be added as a punishment to one of the circles in Dante's *Inferno.* It took forever and there was no easy way to get the job done. I spent most of the time scrubbing the trough trying to get through layers of muck. Had it even been cleaned in the last five years? I scrubbed until my hand and arm ached. I tried switching hands, but my left lacked scrubbing power.

Rocking back on my heels, I ran my arm across my forehead. My eyes burned from the dripping sweat. I glanced at my feet. My sneakers were probably ruined. I wished I'd remembered to put on galoshes before entering the pen. I shook my hand to get rid of the cramps, then went back to scouring the trough. I lost track of time. Being tortured by pig gunk would do that to a person.

Sarah's truck pulled in the drive. *Darn.* I'd wanted to finish by the time she returned, so she wouldn't be standing over me telling me how to do the job right. I got to my feet to tell her I was almost done. Stepping forward, I accidentally put my sneaker down on a pig.

It jumped and squealed so loud, it sounded like I was killing it.

Splat.

I lost my balance and fell front first into the slimy mud. It splattered my face when I hit the ground, covering me in stinky, gooey, gross sludge. It squished between my fingers as I struggled to my knees. Trying to brush it off my shirt was useless. I was coated from my chest to my feet.

Sarah covered her mouth, but her fingers didn't hide the corners of her grin. "If you do that again, I'll take your picture." She hiked her purse back up on her shoulder. "Maybe I should take it now anyway."

I struggled to my feet. I had a choice—I could either get mad, or I could laugh with her. Getting mad wouldn't change anything. I'd still be covered from head to toe and stinking worse than a skunk in a hot box. "If you do, I'll pull you in here with me. How long since you last mud wrestled?"

Sarah laughed. "I'm sorry. I can't help it. You look like Brer Rabbit's tar baby."

I tromped over to the fence. "Very funny." I grinned. With my slimy finger, I put some goo on her nose.

She pulled her head back before I spread it.

I held up both hands. "What? Don't you want to try a mud pack? It's always in fashion, and it's supposed to be excellent for the skin."

She backed away. "I'm going into the house before we both end up covered in guck. I'll put some clean clothes in the bathroom for you. Use the back door so you don't track dirt all through the house." She studied my feet. "Leave your shoes outside. I'll put a towel by the door. Use it to slide your way down the hall."

After she left, it didn't take long for me to finish. I went around to the back of the house, took off my shoes, and tiptoed into the bathroom. I didn't want to reclean it after working so hard on it. Wrapping my clothes in the towel, I bundled them into the hamper, then turned the shower on as hot as I could stand it. As the water ran over my body, all the jobs I had to do because I'd hit Denton flashed through my mind, followed by the things he'd said and the way he'd said them. Hitting him had been worth every minute—even falling in the pigs' slop.

After getting cleaned up and putting my filthy clothes in the wash, I went for a walk. I needed to be alone and not bothered by anyone. A rock lay in my path, and I kicked it as hard as I could.

I wanted to go home, with Daddy out of the hospital and healthy, and have things back the way they were. At home I had friends, things to do, people who loved me. Here, I had nothing. I didn't fit in. The back of my throat burned like the tears I'd been trying to avoid all day were going to catch up with me.

I ran past the barn, then alongside the pasture fence and out to the creek. I ran until I reached the clearing in the woods. My chest ached and heaved with each short, raspy breath. My heart pounded in my ears and sweat trickled down my forehead. Staring into the distance, I sagged against a tree and slid to the ground.

I missed Daddy. I missed the strength of his arms hugging me, comforting me. Why was this happening? I should've known he was sick, so why hadn't I seen it?

A few rocks were scattered near the base of the tree. I dug one out of the dirt and hurled it into the creek. Angry with Daddy for not telling me sooner ... I grabbed another stone and threw it as far downstream as I could. Angry with myself for not noticing ... I snatched a rock hiding under some leaves and flung it into the water. And most of all, angry with God for making Daddy sick ... I clutched the biggest stone and heaved it with all my might. The splash rose three feet in the air. I got up and tramped through the woods. Homesickness, anger, sadness, and fear fought with the weak glimmer of hope Daddy would recover.

I followed the creek, kicking rocks in my path. Wave after wave of helplessness washed over me, but I chased it away with anger. Feeling helpless made me want to cry and I refused. Crying would mean I'd given up. And I couldn't give up on Daddy.

Rage was better than helplessness.

The sky darkened. *Crap.* How long had I been gone? I turned around and hurried along the creek bank in the waning dusk. The porch light shone in the darkness and Sarah rigidly stood in the doorway, peering into the falling night.

When she saw me coming, the worry lines relaxed, and she released her grip on the door frame. "Where've you been? I've been worried sick about you."

"Walking around." A spurt of anger flared in my gut, and I clenched my jaw so tight my teeth hurt. "Do I have to tell you every little thing?"

I strode past her and into the house. I didn't stop to talk to anyone but kept going until I reached my room and flopped on the bed. I had a difficult time putting into words the way I felt.

Angry, hurt, lonely. Afraid.

A few minutes later, Sarah came in and sat beside me. "Katie, honey, I can tell you're upset about something."

I scowled at her.

"I know you don't want to talk about it. But when you do feel like talking, I'll be ready to listen." She stroked my hair as she spoke. "It's not good to keep things bottled up inside."

I wanted to throw my arms around her and sob. She patted my back and got up to leave.

I grabbed her hand. "Don't go." I didn't want to talk, but I didn't want to be alone either. I wanted someone to hold me but would never ask.

Sarah sat with her back against the headboard. When I moved next to her, she put her arm around me and gave me a squeeze. Then she quietly hummed.

Tears stung my eyelids and I tried to fight them back. One by one, they welled up, flowing over the edge, and made silent, salty tracks on my cheeks. I raised my hand and brushed them away, grateful to Sarah for pretending she didn't notice. She kept humming and stroking my hair, staring at the wall.

I took a deep breath, swallowed hard, and managed to stop the flow. "Sarah? Why doesn't Daddy want me with him? I could sleep in a chair next to his bed."

She turned her head for the first time and gazed into my eyes, pausing before answering. "Honey, your daddy loves you, but the hospital won't allow you to stay with him." She took a deep breath. "You're not here because he doesn't want you."

More tears fell. She'd answered the one question I'd been too afraid to ask. Was he too sick to want me anymore?

She rubbed my arm. "He wants the best for you."

He'd said the same thing right before he put me on the bus. "How am I supposed to know if it's true?" I sobbed. No one had told me why this was supposed to be the best for me. In my mind, the best was to be with Daddy, not to be so very far away.

Sarah leaned away from me for a moment. "How does your daddy feel about the truth?"

The question surprised me so much I regained a little control. "He's a stickler for it." I'd told him a lie once, and he'd made sure there wasn't anything I'd think worth lying about ever again.

She raised her eyebrows. "Well then?"

I glanced away. "He'd tell me the truth." I paused for a moment. "I goofed up big time right before he sent me here. It bothers me I left on such a bad note. I wouldn't tell him goodbye."

Sarah patted my leg. "Sweetie, no matter what you did, it doesn't change your daddy's love for you. It's unconditional. You've had a few very tough days, and there will be more ahead." She cupped my chin and turned my head so our eyes met. "The only thing I can tell you is we will be here for you to help you get through it." She ran a hand down my back, then swung her legs over the edge of the bed. "I saved you some supper. All we have to do is heat it up."

"No, thanks. I'm not hungry." It surprised me she hadn't told me I had to eat. "If you don't need me to clear up or anything, I'll sit here for a while and read."

She stood. "All right. If you need to talk any more, about anything, let me know."

"Sarah?"

She paused at the door and turned.

I gave her a brief smile. "Thanks."

When Sarah left, she didn't shut the door all the way. I grabbed my book and leaned back, settling against my pillow. Opening the pages, I dove into the story, trying to forget the pain in my heart.

Voices from the next room came through the open door, and my ears pricked up at the mention of my name.

Sarah lowered her voice, so I had to strain to hear her. "Uncle

Charlie, we have one very upset girl in the next room."

Great. Now she'd tell all about my crying scene. Just when I'd thought I might be able to trust her.

A chair scraped against the floor before Sarah spoke again. "Katie needs to see Uncle Ronnie."

I put down the book. I had to hear this conversation. But the murmurs coming from the other room frustrated me. After making sure the door didn't squeak, I sneaked into the hallway.

Sarah's voice was much less muffled. "Right now, she's scared, lonely, feeling a little guilty and angry, because she feels like she's lost control of her life."

Sarah seemed to understand my feelings even better than I did. I hoped Uncle Charlie would listen. I could be ready to leave in five minutes.

"Sarah's right, Dad." Mark took my side again. "I'd want to be there if—."

Uncle Charlie interrupted him. "Now hold on a minute."

Uh oh. This wasn't good.

After a moment, he continued, "Ron's tests should be finished tomorrow and then he'll come stay with us."

Tomorrow? I tipped my head back and closed my eyes. I could wait until then. I moved to the side of the hall door and peered toward the living room.

"Even if we took Katie to see him, she wouldn't be able to stay for more than five minutes." Uncle Charlie cleared his throat. "Ron doesn't want Katie to see him in the hospital."

Matthew paced by the mantle. "Dad, don't you think his judgment might be a little off?"

"No, I don't." His tone sharpened. "Ron has always put Katie first, and no matter how sick he is, he always will."

Sarah's voice rose. "But Uncle Ronnie doesn't know how much she's hurting."

They stopped talking for a moment. The only sound was creaking leather as Uncle Charlie shifted in his chair.

"Let me explain something to all of you." Uncle Charlie sounded somber now. "From the time Marie died, Ron's whole life has been wrapped up in Katie. He'd do anything to protect her and spare her from pain. They have as close a relationship as any two people I know, and if she is feeling pain, he knows it and feels it too."

True. Daddy and I had always been very close. Even with my recent restlessness.

The silence in the next room grew except for the scratching of the chairs on the floor as someone moved.

Sarah disrupted the quiet. "I have things to get ready for the picnic tomorrow."

I sped back to my room, grabbed my book, and buried myself in the story. After reading for a while, my eyes refused to stay open. I turned out the light and went to sleep.

Town Picnic

13

I woke up early to get all my chores out of the way. The morning held the promise of a beautiful day. We had the picnic, one of the town's major events, and my new friend Logan might be there. And although I tried not to get my hopes up too high, I might get to see Daddy today.

By the time I returned to the house, Sarah had breakfast started. "I'm glad you're up early. We have a lot to do. I laid a dress out for you."

"Dress? I'm not wearing a dress to a picnic." We weren't going to church, for crying out loud. "I planned to wear jeans."

She tilted her head. "It's a summer dress. You want to look nice, don't you?"

I gave her a deadpan stare. There were other ways to look nice than wearing a dress.

Sarah arched an eyebrow. "You're not going in scruffy jeans."

I frowned. I wasn't wearing a dress either.

Her eyes got a mischievous glint. "But you'll want to wear an outfit that'll make a good impression on the guys at the picnic." She smiled. "We'll check the closet and pick out something we can agree on."

What a relief.

Under Sarah's direction, I gathered baskets, blankets, and anything else we might need. Matthew came out with a clipboard and sat at the table.

I piled the blankets on the breakfast counter, then leaned against it. "What're you doing?"

He tapped the pencil eraser against the paper. "Making the sign-up sheets and schedule for the boat race."

I peered over his shoulder. "What kind of schedule?"

Matthew continued scribbling on the page. "For the heats."

A boat race sounded fun. "Do you have age divisions, or is everybody racing for the best time?"

"There are three age divisions." He turned his head. "How come you're so interested in this?"

I shrugged. "Maybe I'll compete."

A smile crossed his face. "You?" He laughed.

"Why not me?" I didn't think it was funny.

He smirked. "This is a race of strength and stamina."

I rolled my eyes. "Don't be such a chauvinist. Is there any rule that says a girl can't sign up?"

Still chuckling, Matthew scrawled another line on the page. "No, but do you have a partner? Most of the people who are competing are already paired up, so it won't be an easy job to find one. They've been practicing together all summer."

I didn't think I'd have as much trouble as he made out. "If I find someone, can I be in the race?"

"Sure. Don't count on it though." His eyes twinkled.

I lightly punched his shoulder. "Don't be surprised when I enter."

He shrugged. "Suit yourself."

I imagined his surprise when I not only found a partner but won the race. Sweet.

Uncle Charlie came out with a handful of numbered cloth squares and a piece of paper. I peeked around him. He held a map of the park by the lake. "What's the map for, Uncle Charlie?"

"It's for the obstacle course." He folded the map and tucked it under his arm. "I'm going over early and lay it out."

A thrill of excitement ran through me. "Can I go with you?"

He shook his head. "You stay with Sarah and get everything else ready to bring."

Stuck at the house again. This was my chance to meet most of the kids before school started, and I didn't want to waste a moment. "All right." My head drooped.

Uncle Charlie patted my shoulder. "Don't worry. Sarah has to be there early to set up her booth."

I'd almost forgotten. I smiled at him.

"You sure change moods fast, don't you?" He looked around the room. "Isn't Mark up yet?"

"I called him when I got up, but he rolled over and went back to sleep." Matthew turned back to his schedule.

Uncle Charlie briefly frowned. "Katie, why don't you go pound on the door and tell him as soon as we've eaten, Matthew and I are going to leave. With or without him."

I walked along the dark hall toward the back bedroom. Mark nearly knocked me over when he flew out the door, still putting his shirt on.

"Hey, watch where you're going." I rubbed my arm where he ran into me.

He finished tucking in his shirt. "Sorry, Kit-Kat. I didn't know you were there." He grinned. "I'm late. Matthew and I are helping Dad set up."

I nodded. "You'd better hurry."

It seemed like we'd never get everything ready and get out of the house. Sarah always had one last thing or another to do. Whatever it was brought something fresh to mind. At long last, we were ready, and I couldn't contain my excitement as we pulled out of the drive.

Sarah glanced over at me. "What has you so wound up today? You haven't stopped moving since you got up this morning."

"I don't know." I thought for a moment. "I guess it's because this is the first town picnic I've ever been to."

"You never went to any of these with your daddy?" She looked surprised.

"Nothing this big." Sometimes Daddy, Tommy, and I would picnic at the river. I sighed. "My hometown is microscopic."

When we arrived, several men were putting up booths and setting tables all over the place. Uncle Charlie stood on the top of the hill, waving his arms at something on the other side. When Sarah parked,

I grabbed what I could from the truck and schlepped it across the grass. My arms felt as if they were going to break before Sarah called out to let me know I'd gone far enough. Thankfully, I put everything down on the ground.

Sarah stopped right behind me. "I couldn't carry the juice jugs. Will you please go get them?"

"Sure." One more thing to break my arms with. The juice came in two four-gallon jugs, and I stopped several times to give my arms a rest. They were so full they kept sloshing over the side.

"Can I give you a hand?" Logan came up behind me.

He came looking for me. Inside, I squealed like a little kid, but I played it cool on the outside. "Grab one."

"Yes, ma'am." He gave a mock salute before bending to grab the handle of the jug. "What contests are you going to enter?"

"Any I have time for, and I'm allowed to be in." I wasn't paying attention to the way I carried the jug, and it swung out to the side, then hit me on the back of the knee. I winced and tried to keep from falling. I put the jug down fast to give the pain in my leg a chance to stop.

"Having some trouble?" Logan bit back a grin.

"A little." I limped around in a circle "Give me a sec and I'll be fine."

Logan set his jug beside mine. "You sure would look nice if you hadn't spilled punch all over yourself."

"Where?" I quickly searched my clothes for any stains. I thought I managed to get any spillage on the grass.

Logan laughed. "You shoulda seen your face."

"Ha ha." But he'd said I looked nice, in a kinda backhanded way. If it got Logan's attention, I was glad Sarah and I had finally agreed on a pair of light-blue overalls and a pink and blue plaid blouse.

"Well, Gimpy, looks like you're ready for the three-legged race." He shoved a hand in his pocket. "Gotta partner yet?"

This sounded hopeful. "No, do you?"

He picked up his jug. "I do now."

Sarah called me, and I hastily grabbed my jug and traipsed toward our site.

"Are you rowing in the boat race?" I tried not to sound too interested. If he already had a partner, then that'd be the end of it. I'd have to cheer him on from the sidelines.

He stared at his feet. "I wanted to, but my buddy broke his arm during football camp. He's still doing physical therapy."

Now came the tricky part—getting him to ask me to be his partner, without making it obvious. "I talked to Matthew, and he said I could sign up. Do I have to partner with another girl?"

Logan shook his head. "I don't think so. Most girls don't want to compete in the race."

Why not? Tommy Wolff and I challenged each other all the time. Had I made a mistake?

"It's kinda silly." He shifted the jug to his other hand. "It takes hard work, but some of the girls around here kick butt when they want to."

Phew.

Logan glanced at me. "Do you wanna be partners for the race?"

I hid my glee. "Sure. It'd be great." *That's it, Katie. Go for the casual approach.*

Sarah had laid our stuff out on one of the tables, so Logan and I toted the jugs over. We'd brought enough food to feed an army and it looked delicious.

After setting down the jug, Logan hesitated. "I have to help put up some booths. Where will you be in a bit?"

"I don't know, probably somewhere around here." I'd be doing hard labor, with Sarah giving out the orders. "Sarah's in charge of some booth. If I'm not here, I'll be helping her."

"All right. I'll see you around." He gave a wave, then sprinted off.

I watched until he joined the men moving boards around. I'd rather go help them than be stuck here.

Our table overlooked the lake and sat in the shade of a huge tree. What a great vantage point to see all the activity. Everything had been a mess when we arrived, but now it took on a carnival atmosphere. It didn't seem long before people arrived carrying boxes, bags, and coolers.

While arranging the food, I glanced across at Sarah, who was putting the sign up at her booth. A big man in uniform walked up behind her and put his arms around her waist. She gave a slight jump and turned around. Then she flung her arms around his neck and kissed him.

Wow. Sarah hadn't told me she had a boyfriend. Of course, I hadn't exactly given her the chance. The man hauled some steel fencing out of a box and put it up at the back of the booth.

Sarah motioned for me to join her. "Katie, I'd like you to meet my boyfriend, Jim Baines."

"Hello, Katie." He stretched out his hand.

"Hi." He certainly had a firm grip.

Sarah couldn't keep a smile from pulling at the corners of her lips. "Jim works for the police department."

As if the uniform wasn't a dead giveaway. His light-brown hair was cut short, and his biceps bulged out of his short sleeves. He wasn't as tall as my cousins, but he and Sarah looked good together, like a matched set.

He took Sarah's hand. "I need to talk to your uncle. Do you know where he is?"

Sarah shaded her eyes from the sun. "He's on the other side of the hill setting up the obstacle course."

Jim whipped his mirrored sunglasses out of his breast pocket and covered his gray eyes.

"Will you stop back by before you leave?" Sarah sounded a little anxious.

"Of course." He leaned over and gave her a quick peck on the cheek before striding off to find Uncle Charlie.

I waited until he was out of hearing. "He's cute, Sarah. Where'd you find him?"

Her cheeks flushed a little before she answered. "Jim and I were in high school together. He graduated a couple years ahead of me, and I always had the most terrific crush on him."

She still did. "Do you love him?"

She smiled and nodded. "Now help me sort these prizes. They came all jumbled together."

Sarah oversaw the baseball-throw booth; all the little plastic animals, false teeth, and other prizes were thrown into a big box and looked hopelessly tangled. It took me a few moments to figure out what all the prizes were. The only things to separate easily were the stuffed animals for the grand prizes.

"Hello, Sarah. How are you this morning?"

I spun around. A girl about my age stood there with her hands clasped behind her back. She wore a lightweight sundress with sandals so white they looked brand new. Her long, black hair was held back with a ribbon tied in a bow on the top of her head.

Sarah continued to segregate the prizes. "Hi, Emma."

Emma rocked forward on her toes. "Who is your little friend helping you with the booth today?"

Little friend? Her voice sounded so sweet it about made me sick. Besides, I stood taller than Emma. *Who does she think she is?* She reminded me of some kind of *Little Miss Perfect*.

Sarah stopped for a moment and tucked a loose lock of hair behind her ear. "This is my cousin, Katie."

"Hi." This had to be the worst part about introductions. You were forced to talk to people you didn't want to be caught dead near.

"How do you do, Katie? I'm Emma Carter." She nodded as she spoke, and her hair bounced on her shoulders with each bob of the head.

"I'm fine." What else could I say?

Sarah gave me a strange look. I think she wanted me to try harder to keep the conversation going.

Fine. "Are you entered in any of the events today, Emma?"

"Of course." She gave a fake little laugh. "I'm a participant in the junior bake-off with my lemon chiffon cake."

It probably tasted like sawdust. A bake-off wasn't exactly the type of contest I meant either.

Her smug expression radiated superiority. "What do *you* have entered?"

Was it a law around here that every girl had to enter the baking contest? The only things I baked came prepackaged at the grocery store.

Sarah came to my rescue. "She only got into town two days ago, Emma."

"Awww." She gave me a sarcastic frown. "Then you didn't have a chance to prepare anything. I'm sure you'll be in the running next year."

Hypocrite. As if I'd think of nothing else for the entire year. If I had my way, I wouldn't even be here.

"If you bake anything like Sarah, you'll give me stiff competition." Her voice took on an even more syrupy tone. "She makes the best pies and cakes I've ever eaten."

What a suck up. But why? It didn't make sense. "It was nice talking to you." The words almost stuck in my throat. "But I have to help Sarah with this booth. Maybe we can talk later."

After about six or seven years on a deserted island with no one else around, maybe. But not until then.

Emma fluffed her hair. "I hope we'll see each other later today. Then we can have a nice chat."

I couldn't think of anything to put a bigger damper on my afternoon.

She spun quickly to make her skirt twirl out, and her hair bounced with every step.

My face crunched like I'd tasted something sour. "Is she like that all the time?"

Sarah tilted her head. "She is around me. Why?"

I didn't think asking how she could stand Emma would go over too well. "She sounded a little fake to me. I almost wondered where the cameras were."

Sarah nodded thoughtfully. "I thought you didn't like something."

No kidding. Try everything.

She shrugged. "I don't know what to tell you. That's the way she is."

Did she really believe that? From what I knew of Sarah, she wouldn't be taken in by such phoniness. But sometimes adults were blind to the oddest things.

She handed me a basket of sorted prizes. "I don't expect you two to become best friends."

Thank goodness for small favors.

Touching my shoulder, she looked straight into my eyes. "All I ask is you be civil."

She might as well ask for the moon.

People were milling all over the place. The official opening of the picnic couldn't be far off. "Can I go look around?" I wanted to find Logan and help him work if he wasn't done yet. Anything'd be better than hanging around here.

Sarah checked her watch. "I want you back in half an hour. Matthew and Mark should be done then too."

I grinned. "Thanks."

As I walked off, I saw Uncle Charlie and Jim Baines coming over the top of the hill. Motioning with his hands, Uncle Charlie kept his eyes on the ground. They were in the middle of a deep discussion. Past the hill on the lake side, I saw Logan, so I made straight for the path around the lake.

When I took my eyes off Logan, my heart nearly stopped. Denton had set a lawn chair next to the path. If I passed, I might have to stop and talk to him, and I couldn't think of anything I'd rather do less.

Changing direction, I took the scenic route over the top of the hill so there wouldn't be any chance he'd talk to me. I couldn't avoid him forever, but any time I spent away from him was better than nothing.

As I crested the hill, someone called my name. *Shoot.* I stopped but didn't turn around. Who wanted me now?

"Hey Kit-Kat, I need a little help. Come here." Mark held up some tangled rope.

I put my hands on my hips. "All right but remember this when I need a favor." I grabbed one end and worked with him to undo the knots. "Now what do we do with it?"

Mark grinned. "I'm glad you asked."

Uh-oh. Why did I have to open my big mouth? As much as I liked Mark, I didn't want to spend all my *free* time helping him.

Mark tossed one end of the rope at me. "We need to make the boundary for the obstacle course."

But I hadn't even talked to Logan yet. "Where's Uncle Charlie? I thought he was supposed to be doing this?"

"He's busy right now." He pointed clear across the hill. "Take your end and tie it to the pylon over there."

I crossed my arms. "What're you gonna do?"

He smirked. "After you get your end tied down, I'll tie this one."

Great. I got to do all the legwork. "Don't overexert yourself."

By the time I got through helping Mark, my time had run out.

Mark clapped a hand on my shoulder. "Matthew and I are monitoring a couple of the contests. If I can sneak away from them for a little while, how'd you like to be my partner for the piggyback races?"

"I don't know." I pretended to think about it for a moment. "You might not have enough energy after all the work you've done this morning."

"Sucks to be you." He stuck his tongue out, then laughed. "C'mon. Let's get back to the table. I'm famished."

I rolled my eyes. "Are you ever not hungry?"

"Now you're starting to sound like Sarah." He rubbed his flat stomach. "Can't help it if I burn it off faster than everyone else."

I snorted. "Yeah. I'm sure you burn a lot of calories doin' nothing." I sprinted ahead. "Race you."

Even with the head start, I had to run full-out and we arrived at the picnic site in a dead heat.

Sarah didn't even give me a chance to catch my breath before she started in on me. "It's about time. What took you so long?"

Questions. Too many questions. Daddy didn't want to know where I was this much.

"It's all right." Mark plucked a grape from the bunch and popped it in his mouth. "The boundary rope got tangled and we had to get it sorted out. I saw Katie and asked for her help."

Thank goodness he'd answered. I wouldn't've been very nice.

Matthew arrived from the lake path as I mopped my face with a napkin. "Hey, Matthew. Put my name down for the boat race."

He raised his eyebrows. "You have a partner?"

"Logan Cruz."

Matthew picked up the clipboard and wrote the name down. "You're sure you want to do this?"

I popped out my hip and settled a hand on it. "Why not?"

He shrugged. "Don't complain to me when your arms hurt."

Off to the Races

14

Amid the smells of grilling meat and carnival-like sounds, we sat down to eat, but Uncle Charlie hadn't come back yet. Sarah said he wanted us to start without him, and he'd be there as soon as possible.

When we finished, I ran off to find Logan so we could start winning contests.

With my legs being shorter than his, we got tripped up twice in the three-legged race. Then we got into the swing of things and nothing could've stopped us. If we'd had a chance to practice before the start, we would've won. But his arm around my waist as we ran toward the finish line felt so good, I didn't care about coming in second.

We stopped back by our picnic table for something to drink afterward. The heat from the day coupled with the exercise made me thirsty. As I downed some water, I saw the boys in the distance, while Sarah organized volunteers over by the booths, but Uncle Charlie was still nowhere to be seen.

Logan put his hand on my shoulder. "Cheer up."

Cheer up? I wasn't sad.

"Next time Ted gets in front of us, I'll tie his shoelaces together." He winked.

I smiled. "His partner won't be too happy when he trips and brings her down with him."

Logan put his cup down. "You're right. Debbi wouldn't think it was funny."

We strolled along the path. Every time we passed someone, Logan waved and had something to say. He must've known everyone at the picnic.

I nudged him. "When are you going to introduce me to all your friends?"

He surveyed the crowd. "Who? The people I've been talking to?" I nodded.

Logan shrugged. "They're not really friends. Just people I know. Mike and Pete are the guys I hang around with the most. You already know them."

I'd met them but couldn't say I knew them. I hadn't known Logan for very long either, though. A trickle of excitement ran through me just being close to him. I wanted to hold his hand but wasn't brave enough to make the move. "Do you hang around with any girls?" I gave him a mock innocent look. "Or don't you like them?"

He glanced at me sideways. "You're wicked."

A smile crept across my face. "Just making sure you don't have a girlfriend stashed away somewhere."

He laughed. "Well, judging by the bruises on the face of your last boyfriend, I certainly don't want to get on your wrong side."

Pretending to be outraged, I bumped against his shoulder. "I don't have a boyfriend."

"Yeah. You brutally assaulted your *last* one, so he dumped you." Logan sprinted a few steps, cackling the whole way. "Have you seen Denton's face today? It's black and blue."

"Denton, for your information, falls into the category of the last person on the face of the earth I would have for a boyfriend. I've been trying to stay away from him."

Logan rubbed the back of his neck. "Why?"

I gave him a half shrug. "I didn't think he'd be very nice. I got into enough trouble for hitting him and didn't want to tempt fate." The whole incident embarrassed me horribly. I wanted to forget it ever happened. I'd avoided Denton earlier, because I wanted to wait until the damage was only a memory. Not something the whole world could see.

"Katie." Mark signaled from the top of the hill.

"Will you have to go slog away at something else now?" Logan's wistful tone made me feel good. He didn't want me to leave.

"I don't think so. I promised Mark I'd be his rider for the piggyback race." I raised my eyebrows. "Will you stay and cheer us on?"

"Are you kidding? I wouldn't miss this for the world." Logan slipped his hand in mine, and we climbed the hill hand in hand.

Logan Cruz is holding my hand. I wanted to pinch myself. Could this day get any better?

When we got to the top, Mark held his hand out. "Hey, Logan. It's been a while. How are things going?"

Logan dropped my hand to shake Mark's. "I'm doing great. You should've seen Katie and me in the three-legged race. We'd've won if she would've stood up for half of it."

I stared at him and tapped my foot on the ground, waiting. Logan and Mark laughed.

"What? Did I say something wrong?" Logan feigned innocence like *I'd* wounded *him* somehow.

"I could always say the same about you, you know." I mimicked his innocent look.

Mark ran a hand through his dark hair. "That must've been some race."

"It was." Sarcasm colored my words. "For all my clumsiness, we still came in second."

Mark rubbed his hands together. "Are you ready to triumph in the piggyback race, Kit-Kat?"

"You bet." I always wanted to win.

Logan leaned over and whispered in my ear, "He calls you Kit-Kat?"

All I could do was shrug. Mark's nickname for me wasn't explainable. Unless I wanted to blush.

Mark knelt at the starting post and Logan waved from the finish line. I almost laughed out loud when I saw DL Dunn. He'd dressed in what had to be his "Western Wear"—a plaid shirt, blue jeans tucked into boots, a kerchief tied around his neck, and a cowboy hat topped everything off. Being the official starter of the race, he even had a holster for the starter gun. Daddy wore a Stetson with his uniform, but it gave him an air of authority while DL looked goofy.

DL checked each of the contestants in on a clipboard. "Mark McCabe with rider Katie McCabe?"

Mark answered for us. "Right here."

DL lifted his eyes from the clipboard, and they met mine.

A shiver ran through me. The way he looked at me frightened me. Like he hated me. Maybe he was upset I had hurt his precious son.

His eyes narrowed.

Was he trying to intimidate me? Stare me down? I stared back. His eyes were dead. Like he had no soul.

When I thought I might cave and look away, he glanced at his clipboard and called the next team on the list. When he finished, he scanned the starting line. "Riders, mount up."

I climbed on Mark's back, and he stood.

"Am I in a comfortable spot for you?" The last time I'd been carried piggyback was by my daddy, and I think I was five.

"You're a little high. See if you can slide down a smidge." He grabbed ahold of my legs as I slid down his back. "There. Perfect."

"Where do you want my arms to be?" Something I'd never thought about as a child.

"Hold on to my shoulders." He shifted my position a bit more. "And lean forward while I'm running." He walked to our lane. "If you lean back, it'll slow me down."

Matthew walked up to the line with Sarah as his rider. Sarah waved. I hadn't known they'd be in the race too.

Matthew turned and yelled at us. "Hey, Mark. You two are going to eat our dust."

"No way. By the time you cross the starting line, we'll be halfway home." Mark stepped across the line to face him. "Let's say we make a little wager on it."

Matthew walked over to the lane beside us. "You're on. Loser pays ten bucks."

Mark nodded. "It's a bet."

DL called the racers to order, raised his pistol, and slowly pulled the trigger. As soon as the gun fired, Mark took off running. I leaned forward and tried to stay as close to him as I could. I didn't want to take the blame if we lost. He and Matthew ran neck and neck most of the way. It almost seemed as if they were the only two in the race, because everyone else fell so far behind.

At the end of the race, Mark found an extra bit of energy. When I didn't think he could run any faster, we flew past the finish line, split seconds before Matthew and Sarah. He came to a stop and let me slide off his back.

Mark strutted toward Matthew and slapped him on the arm. "Good race." He held out his hand. "Now pay up."

Sarah shook her head. "I don't know about you two. One of these days, you're going to kill yourselves trying to outdo each other."

While they continued talking, I slipped away with Logan. "Oh no." I stopped walking.

His eyebrows drew together. "What's wrong?"

"I forgot to ask when it's our turn to do the rowboat thing." The last thing I wanted to do was go back. Sarah might find something else for me to do.

Logan took my hand and walked forward. "Don't worry about it. I already checked with Matthew. We're in the second to the last heat."

Trust Matthew to make us wait until the last part of the day when we'd be all tired out. I scowled. "I'd hoped we'd be able to go sooner."

"Why? We've got one of the best heats there are." Logan rolled his eyes toward the sky. "Look. By going second to the last, we know who to beat, and we'll have a general idea of how fast everyone is going."

Made sense.

Sweet Revenge

15

Logan and I strolled past all the picnickers. The park had filled up—everyone in town must have been there. Most of the food had been packed away, but the party atmosphere remained.

Logan stiffened and stopped walking. "Don't look now, but Denton's headed this way, and Emma is with him."

From the way he said Emma's name, I got the feeling Logan didn't like her any more than I did.

He turned toward me. "Do you want to go the other way? Since we're stopped, we can pretend we were headed another direction to begin with."

"No. I might as well face him now, while I have one of my Musketeers with me." I turned to wait for the inevitable and let go of Logan's hand in case I had to greet Denton with a handshake. What a disgusting thought.

As they approached, a feeling of revulsion ran through me. Denton's frizzy hair drooped across his eyes. His half-untucked collared shirt had a mustard and ketchup stain on it and his untied shoelaces flopped on the ground with every step. *Did the boy not know how to tuck in a shirt or tie his shoes?* They made a mismatched couple—Emma's sundress didn't even have a wrinkle.

Things might not be so bad if I got the first words in, so I forced a smile. "Hey, Denton, how are you? Hi, Emma."

Emma curled her upper lip. "Hi yourself."

Was this the same girl who'd been so sickeningly sweet this morning? Instead of being prissily over-polite, she was obnoxious.

Emma clasped her hands behind her back and twisted her torso to make her skirt sway. "In case you're interested, Logan, I have a lemon chiffon cake entered in the baking contest. You should get yourself a piece after the judging is over."

Was this her idea of flirting? Not that I had a clue about how to flirt, but even I'd do a better job if I tried.

Strange. Denton's face wasn't nearly as bad as I remembered it. Maybe the excitement of hitting him had made it look worse than it was. I'd expected it to still be swollen and distorted. A round, discolored patch wasn't bad. My arms hung awkwardly at my sides as we stood there in silence.

Denton glared at me, then turned his head toward Logan. "I heard you and Katie are going to be a team for the rowboats."

He talked to Logan as if I wasn't there, and his voice sounded as repulsive as ever.

Emma giggled and laid her hand on Denton's arm. "Can you imagine Katie in a rowboat? How ridiculous."

I bit the end of my tongue. I wanted to tell her off in the worst way, but if I did, she'd get me in trouble somehow. I took a deep breath. "Ridiculous? I'm surprised you and Denton aren't going to be a team." How cool I sounded, while underneath my anger rose.

Emma flushed and bit her lip. "Trying to compete with boys is vulgar." Every word aimed to taunt.

I wanted to slam her back, but I had to maintain my calm. "I'm sorry. I forgot." Mockery wove its way through my words. "Little girls don't always understand playing with boys is a way of life. Maybe you'll learn how when you grow up."

Her face turned bright red, and anger choked her. "Well, I never!" She sputtered like a fish, her mouth snapping open and shut.

I gloated. "And you probably never will."

Logan's hand flew to his mouth to hide a snicker.

"Didn't anyone warn you?" I gave her an evil grin. "No amount of kissing that toad ..." I hooked a thumb toward Denton. "... will ever make him a prince."

Emma stomped off with Denton following her like a puppy dog. What a perfect couple.

"I can't believe how you handled her." Logan's grin spread clear across his face. "I was right when I called you wicked."

Wicked as a compliment—I'd take it.

"I thought for a minute you were gonna lose it." He winked.

"I almost did, but this felt better." I laughed. "I can't believe I stayed in control and chewed her out at the same time."

His brown eyes twinkled. "When did you meet Emma? You haven't been in town for too long and she isn't exactly the social butterfly she likes to think she is."

"She trapped me over at the baseball-throw booth." Even remembering it made me shudder. "She wore her phony 'nice' face around Sarah." I paused for a moment. "I think Emma likes you."

Logan gave a slight start and took a step back. "What?" He grimaced and shook his head slowly. "Where'd you get such an awful idea?"

I shrugged. "I don't know. It seemed like it to me."

"She does try to impress me sometimes, but it makes me sick." He cringed. "What a nightmare—Emma after me."

I raised my eyebrows. "You mean I don't have to be jealous she tried to tempt you with lemon chiffon?"

Logan laughed and took my hand. "No worries there."

We walked down by the lake. Kids in shorts and rolled up pants splashed along the shore. Others had bathing suits on and were swimming out to the float and diving off the edge. As we stood gazing at all the people, Logan slipped his arm across my shoulders. It startled me, and I jumped.

He quickly dropped his arm to his side. "This school year's gonna be great. You and Emma are going to be the best of friends. I can tell already." His forced words were rushed.

My cheeks burned. I hadn't meant to jump, but it was so unexpected. It felt nice, and I didn't mind his arm around me. I'd have to wait for him to work up his courage to try again and hope I'd be ready.

Logan checked his watch. "It's almost time for our race. Let's go see about a boat and some oars."

We picked out a nice boat with cushions on the seats. It was a beautiful day and I almost wished we hadn't signed up for the race. It'd be nice to drift on the water and chat.

"What we need to do is get a rhythm going and keep it up." He tossed me an oar. "We won't go anywhere unless we pull together."

The boats had to stay half onshore, and one member of the team had to push it off and then jump in. Logan volunteered to give us the push. We had the outside starting position and got off to a great start. We glided through the water. As we approached a nice shady cove to our left, a boat sailed out, angled to cross our bow and cut us off.

"Logan! To our left."

He snapped his head around. "Outrun them."

I didn't see how—the other boat skimmed ahead and going faster would make us crash into it. I craned my head around to see who was in the boat. Denton and Emma. The King of the Toads and Princess Wannabe had hidden in the cove waiting for us to pass.

I kept pulling hard, hoping against hope we'd outdistance them. If they cut us off, we'd lose the race for sure. My arms burned as I rowed.

The boats collided. The jolt sent me flying forward out of my seat.

Jeering laughter came from the other boat.

Logan jumped up. "What in the world do you think you're doing?" He punched the air as he yelled.

Denton plastered a smug smile on his bruised face. "We're sorry. We didn't mean to bump into you."

I crawled back to my seat. He had zero remorse.

"I guess it doesn't pay to have a girl for a partner, does it, Logan?" Emma's words dripped with acid honey. "She gets you into wrecks, and you lose."

"Since you're in a rowboat, Emma, you shouldn't talk so high and mighty." My temper flared. "As I recall, you're the one who said girls in rowboats were ridiculous." I spat the words out of my mouth. "And I think you used the word *vulgar.*"

Emma stood. "How dare you." Her voice shrill, she took a step forward.

"I only used your words."

As she took another step forward, I pushed the side of their boat down and away. Emma lost her balance and toppled toward the gunwale. She probably would've fallen into the bottom of the boat if Denton hadn't stood. The boat rocked so hard it threw her up against the side. As she went over, she clutched at Denton and pulled him into the lake with her.

When she came up, her face turned into a waterlogged picture of fury. They both looked exactly like what they were—a couple of drowned rats.

Logan and I laughed so hard, we almost split our sides. Denton yelled, but the words got lost in all the splashing. Every time one tried to climb into the boat, the other tried from the other side. The boat bobbed up and down, and they lost their hold, sinking back into the lake.

Denton swam to our boat and tried to climb in. Logan waited until he reached for the edge, then pushed Denton in the chest with the paddle. Denton went under. In seconds, his head emerged, and he took a stroke toward us.

"Start rowing." Logan held the oar ready in case Denton tried to board our boat again.

I grabbed the oars and dipped them in the lake. A sharp tug almost wrenched the paddle from my grasp. I'd forgotten about Emma while Logan and Denton scuffled. Since she still had a hold of the oar, I gave it a big push.

Crap. It hit her in the face and she went under.

I held my breath and my legs tensed. What if I had knocked her out? I half stood, ready to jump in when she broke through the surface, sputtering. I breathed a sigh of relief and rowed—fast.

When Logan and I left them, they were trying to get back into their boat.

Laughing, I grabbed Logan's arm. "Well? Did capsizing them

make up for not winning the race?"

"It'll do. 'Sides, we owed Denton for sticking us with that check." Logan grinned with a glint in his eyes. "I'll treasure the memory of the two of them hanging on the boat." He brushed his hair back. "They looked as stupid as Beach Bobbing Bob when he falls into the water."

I jerked my head back in confusion. "Who?"

He snorted. "It's an old online game where you have to get Bob, a monkey, to leap across the water, jumping on barrels to bring coconuts from one side to the other. Sometimes the barrels sink or blow up and Bob gets dunked."

We explained to Matthew what happened, and he marked us down as a disabled boat. With Logan as a witness, maybe I wouldn't get in trouble if Emma showed up with bruises.

Matthew stopped us before we left. "Sarah's been looking for you, Katie. She says it's time to start packing things up."

When I turned toward our table, I saw Uncle Charlie talking to Sarah. *Excellent.* A few extra minutes to spend with Logan. We stopped underneath the shade of a tree. "I had a great time today."

Logan nodded but seemed a little distracted.

I shrugged. "I probably should go before Sarah sends out a search party." Had I done something to make him not like me? "I can't believe I have to leave already."

Half turned, I took a step when Logan grabbed my arms and swung me toward him.

He pulled me in close and kissed me quickly on the lips. "Today was special because of you."

My eyelids fluttered as I stood rooted to the spot, unable to speak. Logan kissed me again, longer this time.

He let go of my arms and stepped back. "I'll see you around." He turned and ran off.

My mouth tingled from his kiss as I walked slowly to our table, a warm cozy feeling spreading through my body.

The News

16

After packing up all the things from the picnic, Sarah and I got into her truck to go back to Uncle Charlie's. Though I was tired from all the activity, my mind raced. "I had so much fun. Today was great. Don't ya think?" The best part was my first kiss, but I wasn't going to share that with Sarah.

She kept driving, like she hadn't heard me, with one hand on the steering wheel while the other clutched her infinity heart pendant as if her life depended on it.

"Sarah?"

Still no reaction.

"Sarah." I raised my voice to get her attention.

She briefly turned her head. "What?"

"Wasn't today fun? I had such a good time." My mouth dried. Her lackluster response unnerved me.

"Yes." She didn't even sound sure about it, gripping the steering wheel so tightly her knuckles were white.

Had I done anything wrong? I didn't think so … unless she'd found out about Denton and Emma getting dumped into the lake. If half-drowning those two was bothering her, she would've jumped on me for it right away. She wouldn't wait until we got to the house. No, it had to be something worse.

She held herself rigid and her teeth were clenched. I wanted to help somehow, but I didn't know what to say. After all, she'd helped me feel better when I felt homesick. How did I start? *Awkward.* "Sarah? If it's something I said or did …"

I trailed off as she bit her lip and shook her head. Tears trickled down her cheeks.

"I'm sorry." Exactly what I'd wanted to avoid. "I didn't mean to upset you." Whatever happened must've been bad. Worse than I'd thought, and I had to go stick my foot in my mouth. "Is there anything I can do?"

"No." The word barely came out. She took a deep breath. "Honey, be quiet until we get home." Her soft voice shook.

Had Jim broken up with her? Although they looked far from breaking up when I saw them together. Fortunately, the house was only a couple of minutes away. When we got there, I'd bring in all the dishes and baskets and put them away, without being asked. I didn't know how else to help.

When we arrived at the house, Sarah went straight into the bathroom and turned on the water. I carried in everything from the truck, and almost had it all put away when she came out. She helped me put the rest away, and we washed the dishes, working side by side in silence. She obviously didn't want to talk, and I didn't want to say anything, because I didn't want the flood to start.

I put the last dish away as Matthew, Mark, and Uncle Charlie drove up. They came quietly into the house, and for once, no one was smiling. They only looked at me through sad eyes.

It scared me. "What is wrong with everyone? We get back from a great picnic and you're all acting like Old Yeller died." I had to get someone to smile. Panic filled me. "Boy, this family sure is weird. Most people are happy and relaxed after a picnic."

"Katie." Uncle Charlie spoke softly, but the one word pierced straight through me. He stared for a moment at the pictures on the mantle before continuing. "Sit down. I need to talk to you."

Something was terribly wrong. He had been less upset when I hit Denton.

Mark put his hand on the doorknob. "I have to tend to the animals."

Uncle Charlie flicked a look at him and opened his mouth but didn't say anything. His gaze left my face for less than a second. I backed toward my chair, felt it with my hand, and sat. Sarah came in from the kitchen and sat in her chair. Matthew stood by the door, tapping a pencil on his clipboard, carefully avoiding my eyes.

"Katie, I'm afraid I have some bad news." Uncle Charlie's eyes filled with pain.

Fear squeezed my heart. Not Daddy. Anything but that. "If Daddy's worse, he'll want to see me." I stood. "I'll go pack some things, or we can leave right now. I don't need to take anything."

He swallowed hard. "Katie, hear me out."

I sank slowly into my chair. The grief in his voice was plain. I didn't want to know the rest.

Uncle Charlie stared at his hands for a moment before looking directly into my eyes. "He had cancer and it spread to his liver."

Had? What did he mean, *had*?

His voice grew rough and gravelly. "The doctors did all they could."

Sarah wept silently and Matthew turned his head.

My brain had been frozen, not taking everything in. Then it snapped. "No, I don't want to hear any more." I sprang to my feet, tears blurring my vision. "Take me home to Daddy. I need to see him."

Uncle Charlie knelt next to me and took my hands. "I'm sorry, Katie. I got the call while we were at the picnic. Your daddy died this morning in his sleep."

No. It had to be a mistake. Hot tears slid down my face. Daddies were supposed to be there when you grew up. My daddy was too big and strong to give in to death.

The sobs sent shudders through my body. I wished everyone would stop staring at me. They looked as helpless as I felt, and it hurt. Everything seemed to be happening in slow motion.

Sarah touched my shoulder. "Katie."

I jerked my shoulder away from her touch and pulled my hand back from Uncle Charlie. "Leave me alone!" How loud my voice sounded. I had to get out of there. I couldn't stand their staring anymore. Running blindly, I bumped into Matthew. I pushed against him and continued out the door.

Uncle Charlie spoke to Sarah and Matthew as I left. "Let her go.

She needs some time alone."

Time alone? I needed Daddy.

Mark came out of the barn, Günter at his side. I didn't want to talk to anyone. Mark leaned down and spoke to Günter. As I ran toward my special place in the woods, Günter followed.

I wanted to yell and scream. I wanted to hit something, break things.

What would happen to me now?

Abandoned, alone in the world, I was an orphan. Those people in the house were strangers. They didn't know anything about me.

But I had nowhere else to go.

Falling to my knees, I put my arms around Günter's neck and buried my face on his back. I cried until not another tear would fall. Sitting back against a tree, I waited for my breath to slow, and to stop jumping in my chest. My throat closed and swelled until it wouldn't let another sound pass through.

As I sat there, thoughts of Daddy kept popping into my head. I didn't want to think about him. It hurt. But there he was, tucking me into bed, telling me a story, and kissing me goodnight. His arms hugging me when I hurt myself. The stern expression on his face when I had done something wrong. Sitting on his lap in the evening, talking about our day.

My nose ran, even though it felt stuffed up. I didn't have any tissue either. I crawled to the stream and washed off my face. It made me feel a little better, but not much.

I had to go back to the house, but I didn't want to. I never wanted to go back. If it hadn't been for them, I would've been with Daddy when he died. Tears filled my eyes again. I didn't see how I had any left.

I slowly stood. The dark woods shrouded me, making it difficult to see. With each reluctant step, I made my way toward the house. Günter stayed by my side, not running off like usual. When I reached the edge of the woods, I hid behind a tree and stared at the house for a long time.

Everything would be different now. I had a new family, and I didn't want them. The porch light and the half-moon were the only things breaking the darkness. How cozy the house looked, and how outside and alone I felt.

How would I fit into the cheerful, white house when I felt like half of me was missing? The house was full of warmth and happiness, and I was hollowed out, and pain filled the hole.

A gentle breeze blew, and the porch swing creaked as it moved. With leaden feet, I walked over to the swing. I couldn't go inside.

After a few minutes, Uncle Charlie came out and sat beside me. He must have been watching from the window. He didn't try to give me false comfort or say anything. We swung back and forth with no sound except the soft creaking of the swing.

I broke the silence first. "What happens now?"

He didn't say anything for a moment and stared straight ahead. "We'll have the funeral shortly."

I crumpled against the side of the swing.

"Ron didn't want a fuss or things drawn out. He set everything up when he went into the hospital." Tears sprang into Uncle Charlie's eyes. "He didn't want us to deal with having to make the arrangements."

The words barely reached my mind. Everything felt unreal.

"After the funeral, we'll go back to the house and pack your things and bring as much as we can back with us."

I didn't want to go to a funeral or pack. I wanted to be home with Daddy's things all around, not putting my life in boxes. At least then I could pretend he'd come through the door at the end of the day, and everything would be all right.

Nothing will ever be right again.

"I'm your legal guardian now, and you'll always have a home with me." He patted my hand.

He tried to be nice, but all I wanted was Daddy.

Uncle Charlie stood. "You come in when you're ready."

I didn't feel like I'd ever be ready to go back into that house. My brain went numb—no thoughts, no emotions. All I could do was swing back and forth.

The night air grew cold, and goose pimples rose on my arms. But I stared into the night, an empty shell. Sarah brought out a blanket and put it around my shoulders, then went back inside.

The screen door creaked again. She came out with something hot and steamy in her hands. "I brought you some tea. I thought you might need it."

She sat beside me and when I didn't take the cup, she pressed it into my hands.

I brought it to my lips and took a sip. The warmth felt good. I'd been colder than I thought. As I drank my tea, we swung silently. Only the creak of the swing and the occasional night bird marred the stillness.

I bit my lower lip and felt like crying again. The numbness faded and one thought ran through my head like a nightmarish song. *Daddy is dead.* Each salty tear followed the next down my cheeks. I gulped the tea to try and stem the flow.

I set the cup on the porch floorboards. The tears came faster and faster. Sarah reached over and stroked my hair. I turned and flung my arms around her. She held me and rocked slowly while I cried myself out.

"I'm sorry." I pulled back. I felt like I'd cried more since coming to this house than I had cried in my whole life.

She looked puzzled. "What're you sorry about?"

"I didn't mean to cry anymore." I touched her shoulder. "And I got your blouse all wet."

Shaking her head, Sarah patted me on the back. "There's nothing wrong with tears, and this blouse has to get washed anyway." Her eyes turned grave. "I've shed a few myself."

I took a deep, shuddery breath and held it for a moment. Then I swallowed hard to force the tears back. "I don't want tears to make me weak ... I have to be strong now that Daddy is gone. It's just ..." I bit my bottom lip, and my face scrunched up. "Just ..." A mewling whine escaped my lips.

Sarah slipped her arm around me and squeezed. "Honey, tears don't make you weak. They're grief's way of rain falling on embers. All your emotions are swirling around, and tears help soothe the pain for a bit." A tear rolled down her cheek. "When I was young, I used to stay with Uncle Ronnie and Auntie Marie a lot. They were very special to me."

That's why she cried on the way home from the picnic.

She reached over and picked up the cup. "Why don't we go in before we freeze out here?" She stood and waited. "It can be hot during the day, but once the sun sets, it gets downright chilly."

I still didn't want to go in, but I couldn't spend the night on the porch swing either.

Going Home

17

I awoke early in the morning after a fitful night's sleep. My head ached, and my eyes were gritty from all the crying I'd done. No one said much while we were getting ready, and it wasn't long before we headed out the door.

With each passing mile, I wished they would multiply. It'd take a lot longer to get home then. In one way, I wanted the trip to take forever. In another, I wanted it over and done with.

I didn't want to deal with what would happen when the truck finally stopped.

Sarah drove without speaking for a while. I didn't mind. I had nothing to say. Matthew's car sped along in front of us, kicking dust at our faces. Somehow that seemed right, a metaphor for how I felt—like dirt. And uncomfortable in the borrowed blue, white, and black plaid dress, though it was the only appropriate thing that fit me for the funeral.

Funeral. What an awful word. I couldn't remember ever having been to one before, but I supposed I'd gone to my mother's. Now who'd tell me stories about my mama? No one else had known her like Daddy, and I didn't know enough about her.

Sarah rubbed the key pendant around her neck, then looked in the rearview mirror, our eyes meeting. She broke the silence. "How're you doing, Katie?"

If I told the truth, I was on the verge of tears again. "Hanging in there." I glanced out the window. We were getting close. I'd made it out this far on one of my runaway attempts. Daddy had found me right after, though. He always found me.

Not anymore. I'd wanted to come home, but not like this.

The cars rolled to a stop in front of the church. Sarah got out.

"Are you coming?"

"In a minute." If I had my way, I'd sit in the truck for the entire service. I stared straight ahead, trying not to think about what came next. Staying put made it easier to delude myself and kept it from being real. If I sat and waited long enough, Daddy might drive up and walk in with me. The moment I stepped foot in the church, the casket, flowers, and all the mourners meant I couldn't pretend anymore.

Several men greeted Uncle Charlie with a hug. They must be the brothers ... the uncles I'd never met. A woman, wearing her brunette hair in an updo, walked up behind Sarah and placed a hand on her shoulder. Sarah turned, then gave the woman an awkward hug, like one given out of duty. The woman pointed to her cheek and Sarah gave her a brief kiss. Was that Sarah's mother?

Sarah gave the man at the woman's side a genuine smile and embraced him warmly. *Is he her father or an uncle?* The man said something, and Sarah glanced toward the truck where I sat. The woman frowned and took a step toward me, but Sarah moved in front of her, and the man took hold of her arm and walked her into the church. *They must be her parents.*

After a while, Uncle Charlie came out of the church, over to the truck, and opened my door. "It's time, Katie."

My legs felt like lead as I swung them around. Each step seemed harder than the last. People were arriving. I didn't want anyone to talk to me. I kept my head down so I wouldn't meet their eyes.

After the service, I couldn't remember any part of it except stupid little things. Like Reverend Archer having a cold, making his words sound funny. Throughout the ceremony, I stared at a hole someone had dug into the rail in front of me. When everyone came out, we stood by the door for people to pay their condolences. The only reason I made it through was Uncle Charlie's hand on my shoulder, which comforted me.

It felt bizarre to have people I'd known my whole life talking to me like I was a stranger. Everyone said the same thing over and over. *I'm so sorry for your loss. Your daddy was such a wonderful man. We will all miss him so much.* And worst of all ... *Let me know if you need anything.*

No one could give me the one thing I *needed* ... my daddy alive and well.

Several of my classmates had come and none of them could look me in the eye. They mumbled out a brief, *sorry*, then moved on. I could almost smell their relief when walking away. Even Tommy muttered a brief, *sorry, Katie*, before he sped off, but at least his eyes briefly connected with mine.

The graveside service came next.

"Katie." Uncle Charlie's voice was quiet. "Would you like to pay your last respects before we go to the cemetery?"

I nodded, numb. Last respects. How final and unyielding those words sounded.

The smell of flowers almost overpowered the room. The dim light helped create a sense of peace, and the quiet gave me a chance to shut everything else out. I walked toward the plain pine casket, but halfway down the aisle I froze and couldn't catch my breath.

Instead of being covered in a spray of flowers, or draped in a flag, Daddy's Stetson adorned the coffin. My knees buckled and I fell into the nearest pew. I hadn't looked at it during the ceremony. I couldn't. The hat—the thing Daddy never left home without—made his death real. Final. And I'd never recover from the loss.

After a few moments, I strengthened my resolve and made my way to the front of the church. The ceremony had been closed casket in accordance with Daddy's wishes. He wanted me to remember him the way he was, not laid out in fine clothes, not moving, not breathing. I rubbed my hands across the polished top. Even the wood felt cold and lifeless.

Tears gently streamed down my cheeks. Not the sobs of the day before, but simple grief. For the first time I could remember, crying didn't matter. As I stood there running my hands across the top, I felt Daddy's presence, felt his love.

"Daddy?" My voice echoed in the empty room. "If you can hear me, I have something to tell you." I waited for a moment, half expecting to hear his voice. "Find Mama, so you can take care of each other." My throat burned. "I miss you so much. I'll love you ... forever and ever." My voice shook, but I regained control. "Watch over me, Daddy. You said you always would." I paused to swallow the lump in my throat. "All I want to know is why? You mean too much to me to be dead." I hit the top of the casket and dashed down the aisle and into the bathroom to dry my tears before joining the others.

Now I had to face the hardest thing of all—the graveside service. I didn't want to stand there while men threw dirt over what used to be my daddy. He had to be able to hear me, to know what I felt, and what I was thinking. I stood back a ways from the crowd.

Matthew came over to me. "Wouldn't you like to move in closer, Katie?"

"No." The word exploded from my lips. "I'm sorry. I didn't mean to say it that way."

Matthew gave me a quick hug. "It's all right. I understand." He stood for a moment, looking toward the grave. "Would you like me to stay, or would you rather be by yourself?"

I grabbed his hand. "Stay."

He gave my hand a squeeze and put his arm across my shoulders. I didn't listen to any of the words being said. I watched the people who'd come to say goodbye. Everyone looked strange, different somehow, even though I had seen many of them just a few days before. Maybe I was used to seeing them in everyday clothes and acting like themselves. Tommy looked funny in a light brown suit that was two inches too short for him. His hair had been neatly combed and slicked down, something I'd never seen before. Mr. Pickford wore a dark blue suit. I hadn't known he owned such a thing. His shoes were spit-polish shined. The Reverend's white socks slowly inched down.

The shovel scraped against the ground as the sexton picked it up. He placed his boot on the blade and shoved it into the pile. I covered my eyes and squeezed Matthew's hand tight.

Reverend Archer reached the culmination of the service. "... ashes to ashes, dust to dust."

Next, the expectant pause as the sexton aimed. Then a shower of dirt hit the casket. I felt as if every lump and particle pierced through my body.

I turned toward Matthew and buried my face in his chest. "Take me home. I want to go now."

He put his arms around me. "It's all right, Katie. We'll leave." He took me by the hand and led me to the car. "Let me tell Dad we're leaving."

I sat in the car and waited staring straight ahead, not really seeing anything. He came back sooner than I expected. "We'll take Sarah's truck. She'll ride back with Mark."

The short trip home went by way too quickly. A feeling deep down inside told me this might be even harder to cope with than the graveside service.

Boxing Life

18

When the truck pulled up in front of Daddy's house, I made no move to get out. "Go ahead. I'll come in later."

Matthew gave me one last look and went inside. I didn't want to pass through the door and have Daddy not be there. Funeral or not, I longed to preserve my fantasy that he wasn't dead.

If I walked into the house, and he wasn't there, I'd have to face reality. I didn't want to be in the truck when the rest of the family arrived, though. Facing people was an ordeal I'd rather avoid. Especially if all the uncles and their wives showed up.

I unglued my legs from the seat of the truck and trudged to the door. Standing outside for a moment, I gathered my courage. I walked through the doorway and took a deep breath.

Everything was the same, like Daddy would be coming home any minute. A footstep sounded from his bedroom.

I swallowed hard when I saw Matthew moving around inside. He looked so much like Daddy tears came to my eyes. If I cried here, I might not be able to stop. Memories of all the good times we'd spent together came flooding back, so I ran into my room and grabbed my teddy bear, Rupert, off my pillow.

Here I might find peace. Not as many memories to pester me. I sat on the edge of my bed and stared at the wall, stroking Rupert's cinnamon-colored fur. I'd only been gone for a few days, but it seemed like forever.

The bush outside my window tapped against the pane, and I tried to force all thoughts from my mind. *Focus on the leaves scraping the window.* I hugged Rupert tight. *Don't think about anything.*

Why couldn't I make time stop and go backward? Maybe things would work out differently. Maybe Daddy wouldn't have died.

The front door squeaked open, and feet shuffled from room to room. Murmuring voices filtered through my bedroom door. Grunts mingled with the sound of furniture sliding across the floor, and murmurs were masked by the clink of dishes being taken out of the cupboard and set on the counter. Picture frames clanked against one another as the pictures by the mantle were stacked.

My life was being torn down and packed up.

The door opened and Sarah stuck her head around the corner. "Mind if I come in?"

"No."

She entered and sat beside me. "It was a nice service, wasn't it?"

I gave a nod, even though I disagreed. How could it be a nice service? Daddy was dead.

A high-pitched voice called through the door. "Sarah? How many boxes do you need?"

She stiffened and twiddled her heart-key necklace rapidly back and forth by the key bit. "Good grief, Mama. Give me a minute." Sarah muttered the words under her breath, then patted my hand. "We need to get started in here, Katie. We don't have a lot of time to pack today. And the last thing we want is for my mama to come help." She grimaced. "I'm sure you don't remember them, but your uncle Shane and auntie Delia are my parents. The last time you saw them, you were probably around two." She stood and walked to the door.

So the brunette with the updo at the church *was* Sarah's mother and I hadn't been wrong about the awkwardness of their hug. The relationship between Sarah and her mother promised a story. Any other day, I'd have been dying to know what'd happened between them.

At the door, Sarah stopped and glanced back. "I'll grab a couple boxes. Why don't you start getting something ready?"

I didn't want to box anything up. This house was my last tie to Daddy, and they wanted to tear it apart, pack it up, and sell it. Didn't they understand this was my home?

It was my life.

"I'm sorry, Shane. It wasn't right." The same shrill voice that'd called to Sarah came through the cracked door. "Ron's girl should have stayed and thanked everyone for coming instead of being so disrespectful by leaving early."

Ron's girl? Couldn't she call me by my name?

"Now, Delia ..."

A sour taste filled my mouth as I rubbed the tail of Rupert's purple and yellow plaid bow between my thumb and forefinger. Auntie Delia and I were *not* going to be friends.

Sarah hurried into the room and put the boxes on the floor. She had a small wooden chest tucked under her arm that she placed on the dresser.

I hadn't moved. She didn't say anything, but opened my closet, took out some clothes, and laid them on the bed next to me.

"I know this is difficult, Katie, but I need your help." Her voice came out gently, and she didn't sound upset.

Maybe she understood how I felt. After placing Rupert back on my pillow, I went over to the bookcase and ran my hand along the backs of the books. I pulled a few off the shelf and put them in the box. Without them all over the place, my room wouldn't look like it belonged to me anymore. It wouldn't be mine.

"Do we have to do this today?" If we didn't, I wanted to leave.

"I'm sorry, sweetie. It's just that we live so far from here we won't be able to work on it a little at a time." She moved on to packing what I'd left in the dresser. She never once stopped working. "The whole family came to help, and it'll be easier to get as much as we can done now."

Easier for them maybe, but not for me. I put a few more books in the box.

Auntie Delia's voice pierced through the door. "Everyone was saying how disgraceful it was that she came into the church late and didn't greet anyone ... not even family. After we closed the store and came all this way. All I can say is Ron must not have brought her up very well."

I felt as if I'd been slapped. The book I'd pulled from the shelf slipped out of my hand and fell to the floor.

"Enough, Delia." Uncle Shane's voice was stern as he rebuked her.

Sarah hurried to the door. The voices became muffled when she closed it. Then she gathered me into her arms. "Don't pay any attention to what Mama says. I don't. She gets too hung up on appearance and what other people think." She patted my back. "And no one but Mama cared what you were doing ... they only cared how you were."

When Sarah went back to packing up my closet, I picked up the book I'd dropped and stared at it, swallowing hard. Taking apart my life bit by bit was too much. I needed to get out.

I caught Sarah by surprise as I snatched Rupert from the bed, strode to the door, and slammed it behind me.

Saying Goodbye

19

Once outside, I broke into a sprint. My feet flew along, without any thought about where I was going. I automatically ran to my place by the riverbank. Slowing to a walk, I gazed across the river.

Daddy and I went fishing in the river a lot. It was one of our favorite things to do together. When I came to my favorite tree, I looked up. The oak planks across the branches were hidden from view. I tucked Rupert into the bodice of my dress, using his arms as an anchor. Glancing around, I climbed into the tree. I sat on the platform and peered between the leaves. The river shimmered in the sunlight, and I wanted to stay in the tree forever. No one would find me, and I wouldn't have to go back to Uncle Charlie's house. They were nice to me, but I didn't belong.

The late afternoon heat made me drowsy. Hugging Rupert, I leaned up against the trunk and fell asleep.

A scratching noise jerked me awake. Someone was climbing the tree. How had anyone found me?

I stood, ready to climb higher, when I saw the top of Tommy's head. "What're you doing here?"

"I could ask you the same thing." He hauled himself the rest of the way up. "Your family is looking for you."

Dressed in a pair of ragged jeans and a T-shirt—I ought to have known a suit wouldn't last long on him—Tommy scooted away from the edge.

"I figured you'd be here." He stared at the boards.

Had Tommy gotten skinnier? He couldn't have, could he? I'd only been gone for a few days but was glad to see such a good friend. The only person left in my life who really knew me.

He sat there, silently.

"Tommy?" My throat was sore from choking back all the emotion of the day.

"What?" He didn't even glance at me.

"What did you think about the funeral?" I couldn't call it *my daddy's* yet.

"I dunno. What did you think?" He still wouldn't look at me.

"Don't do that." I pressed my lips tightly together.

Tommy hunched his shoulders. "Do what?"

A knot of anger formed in my stomach. "Everyone I know is treating me differently, acting like I might break or something." He hadn't even teased me about bringing Rupert with me like he used to. "I need someone or something to be the same."

He finally turned his head. "I don't know what to say. I don't want to upset you."

I threw my head back. The leaves overhead swayed in the breeze. "I'd rather be upset than to have you be different too." I sat beside him.

"You said it yourself ..." Tommy's voice cracked. "Things have changed, and I don't know how to act."

"You never worried about how to act around me before." My lips trembled, so I hugged Rupert tight and took a deep breath. "You're my best friend. I don't want that to change."

Tommy traced the grain on the plank with his index finger. "I couldn't believe it when you left." His voice got quiet. "One minute we were together burning down sheds, and the next you were gone."

I had to strain to hear.

"I thought your dad was joking when he told me you'd left." He hung his head. "The Katie I know would never stand to be sent away."

I rested my hand on his arm. "I didn't want to go, but I had no choice."

A pang of sorrow hit me. So much had changed for Tommy, too. I was his only friend, and he always felt welcome at our house, and not many other places. With me and Daddy gone, he didn't have anyone except his worthless father. Guilt burned in my stomach. I'd overlooked how much he'd be hurting. His life had been turned upside down, just like mine.

The river glistened through the branches. Tears filled my eyes and I blinked them back. Regret about how I'd treated Daddy before I left gnawed at me. I needed to tell someone before it ate me alive—and I could always tell Tommy anything. "You know what bothers me the most? The last thing we did was argue, and I never told him how much I'd miss him."

The silence grew for a moment. "You didn't have to tell him. He knew."

I stood and walked to the edge. "I wish I'd said it, that's all. I wouldn't even look at him when the bus pulled out." I hit a branch. "I'd give anything to do it all over again."

"You can't go back." Tommy put a hand on my shoulder. "You'll have to go forward."

I opened my mouth, ready to argue, but he stopped me.

"I know. It's easy to say." He sniffed. "What'll happen now?"

I turned toward him. "I'll live with Uncle Charlie and go to school. It's the way Daddy set things up." The sky turned pink and gold as night approached. "As much as I wanted to get out of this place and experience life, this isn't what I wanted."

Tommy glowered at the darkening sky. "I suppose you have to go. They'll really be searching for you now."

I jutted my chin out. "Let them."

He peered at me. "Katie, you have to go back with them."

I sat in front of him. "I don't wanna go home." I swallowed to keep my voice from rising. "I don't want to walk in and see everything gone. I want to remember it the way it was." I picked at my skirt. "That's not too much to ask, is it?"

He reached a finger out and stroked Rupert's nose. "No."

His voice soothed me. I'd miss him so much it hurt.

He touched my hand. "We have to leave sometime, though."

"Give me five minutes." We sat in silence while I got ready to go back to the house. With Daddy gone, I couldn't truly call it home anymore. Darkness had fallen by the time I forced my way down the tree.

Tommy walked me back to the house. The silence was nice, comforting.

He gave me a hug. "You better write and tell me what kind of mischief you get yourself into." He gave me a little punch on the shoulder. "The one thing I'm sure of in life is wherever you are, you're probably making trouble of some kind."

As he left, I turned my back to the road, so I didn't have to see him disappear. I thought we'd always be together. He was the closest thing to a brother I had. Everything had been stripped from me in one blow. I lost my daddy, my home, and my best friend.

They weren't finished packing yet, but I couldn't go inside. So I opened the door of the truck and climbed in to wait. I put Rupert on the dash to watch over me.

After what seemed like forever, Mark came out. "Have you been here long?"

My legs had gone to sleep. "A little while."

He cocked his head toward the house. "You sure you don't wanna come in and meet all the family?"

I shook my head. If going inside meant I had to be civil to Aunt Delia, then noooo thank you. Besides, why should I go meet the people who had never bothered to come see how Daddy and I were getting along?

"Nice bear." Mark nodded at Rupert. "So what's the story?"

A brief smile flitted across my face. Mark's snarky tone comforted me. It was something normal in the middle of my life being torn apart. "When I was really little, Mama used to read me the Rupert Bear stories. Apparently, they were my favorite. One day, about a week before she died, we were shopping and I saw this bear and yelled, *Rupert!* She put him in my arms and I'd hugged him as if I'd never let go."

The air had cooled off, and goose pimples covered my arms. "I don't remember any of it, but Daddy told me the story hundreds of times. So the teddy bear is the last thing Mama gave me—he's my connection to her." I stared ahead, unblinking, and gently touched Rupert's paw. "Sometimes, if I try really hard, I can remember Mama reading the stories to me. But the memories are make-believe." I used to stare at her picture and imagine what her facial expressions would be, but it was all a fantasy.

Mark blinked a couple of times, then stuck his hands in his pockets and leaned against the truck. "Looks like you need a jacket."

I shrugged one shoulder. "I'm all right."

He glanced at the house. "We'll be leaving soon. They're about finished."

My whole life packed up and ready to go. The back of the truck was already filled. I didn't check to see what was in it. I didn't want to know.

"I'm going inside to help finish." He stood upright. "Wanna come?"

My mouth dried at the thought. "No. I can't."

He nodded. "We'll all be out in a few minutes." He reached through the window and patted Rupert's head.

When he went in the front door, I saw the passageway and how empty it looked beyond. I only caught a glimpse before the door closed, but it was enough. I closed my eyes, leaned my head all the way back, and took a deep breath.

A few minutes later, the truck door opened, and Sarah tossed my jacket on top of me. "It's a long trip back. You should wear it."

I slipped it on and closed the door.

Sarah got in, took Rupert out of the window, handed him to me, and started the truck. "Uncle Charlie said we should go home now so it won't be too late when we get back."

I scrunched up in the seat to prepare for the long trip. As I sat staring into the darkness, a flicker of anger ignited in my gut. The flicker turned into a flame and grew with each passing mile. It felt like a fire inside me, raging out of control.

I was angry. Angry with God for taking Daddy away from me.

How could He, when I still needed Daddy so much? Angry with myself for not realizing he was sick and making him get help. Angry with Uncle Charlie because he'd known Daddy was dying when I arrived—that's the only reason he took me in. And angry with him for keeping me from being with Daddy at the end. It was Uncle Charlie's fault he'd died in the hospital alone, and I'd never forgive him for it.

Even though it wasn't rational, I was angry with Daddy for leaving me with a family who didn't want me. I'd been forced on them, and they'd taken me out of pity. Well, I didn't want or need them either.

A charity case. A stupid charity case was all I was to them. I hoped they felt righteous and holy about it. It was the sort of thing McCabes did. Taking in the homeless and unwanted made them feel good. It'd be a bad reflection on the McCabe name if they didn't take me in. I'd never felt like a member of the family, and now I felt even less like one. But I'd make them break the McCabe tradition. They could forget about me obeying any rules they set up. I didn't want to live with them, and I'd let them know it.

We drove most of the way through the night without talking. Sarah broke the silence first.

"School starts on Tuesday." She paused to brush a strand of hair out of the way. "Uncle Charlie wants to know whether you want to go or wait a few days."

School wasn't important. If I never went to school again, I wouldn't care. "I don't know." I stared out the window into the darkness.

"Well, it's your decision." She left the end hanging like she had more to say.

I turned toward her. "But you have your own opinion."

She gave a slight nod. "You've had so many changes over the past few days, it's a lot to take in, and you need time to grieve." She hesitated. "But you might feel like you need something to take your mind off it all."

I doubted it. I'd be surrounded by strangers, none of whom

would know what I was going through, and they wouldn't care. I stared out the window again. "Fine. I'll go."

"I didn't mean I thought you should." Sarah sighed and drummed her fingers against the steering wheel. "But I'm worried you might brood too much if on your own."

Sarah's contradictions might bother me more if I didn't feel dead inside. "It doesn't make any difference to me anyway, so I might as well." I could cause as much trouble at school as I could at the house. Maybe more if I worked at it.

Her eyes flicked toward me, then back to the road. "You can always go, and if it's too much, you can give me a call and come home."

Home. Such a small word—but meaning so much. I wasn't headed toward home. I was getting farther and farther away with each passing mile.

School Time Troubles

20

Despite having gone to bed late and not sleeping well, I woke early. My head pounded and my sinuses were stuffy from all the crying I'd done over the past few days. I dreaded going to a school so much bigger than the one at home, but I might as well get it over with. At least Logan would be there.

Somehow, knowing I had a friend at school didn't comfort me. He'd be on a different campus, so I'd only see him during breaks. I pulled on jeans and a flannel shirt to do my chores before breakfast.

It surprised me to be the first one up. Usually, I had to be dragged out of bed and forced to get ready. During the night, I'd tossed and turned, never quite getting comfortable. Relieved to get out of the house into the cool morning air, I took my time doing chores. I wanted to be alone for a while.

When I got back inside, Sarah was awake, dressed, and making breakfast.

She smiled. "There you are." Her voice had a bubbly lilt to it. "I wondered where you'd gone."

I stared at her. What did she have to be so cheerful about?

She turned off the stove and dished the food onto plates. "I laid out one of the dresses we brought back with us for you to wear."

Again with a dress? "I don't want to wear one."

She pressed her lips together. "It's the first day of school and you want to look nice, don't you?"

For some reason, she didn't seem to think I could look nice in anything but a dress. "I have other clothes." Hostility put an edge in my tone. "And where do you get off picking out my outfit, anyway? I'm not a doll you can dress up."

"I don't know why you have this thing against dresses." Her hair swirled as she shook her head. "Putting on a dress makes me feel pretty. A little more feminine after working out here on the farm, I guess."

Sarah didn't need a dress to make her beautiful. She could wear a trash bag and look gorgeous. I frowned. "Dresses make me feel like I have to be on my best behavior."

"Excuse me while I go throw out the rest of your clothes." She winked at me and laughed. "I'm not asking you to walk a plank or skydive from thirty thousand feet. I want you to make a good impression on your first day at school."

"You don't think it'll make me too prissy, or like I'm full of myself?" Or even worse, like Emma. What a horrible thought to stick in my brain.

Sarah arched an eyebrow. "Are you worried about starting a new school?"

I stared at the floor and shrugged. "Maybe. A little."

She handed me a plate and patted me on the back. "What you're feeling is normal. You've had a lot of changes in a short time, and this is another change." She grabbed another plate and poured a cup of coffee. "I remember being apprehensive before my first day of middle school, and I'd grown up in this town and knew all the kids."

I put my plate on the table and sat. If Tommy lived here, I wouldn't care. My best friend would be at my side—even though he'd be on the high school campus. "But what if I can't make any friends?"

Sarah settled at the table, touched the purple stone in her rose-gold necklace, then leaned forward and placed her hand over mine. "From what I've seen, you've already made friends."

True, but I'd made some enemies as well.

She pulled her hand back and took a sip of coffee. "Just be yourself. You're a likeable person—when you're not snarling at everyone." Her eyes twinkled as she grinned.

I laughed. At least I felt a little better about the day ahead.

Sarah tapped her fork against the napkin. "Finish up and get ready. We have to be at school early to get your class schedule."

I rolled my eyes. "Don't remind me."

After breakfast, I showered and hurried to my room. Picking up the dress Sarah had laid out, I felt on the verge of tears. My emotions were in such a whirlwind, I never knew what to expect. One minute grumpy, the next happy as Sarah teased me, and now my heart was so sorrowful it felt like it would burst.

When we arrived, I slid out of the truck and stared. My first day of school without Daddy. Feeling like I'd never be happy again, I took a deep breath.

Sarah put a hand on my shoulder. "We can always go home if you're not ready."

I shook my head and swallowed the lump forming in my throat. It'd never get easier, so best to get this first day out of the way and into the past.

As I walked onto the campus, I didn't feel quite so out of place in a dress. Every other girl wore one, too. If they wore them every day, I'd hate getting dressed for school.

Sarah came with me to check my class schedule.

Principal Conway still wore a bow tie, crooked. It wasn't working for him. He didn't need any help being dorkified.

He leaned against his desk. "We were quite impressed with your test results, Katie."

I opened my mouth, but Sarah gripped my shoulder, so I closed it again.

"Coming from such a small school, I didn't expect you to score as well as you did." His glasses were about to slide off his nose. "With the exceptional level of your results, I conferred with Ms. Freeman, the high school principal, and we agreed to advance you to ninth grade. In fact, you've even been placed in a sophomore class."

I'd have class on the same campus as Logan? I bit back a smile.

"Principal Freeman put together your schedule." Mr. Conway pushed up his glasses and straightened his tie before handing me a sheet of paper. "I'll keep myself informed as to how you are doing. We'll be expecting fine work from you."

Fat chance. I didn't have to do any work, and I didn't want to. He'd be keeping track of me all right, but not because of my wonderful grades. Quite the opposite, in fact. I scanned the class schedule he handed me.

Seven subjects and none of them fun. Ms. Freeman had even enrolled me in a study skills class, and I didn't need to learn how to study. I always did well in classes. In addition to the schedule, my locker location and the combination were printed on the front and there was a map of the campus on the back.

Sarah held out her hand to see the assignments. I tried to guess what she thought by watching her face but failed.

She handed back the paper. "You'd better put your things in your locker and get to your first class."

She didn't look pleased, but I had no idea what she was upset about. I left reluctantly, but Sarah watched me until I closed the door. The murmur of voices started as soon as the door clicked shut, but I couldn't distinguish the words. The bell for the first class would ring any minute, and there were a lot of kids walking around. Everyone wore their Sunday best.

I checked my schedule. At least I had volleyball and track for my last class. I'd be outside and might be able to see the football practice. According to the campus map, my locker wasn't in the big set near the entrance, but against one of the buildings lining the quad. As I studied the map, a shadow crossed me and I looked up.

Logan stood there grinning. "I wondered how long it'd take you to figure out you were being watched."

He couldn't have been there for long. I smiled as I took in his suit and tie. He wore it well, a lot better than Tommy. By the look on his face, he liked my dress. Maybe Sarah hadn't been wrong.

"Do you dress like this every day?" I tugged at his tie.

"No. It's kinda a school tradition for everyone to dress up on the first day. After that, it's jeans every day."

Why hadn't Sarah told me about the tradition instead of arguing with me? If she had, I'd have put on the dress without so much of a fight.

He touched the paper. "Is this your schedule?"

I handed it to him. "Yeah. The weird news is I'm now a freshman."

He frowned. "Why are you taking such a heavy load? You'll be doing so much homework you won't have time for me."

I shrugged. "Ms. Freeman enrolled me. Don't worry about the homework though, I won't do any."

Logan took my things and walked toward the lockers. "I'm sure glad she doesn't sign me up for classes. My brain would suffer from overload." He glanced at my schedule again. "We have the same class right before lunch."

"Really?"

"Yep. Geometry. Not the most fun in the world, but we'll liven up the class." Logan winked.

More than he probably knew.

He stopped at a locker, glanced at the combination, and opened the lock. He put the lunch Sarah made inside and shut the door. "I'll walk you to your first class."

When we got inside the building, he stopped talking and gazed straight into my eyes for a moment.

It unnerved me. "What's wrong?"

He pulled me over to the study carrels. "I tried to call you, but no one answered. I heard some story going around about your father being sick. How is he?"

The tears felt hot in my eyes. My fingers curled into tightly balled fists. I didn't want to cry in front of Logan. "No one answered because we were at his funeral."

Pain filled his eyes. "I'm so sorry."

"Don't be. It happened, and your being sorry doesn't change anything." How harsh. "I didn't mean it to come out that way."

"It's all right, I understand." He grabbed my hand. "Anytime you need to talk about him, I'll listen."

I gave his hand a squeeze. "Thanks, Logan." I wanted to tell him why I hadn't said anything before, and how quickly everything had happened, but my throat closed. Not many guys would honestly care so soon after meeting a girl, and others wouldn't be so understanding. And what had I done? Practically snapped his head off.

I hurried into the room and slipped into a desk at the back. First period went by fast. We all had to stand and introduce ourselves. I felt like saying my name and telling the class this was the last place on earth I wanted to be.

Mr. Whitehall then told us what to expect in his class. Kids kept turning around to look at me and whispering to one another while the teacher droned on. I hadn't meant to cause a disturbance ... this time ... but had simply by being the "new girl."

A guy across the room pulled pages out of his notebook, tore them into strips, and rolled the strips into tight little balls. He then used his thumb and middle finger to shoot paper wads at the other kids. The guy shot one at me, and I flicked it back, and the paper wad war began. I ripped a few sheets out of my notebook and made my own ammunition, as did several others. While rolling the strips into balls, I collected those shot at me and rapid-fire shot them back. Mr. Whitehall kept reading from the rules and requirements page, unaware of the balls flying around.

Unfortunately, a wad hit him and he stopped reading.

Mr. Whitehall bent and picked up the paper ball. "Who is responsible for this?" He glared at the class, trying to stare us down.

I still had three wads lined up on my desk. Seizing my chance while he glared at another section of the class, I flicked them off my desk as fast as I could, as close to Mr. Whitehall as possible. The last one struck him. Pay dirt.

His head swung quickly around. "This behavior must stop." He slammed the roll book on his desk and turned bright red. "If the guilty party does not confess, the entire class will be on Saturday cleanup."

A collective groan rose from all parts of the room. The guy who had started the war stared at the ceiling.

I cast a look around the room and then stood.

Mr. Whitehall frowned. "Does this mean you are the guilty party, Miss McCabe?"

What did he think? I'd stood for my health? I nodded.

He tossed the wad in the trash and scanned the room. "Did you make this mess by yourself, or did you have help?"

I wasn't a snitch, especially not on the first day of school. I'd never live it down.

The entire class waited for me to speak. The instigator of the war threw me dirty looks. As if he'd keep me quiet—*Ha*.

Mr. Whitehall stood with his arms folded, glaring at me.

If I wanted to create some problems, this seemed like the perfect time. "It doesn't matter. You wanted a confession? You got one." He wouldn't be happy with it, but who cared?

He frowned. "Miss McCabe, you are showing a definite negative attitude. I asked you a simple question."

A negative attitude? What a joke. "You asked me to turn in my classmates. I won't. Not for something this stupid."

He walked to his desk and opened a drawer. "Come to the front of the room."

I slowly moved to the front.

Mr. Whitehall pulled out a pad of referral slips. "If you won't cooperate, I have no choice but to refer you to the vice principal."

I gritted my teeth. "Send me. I don't cave to threats."

He handed me the slip, and I left the class, giving a mock salute before walking out the door. Things were working out better than I'd expected. Uncle Charlie didn't want me. I'd show him how much trouble charity cases could be.

The receptionist gave me a friendly smile as I walked into the office. "May I help you?"

I held out the blue referral slip. "Mr. Whitehall sent me to see the vice principal."

She calmly picked up the phone and rang Mr. Segerstrom's office.

"He's free to see you now."

I was a little nervous because I wasn't quite sure what to expect. The vice principal of my old school and I had been good friends, if for no other reason than I'd been to see him several times over the years. Well, they couldn't do anything to me here that hadn't already been done. I turned the knob and walked boldly in.

Mr. Segerstrom surprised me. For some reason, I'd expected him to look like the middle school principal, but he was tall with an athletic build. I handed him my slip.

"You'd better take a seat." He folded his hands on the desk and leaned forward. "I don't know what rules you were used to in your previous school, but throwing paper wads around the room is not acceptable here."

Did he seriously think throwing paper wads was acceptable at any school?

He paused as if he expected me to speak. "Since this is your first day here, I'm going to let you go with a warning." He settled back in his chair. "I didn't expect to have someone in my office quite so soon."

How fun. I got to be the first discipline problem of the year.

"What bothers me more than the incident itself is the note Mr. Whitehall wrote on your slip. He mentioned an uncooperative attitude."

I bit the end of my tongue to keep from laughing. I didn't know whether to tell him why Mr. Whitehall thought I was uncooperative or not.

Mr. Segerstrom sat quietly waiting for me to speak.

I bit my lip and struggled to find the right words. "Mr. Whitehall asked me to turn in other kids and I wouldn't." I shifted uncomfortably. "I'd rather take the blame for the whole thing." I tried to hold back from saying anything more. But failed. "Can you imagine what would happen if I ratted someone out in my first class at a new school? Especially when I'm younger than everyone else? I'd be crucified. How unfair can you get?"

Mr. Segerstrom stroked his jaw while a hint of a smile crossed his face. "I'll accept there would've been some peer pressure involved. I hope this was an isolated incident, and you won't make it a habit."

Exactly what I intended to do.

His face grew stern. "Remember, I am letting you off this time. If there's a next time, I'll have to contact your guardian."

The Note Home

21

Second period had already started by the time I left the vice principal's office, so the receptionist gave me an excuse note. I went straight to the teacher, Miss Phelps, and gave her the tardy slip.

She peered over my shoulder. "Why don't you take the empty seat next to Emma?"

I hoped against hope the Emma wouldn't be the same one I met at the picnic, but no luck. I searched the room to see whether there were any other empty seats, but they were all filled. I'd be on time tomorrow, so I wouldn't have to sit next to her.

As I took my seat, Miss Phelps continued class. "I'm sending around a seating chart. Please write your name where you are sitting. This will be your permanent seat for the semester."

I'd be stuck next to Emma for an entire semester? I hadn't done anything bad enough to deserve such a horrible fate. A girl sat next to me on the other side, too. Not that I didn't like any girls, though I got along better with guys.

When the seating chart was passed back to Miss Phelps, she asked for all the chattering to stop, and pointed to an assignment on the board.

Beside me, Emma hissed, "Katie."

I turned toward her. "What?"

She looked away. "Don't talk to me."

Me? Talk to her? "Don't worry. I don't want to catch what you've got." I didn't want it to get around I'd sat next to her, let alone talked to her.

"What do you mean?" Emma's voice rose above a whisper.

I gave her a deadpan stare. "Something must have happened to make you that ugly. It must be some sort of disease, and I don't want to get it."

Her face turned red, and arms went rigid. "Of all the mean ..." She'd reached shriek level before she broke off and pressed her lips into a thin line.

Maybe I'd gone too far, but she'd started it.

Daddy's voice popped into my head. *A fight takes two people. Be the bigger person and walk away.* A pang hit my stomach as my cheeks flamed. He'd have been disappointed in me. The thought crushed me more than it had when he was alive. I swallowed hard.

A shadow fell over us.

Miss Phelps stood in front of us with her arms folded. "Is there some sort of problem here, girls?"

Emma pulled herself straight in her chair as her face returned to its normal pasty complexion. "Since Katie is new here, I tried to help her out by answering some of her questions."

What a two-faced liar.

Miss Phelps tapped a finger on her bicep. "Not quite the impression I got when I walked up. We'll discuss the matter further when you come back after school for detention."

If Mr. Segerstrom wouldn't send a note to Uncle Charlie, then at least I'd gotten detention. It was a start. I'd also managed to get Emma into trouble. What a happy thought. She shot me several dirty looks and went so far as to write a note telling me she'd get me back. But she didn't open her mouth for the rest of the class. An achievement worth repeating.

I practically slept through third period, bored out of my mind. If it stayed as mind numbing as this, I'd have to find some way to liven it up. I hurried to my fourth class to sit next to Logan. I wasn't thrilled about being in geometry, but I'd make it through somehow.

My jaw went slack when Denton walked in the room. I didn't think he had the brains for it, but I supposed there might be one thing in the world he had a talent for. Besides being a rotten person.

The class started off slow and quiet, the same as any other class on the first day. Mrs. Johnson stood tall and straight in front of her desk, her dark hair tightly coiled on top of her head. A table to her side was covered in stacks of textbooks.

She smoothed the pleats of her mint green linen dress. "We're going to dive right in by starting with some review problems. Denton, will you please hand out the books?"

He lumbered to the front of the room and picked up a stack.

Mrs. Johnson pointed to the board. "Every day the homework assignment will be written in the upper left corner."

Homework on the first day? *Blerg.* This would *not* be a class I enjoyed.

She gave us a broad smile. "And we'll have a quiz sometime this week to check how much you retained over the summer."

When Denton reached me, he slammed the book down on my hand. Without pausing to think, I picked it up and swung it around, hitting him on the arm. I pulled it back, ready to hit the toad, again when Mrs. Johnson interrupted.

"Young lady. Put the book down this instant."

I followed through bashing Denton once more before I put the book on the desk.

Mrs. Johnson's voice rose. "Hitting other students is not acceptable in this classroom."

Acceptable seemed to be the buzz word for the day.

She pulled out her referral pad. "Take this down to Mr. Segerstrom's office, and he will handle it from here."

A second trip to the vice principal in one day. What an accomplishment.

Denton smirked as I walked toward the door.

I glanced at Logan as I passed. His eyes were wide and his jaw slack. Maybe I shouldn't have retaliated, but the smug creep deserved it. But then Logan's eyes narrowed, and he scowled as he watched Denton rub his arm. Denton would have to look out for himself.

The receptionist didn't give the same friendly smile when I walked through the door this time. She didn't even ask what I needed but motioned for me to go into Mr. Segerstrom's office.

"Take a seat, Katie." Mr. Segerstrom frowned as I came through the door. "It's more than a little troubling to have you back in my office today." He held out his hand. "I need your blue slip." He glanced at it but tossed it aside without reading. "We have a zero-tolerance policy for violence. What's your justification for hitting a fellow student?"

Ridiculous. The phrase *zero-tolerance* meant it didn't matter whether I was justified or not, I'd still be punished. "The guy handing out the books slammed one on my hand. On purpose." I shrugged. "I lost my temper."

He leaned forward, glaring. "Someone else's behavior does not justify your actions."

How infuriating. "I never said it did. Do you want to know what happened?"

He took out a sheet of paper. "I'm writing a note to your uncle. Bring it back to me, signed by him, before going to any classes tomorrow." He paused a couple of times, then signed it. "Since you've had two referrals in one day, I've informed your uncle of both incidents."

Uncle Charlie'd be wondering what he'd got himself into.

"Normally, students are suspended immediately for violent acts." Mr. Segerstrom pressed his lips tightly together.

So much for following a zero-tolerance policy.

He sealed the note in an envelope and held it out. "I won't hesitate if it happens again."

I stood and took the letter.

"I don't want to see you for the rest of the day, unless it's passing between classes." He pulled a folder from his inbox and flipped it open.

Sarah would probably think the day had been too much for me and be upset I hadn't called. With a quick glance back, I opened the door.

Mr. Segerstrom looked up from the paperwork. "Tell my

receptionist you need to see me tomorrow morning before your first class, and she'll send you right in.

By the time I got back to class, it was almost over. I flipped to the pages in the book referenced on the board for homework and sighed. Mrs. Johnson had assigned forty problems. If she gave us this much homework on a regular basis, it'd be a very long semester.

Either that or I'd voluntarily flunk. Who wanted to spend every waking hour on geometry homework? *Not this girl.* Flunking geometry might not be a bad idea. More free time for me, and it'd upset Uncle Charlie and Sarah. I'd start with not doing any homework tonight.

The last few minutes of class drug by at a snail's pace. I might scream before the bell rang, releasing us to lunch. Denton cast a look over his shoulder, his smug grin stretching his lips so wide, I half expected his tongue to dart out and catch a fly. Another minute or two and I'd be free to spend some time with Logan. Who wouldn't want that?

Mrs. Johnson erased the problem she had written on the board. "Class dismissed."

Possibly some of the best words in the English language. I grabbed my book and strode toward the door.

Logan took my hand as soon as we left. "So, did Segerstrom go light with you? He usually does the first time."

I shook my head. "It was my second time."

"What do you mean?" Logan stopped.

The crush of students exiting the building swarmed around us.

"I got sent in first hour too." I couldn't meet Logan's eyes.

He led me over to the benches lining the walkway and sat. "How come?"

"For doing stupid stuff. I don't want to talk about it." I'd have to explain too much tonight—I didn't want to start now. "He gave me a note for Uncle Charlie to sign. It doesn't matter anyway."

"Why doesn't it matter?" Logan's brow wrinkled with concern. "Won't you get into trouble?"

"Probably." *Definitely* would've been a more accurate response. "The family doesn't love me—they don't even know me." They'd be upset, but not because I meant anything to them. "I'll get into trouble, but I don't care. What can they do to me anyway?"

Seriously, short of physically restraining me, they couldn't do much. If they grounded me, I didn't have to obey. Or listen to them when they yelled. And if I didn't do the chores, what could they do? More of the same?

Logan and I sat through the rest of lunch not saying much. *Awkward.* A troubled expression kept crossing his face. He didn't understand what it felt like to be living somewhere where you're tolerated and not loved.

I bumped his shoulder. "Don't worry about it. I'll be fine."

"I like you and care what happens to you." He slipped his hand over mine. "Call me tonight and let me know what your uncle says. If you can't call for some reason, come to school a little early tomorrow so I have a chance to see you."

The bell rang, and I didn't want to leave. Time flew every time I was around Logan.

The rest of the day went by quickly. Miss Phelps lectured Emma and me for about half an hour and told us she expected us to learn to tolerate each other.

All I'd learned was how much of a pain Emma could be.

The Fallout

22

Sarah was waiting in the parking lot when I came out. "I was about ready to start looking for you. You're a little late."

I hadn't even gotten into the truck yet when the flood of questions began. "I had to stay after one of my classes."

She scrutinized me as she reached for the key. "Is this something we need to discuss at home?"

I slumped in the seat and crossed my arms. "I don't care if we talk about it now or later."

Her lips pressed into a straight line, and she swatted my leg. "Watch your tone." She started the engine and shook her head.

We pulled into the drive a few minutes later. I didn't wait for the truck to come to a complete stop before I jumped out and ran into the house, heading straight into my room.

Sarah quickly followed me. "I want to know what happened at school."

I studied my nails and picked at my cuticles. "Emma and I got into an argument in my second class, so the teacher gave us detention." I flopped back on the bed. "It was no big deal."

Sarah's nostrils flared. "Since it was no big deal, you can stay in your room until Uncle Charlie gets home. Then you can talk to him about it."

And a few other things. "Won't you need my help in the kitchen?" I tried to be as sarcastic as possible.

"Not tonight I won't." She paused at the door before leaving. "If you have any homework, do it."

Homework? I laughed. No way. A couple hours alone were a blessing. Maybe I should be thinking about what I'd done wrong. Perhaps feel a little sorry about it. Instead, I lay down and went to sleep.

I woke to someone shaking my shoulder. Sarah.

"It's time to eat."

I came out and sat at the table. As soon as grace was said, the inquisition started.

Uncle Charlie picked up his fork and glanced over at me. "Sarah tells me you had a problem at school today. I'd like to discuss it."

I hadn't planned to bring up the trips to the vice principal's office until after dinner, but I decided I might as well throw it at them all at once. "Which problem?"

Sarah shot a glance at me. "You said you got detention."

"So?" I raised a shoulder. "That was one, I had a couple others. You only asked me about being late."

Her eyes narrowed. "I asked you what happened at school."

Uncle Charlie cleared his throat. "Katie, you need to tell us what went on today. All of it."

I jumped up from the table and went into my room to get the note from Mr. Segerstrom. "I'm supposed to give this to you. I guess now is as good a time as any."

I ate hurriedly while Uncle Charlie read the note, his face growing grimmer as he went down the page.

He read to the end then put the letter on the table. "You're excused to go to your room."

I opened my mouth to protest, but Uncle Charlie held up his hand.

"No arguments. Go."

I never got to eat a full meal around this place. It wouldn't be long before he came in to talk to me, so I sat on the edge of the bed and waited.

When Uncle Charlie came in, he was quiet and calm. "I brought a bicycle home for you to use to get to and from school."

I'd expected him to yell at me, not give me a bicycle. "Thanks." I didn't sound very grateful, but I'd been thrown off balance.

He sat on Sarah's bed. "Did you get all your classes squared away?"

"Yeah." I didn't understand his beating around the bush. It put me on edge. "They advanced me into high school, and Principal Freeman put my schedule together." I ran a hand through my hair. "She gave me a heavy load."

"I'm sure you'll be able to handle it." His brown eyes pierced mine. "Do you have anything to say for yourself?"

His hurt expression got to me. "I guess not."

He studied me and waited.

"What do you want from me?" I didn't like being stared at, especially since he wasn't saying anything. "Things sorta happened. I suppose I could've helped it." But I hadn't wanted to. My fingers twisted together. I wasn't going to apologize.

"I want you to clean up the kitchen, and tomorrow when you get home from school, Sarah will have a list of extra chores for you to do." Uncle Charlie stood. "After you're through with the kitchen, do your homework, and get into bed."

It was the same routine as usual, work and then bed. I cleaned the kitchen in silence. Sarah stayed at the table studying, and Uncle Charlie joined Matthew and Mark in the living room. When I finished, I picked up the phone to call Logan.

Sarah stared at me. "What do you think you're doing?"

"I'm making a phone call. What does it look like?" I held the receiver in my hand.

"Put down the phone." Her voice had a hard edge to it.

What was *her* problem? "All I'm going to do is call someone."

Sarah stormed over to the phone, took the receiver from my hand, and clicked it off. "You aren't making any phone calls tonight."

Who did she think she was anyway? "It sure didn't take you long to start giving me orders."

She glared at me.

Uncle Charlie held up his hand before Sarah could fire off a retort. "Katie, it's time you went to your room."

At least he had the right to order me around.

I ran into the room and slammed the door. On the edge of tears, I grabbed my teddy bear and flopped on the bed. I straightened the bow at Rupert's neck. What bothered me the most was that I'd gotten in trouble in front of Matthew and Mark. If they'd jumped on me too, it would've been too much for me. Especially Matthew.

I'd avoided Matthew's eyes when Uncle Charlie had read the letter from Mr. Segerstrom. He would've reminded me of Daddy, and I needed to forget him and what he would have thought or felt about things.

If I could forget, maybe I wouldn't hurt so much. And it'd make it easier to hate these people, and not care about hurting them.

Two days later, morning dawned bright, and the crisp air felt like fall. I looked forward to school because Logan had introduced me to lots of people, and I'd see Mike and Pete between classes. Plus, with the number of times I'd already been in trouble, my reputation for being a rebel had spread.

Sarah turned the radio on while we were getting ready, and the weather forecaster predicted a rainstorm within the next day or so, but the blue sky was clear, except for a few scattered white puff-ball clouds. Storms belonged to another day, not this one.

The bicycle Uncle Charlie bought me rode like a dream, and it got me places so much faster than walking. I arrived at school early, anxious to spend some special time with Logan with no one else around. He was the only person I could talk to ... really open my heart to. He seemed to understand what I was going through and wanted to help me. The only thing we disagreed about was whether Uncle Charlie and the rest of the family wanted me to live with them or not. But he still listened.

As I parked my bike at the racks in front of the entrance, I caught a glimpse of Denton near my locker. He shouldn't be anywhere near it. His locker was against another building. I chained up my bike and peered at him again, but Denton had disappeared. I had only glanced away for a second, and Denton didn't ever move that fast. So maybe I had imagined it. Why imagine something as awful as Denton on such a good morning, I'd never know.

"Did things go better for you yesterday?"

I jumped. Logan liked to come out of nowhere.

"A little." Of course, I hadn't been in any trouble at school either. I'd fix that today.

He took my books. "Are you ready for our geometry test?"

I made a face. "It's ridiculous to have a test the first week of school. What does she expect us to know at this point?" I leaned against the wall. "I wouldn't mind so much if Mrs. Johnson wasn't using it as a part of our grade. What happens if we bomb this test?"

"I don't know what to tell you." Logan shrugged. "You've already helped me with geometry, so you should do fine on it."

I paused for a moment. "What if I don't want to?"

Logan turned away. "Katie, don't do this."

"Why shouldn't I?" I laid a hand on his arm. "If you feel so strongly, tell me."

His face softened as he gazed at me. "You'll only be hurting yourself."

My jaw tightened. "I don't care anymore. School may be important to the McCabe clan, but I don't want anything to do with them." They'd get riled if I didn't make good grades, but only because they cared about how things looked ... not about me.

"You may upset them for a while, but you're the one who has to live with the grades." Logan raked his teeth across his lower lip. "And try to get into a decent college with them."

I hadn't considered college. "Freshman year grades don't go on the transcripts, though, do they?"

He shook his head.

I raised my shoulders. "Well then?"

He sighed. "You still have to get into the college prep classes based on how you do this year."

I wrinkled my nose. He was right. I couldn't afford not to do well. "All right." I rolled my eyes. "I'll do my best on this one."

He gave a huge sigh of relief. "I wasn't sure you were going to listen. You'll be glad you did."

The bell for class rang so we had to leave each other ... again.

Walking into second period, I shuddered. I dreaded the class because of Emma. She either completely ignored me or wrote nasty notes. I preferred being ignored. I took my seat and Emma turned toward me. Today wouldn't be one of the blissful days.

"Hello, Katie, how are you today?" Emma smiled at me.

The two-faced Goody Two-shoes had returned. "Fine, thanks." It took all I had to be civil to her.

Her stretched grin looked etched in stone. "Good. Denton told me you're having a test in geometry. Are you ready for it?"

Why had she turned on the fake charm? "I think so." She made me ill with her insincerity.

"Good luck on it." Class started and Emma had to stop talking. The corners of her mouth turned down before she faced the front.

Thank goodness that ordeal was over. She must've been as relieved as I was.

The morning passed quickly, and geometry class came sooner than I expected. The test went well. I didn't have any problems with it at all. I finished the test first, so I waited in the hall until Logan came out.

"So? How'd you do?" He grabbed my books.

I tilted my head. "I think I aced it. How about you?"

He grinned. "Pretty well. I might have missed one or two, but I'm good with that."

We spent the whole lunch hour talking and joking around. Mike joined us about halfway through, and he teased me mercilessly. It was the most relaxing time I'd spent since coming to this place. I couldn't explain why I felt so comfortable with Logan, but I always felt accepted for who I was. Tommy was the only person, other than Daddy, who had made me feel the same way, and I'd known Tommy all my life.

Study skills seemed dingier than usual. Coming in from the bright sunlight, it took a few moments to adjust to the gloom inside. Class started with its usual dreariness. Lecture after lecture of what the study environment should be and the different learning styles got tiring fast, and I wished we could get on to something a little more exciting. The next topic promised to be as boring; the five methods of note-taking. We'd only been at it for about five minutes when a student office worker came in with a message for the teacher.

"Katie." She walked over to my desk. "Mr. Segerstrom would like to see you in his office."

What did the vice principal want me for? I hadn't done anything wrong. I gathered my things and left class. The secretary waved me right into his office when I walked through the door. It was beginning to feel like a familiar habit.

False Accusations

23

When I entered his office, Mr. Segerstrom motioned to the chair in front of his desk. "Take a seat." He leaned forward, a stern look on his face. "We need to discuss a serious matter."

I hadn't figured he'd called me in to talk about the weather.

The lines from his nose to the corners of his mouth deepened as he frowned. "You've been accused of stealing the geometry test master."

A jolt hit the pit of my stomach.

He folded his hands on the desk. "With the accusation, I had Mrs. Johnson grade your paper straightaway, and you scored one hundred percent. Since you've struggled with the homework, she feels your score is suspicious."

My shoulders twitched. Deliberately not doing homework wasn't struggling—it was a choice. The one time missing a few answers on a test would've been a good thing, and I had to go and get a perfect score.

Mr. Segerstrom gave me a long stare. "I want to give you the chance to defend yourself."

"I didn't do it." Stealing a test master had never even occurred to me. "But I can't prove it. When was I supposed to have taken it?" Not that I'd have an alibi.

He briefly smiled. "The information wasn't specific as to time."

What kind of hogwash was that? Someone could accuse me of doing something, but didn't have to give any details?

He stood. "Let's go search your locker so we can put this complaint to rest."

I wrinkled my brow and pressed my lips together. "Do you honestly think I'd've been stupid enough to put the master in my locker if I did steal it? Which I didn't."

He held the door open. "The sooner we check, the sooner you can go back to class."

"Fine. I don't have anything I shouldn't." I stood.

"Nothing would make me happier than to find exactly that."

As we walked, I felt self-conscious about having the vice principal follow me the entire way. Fortunately, classes were still in session.

Even though I'd said I didn't mind, the thought of my locker being pawed through by Mr. Segerstrom set my teeth on edge. We walked without talking, and when we arrived at the locker, the only sound was the scraping of the lock as I turned it. I swung the door open. "There you go."

He systematically took everything out of my locker, eyeballing each paper, and shaking out the books. Nothing. Even though I hadn't done it, I breathed a sigh of relief. He pulled out the last book, and underneath lay a paper I hadn't seen before.

He looked at it. "If you didn't steal the master, how do you explain this?"

But it can't be. Total disbelief caused my jaw to loosen. He couldn't have a copy of the test in his hand. "I don't know. I didn't take it." It sounded lame, even to my ears.

"Let's go back to my office."

Based on his grim tone, I wouldn't be able to talk my way out of this.

Besides, I didn't know what to say or do. It was hard to argue my innocence when he held the "proof" in his hand. My stomach twisted into knots.

When we got back to his office, he placed the master on his desk and pulled out a sheet of blank paper. Maybe he'd write another note to Uncle Charlie. The silence made me nervous, and the pen scratching the paper nearly drove me up a wall. He signed his name then laid his pen on the desk.

Then he reached for the phone. "I'd like to speak with Mr. McCabe, please."

The note hadn't been to Uncle Charlie then. Who had he

written to?

He leaned back in his chair. "Mr. McCabe, this is Vice Principal Segerstrom. I have your niece here in my office right now."

Uncle Charlie wasn't going to be happy. The walls of Mr. Segerstrom's office felt like they were closing in, and my pulse raced. The chair squeaked as I shifted my weight.

Mr. Segerstrom fixed me with a glare. "She was accused of stealing a test master, which she denied, but I found it in her locker."

Somebody had planted it there. I'd been framed but couldn't prove it.

"I'm sending her home now." He watched me closely. "She's been suspended for the rest of the day and tomorrow."

Suspended? I froze. I'd never been suspended before.

Mr. Segerstrom made a note on his pad. "And I've placed her on Saturday cleanup for a month."

Saturday cleanup ... nothing but a term for unpaid labor. I'd been going out of my way to get into trouble and would've taken it in my stride if I'd done something wrong, but this was different.

"Plus, she will receive a zero for her test score." He scribbled another note.

Indignation burned. I wouldn't have failed that badly if I'd tried. I'd never cheated on a test in my life.

Mr. Segerstrom finished the conversation and hung up the phone. "I wanted you to hear so you'd have no doubts about what your uncle has been told." He picked up the letter he'd written and folded it into thirds. "This is to Mrs. Johnson, so she can revise your grade accordingly."

Should I protest my innocence? I swallowed hard. It wouldn't help. Mr. Segerstrom thought I was guilty and actual guilt didn't matter. I couldn't blame him. If I didn't know for sure I hadn't done it, the "evidence" might have convinced me, too.

He let me go after telling me the Saturday cleanup regulations, but I didn't want to go to the house. Sarah would be there, and if Uncle Charlie hadn't called her already, I'd have to explain why I was back early. It wouldn't be a fun afternoon. As I pedaled down the road, my mind went around in circles trying to figure out how the master got in my locker.

There were only two people who hated me enough to have done it—Denton and Emma. I didn't know anyone else well enough for them to have a grudge against me. The other kids I'd met were friendly, and I didn't think they'd frame someone they barely knew. Emma's odd behavior in class must have meant she was involved. If only I could prove it.

Then I remembered Denton had been near my locker before school. *I had seen him.* But I couldn't prove he'd been there. Whatever it took, I'd make sure he got his just desserts. Revenge would be sweet. It wouldn't be anything as simple as dumping him in the lake this time. That'd be too good for him.

I wheeled my bike up the drive, half hoping Sarah wouldn't be there. No such luck. I parked the bike by the barn, took a deep breath, and went in the house.

Sarah sat at the kitchen table, staring into space, with a textbook open in front of her. When I came in, she glanced at the clock on the wall. "What are you doing home so early?" She brushed tears from her eyes and hastily put something in the wooden chest beside her, then closed the clasp.

Uncle Charlie must not have called. "The vice principal told me to leave school." I steeled myself for the reaction.

She closed the textbook. "What for?"

I crossed my arms. "Mr. Segerstrom thinks I stole the master copy to my geometry test."

Sarah's mouth dropped open. "How could you do such a thing?"

"I didn't." I hated sticking up for my innocence and couldn't keep the irritability out of my voice. I was tired of being falsely accused.

She pursed her lips. "Why did he send you home?"

"Because he found it in my locker and suspended me." My anger reached the boiling point.

Sarah pressed her hand against her collarbone and inhaled deeply.

"There's no need to yell. All I'm doing is asking some questions."

Yeah. Question after question. Daddy would've believed me. "But you don't trust me when I say it isn't true." There. Let her answer that one.

She rubbed her heart-key necklace. "I'm trying, Katie. It's hard without all the facts."

I couldn't convince her on the evidence either. I didn't know the entire story.

"Do you know how the copy came to be in your locker?" Sarah tapped a finger on her textbook.

If I'd been able to prove it, I'd still be at school. "How am I supposed to know? Someone else must've put it there."

If I blamed Denton, she'd think I'd made the whole thing up for sure. I wished my denials didn't sound so phony. If I'd done it, I'd have had better excuses.

Sarah sighed. "You said you didn't do it, and I'm trying to find something to help me believe you."

She didn't, though. "What happened to the accused being innocent until proven guilty?" She didn't respond. "I didn't expect the vice principal to accept what I said, but I hoped you would." I tried to glare at Sarah, but she wouldn't meet my eyes.

She picked the phone up from the table.

"What're you doing?"

Sarah took a deep breath. "Regardless of what you think, Uncle Charlie has to be called." She pushed the buttons.

She couldn't wait to tattle on me. "Mr. Segerstrom already called him."

She put the receiver back on the table. "Katie, you assume I don't trust you, but I'm trying to keep an open mind."

She'd keep it open to my guilt and wouldn't listen to anything I had to say.

"I don't know what to think." She ran a finger around the lid of the wooden chest. "You tell me you didn't steal the test, but Mr. Segerstrom clearly thinks you did. And the test was found in your locker."

Like that pointed to my guilt. "I wish Daddy were still alive. He'd tell you I didn't do it." I clenched my teeth, but my fury leaked through. "I'm not stupid enough to have put the master in my locker. But you obviously think I am."

She pressed her lips together. "Settle down."

Tired of being told to settle down, I turned and stomped out of the room. How did Sarah expect me to stay calm when I'd been accused of something I hadn't done?

"I didn't say we were through." Sarah followed me into the hall.

"You're not listening to me." My control snapped and I yelled. "I'm not perfect, but I don't steal, I don't cheat, and I don't lie."

She put her hand on my shoulder and propelled me toward our bedroom.

I shook her hand off. "It's not fair. You're taking Mr. Segerstrom's side."

She walked back to the door. "You stay in here until you calm down and can talk rationally about this."

I'd be in here forever.

Sitting on the edge of the bed, I crossed my arms to keep from throwing things. Maybe I should decide what to do to Denton instead of wasting my energy on anger. I wanted to get him somehow. If I could get my hands on him, I'd whip the tar out of him. That at least would give me some satisfaction.

But if I beat him up, I'd be in even more trouble. How fair was that? I didn't mind getting into trouble for things I'd done, but this time I hadn't done anything.

I already had a bad mark on my record from it, and I'd have to spend a boring month cleaning up the school. And I'd failed the test I'd promised Logan I'd do well on.

I *had* done well on. I deserved the perfect score.

Flopping back on the bed, I grappled with different ways to get back at Denton for what he had done. I'd include Emma in whatever I came up with. She was involved somehow, otherwise she wouldn't have been so sickeningly sweet during second period.

Bodily harm was out. Denton, the worm, would spin another lie I'd have to confess to. Sabotaging his locker sounded fun. The locks were so cheap, sometimes jiggling the handle allowed the door to open. But if I broke the locker, he'd know something was wrong and it'd ruin the surprise of the booby-trap.

I'd have to think it out a little bit. He rode his bike to school, too. Maybe I'd do a little work on his tires. Fix it so they'd come off when he went to ride it. They both sounded like such good ideas, I couldn't decide which one I wanted to do.

My eyelids got heavier and heavier as I mulled over the possibilities, and I drifted off to sleep.

"Katie. It's time for supper."

Startled, I woke up. Sarah stood waiting for me. I groggily went out to the table. Matthew and Mark must have been told about what happened at school, because neither one looked at me when I came into the room. Still half asleep, I flopped into my chair at the table.

Uncle Charlie started in on me as soon as he finished grace. "Katie, I understand we have something to talk about."

I hadn't even taken a bite of food yet. "Can't it wait until we're through? I'm not all the way awake yet."

Uncle Charlie tapped his fork on the side of his dish. "I suppose we can wait until after supper."

What a relief. I didn't feel like arguing about the matter at all, let alone while we were eating. No one said much, so the meal was over quickly. After I finished clearing the table and washing the dishes, I went into the family room and slumped in my chair.

Uncle Charlie didn't waste any time. "Tell me what happened at school today."

Here we went again ... another ride on the merry-go-round. I'd protest my innocence—they wouldn't believe me.

"I got called in to the vice principal's office during fifth period. Someone said I stole a copy of the master for the geometry test." So far, so good. "I denied it, so Mr. Segerstrom asked to search my locker."

Uncle Charlie sat quietly, listening to my every word.

"I told him no problem and went with him to check it. He found a copy of the master, but I have no idea how it got there."

Matthew looked stricken. I wished he would leave the room. "I didn't do it."

Uncle Charlie silently tapped his finger against his cheek. "Katie, I'm not sure what to say."

But he'd think of something.

"You claim you didn't do it, but the evidence, by your own words, says another." He pressed his lips into a flat line. "You need to come straight home from school for the next few weeks."

I bit my upper lip. He'd believed the evidence and not me.

Mark stood and paced back and forth.

Uncle Charlie gazed directly into my eyes. "Also, you won't be able to attend any social activities at school or in town."

I was grounded until further notice. Totally unfair.

"Don't you think you're being a little hard on her?" Anger lines formed at the corners of Mark's mouth. "She says she didn't do it. You should take her word for it."

At last. Someone who didn't think I was a thief and a cheat.

Uncle Charlie stiffened. "I'd like to, but I have to uphold my position as her guardian."

"That stinks." With a loud huff, Mark folded his arms and dropped into his chair.

"Mark, he's wrong, and so is Mr. Segerstrom, but I can't prove anything." Not yet anyway. "It'd be nice if everyone else trusted me like you." It amazed me how calm I'd become. Thoughts of revenge helped. I got up. "Are we done? I have homework."

Uncle Charlie nodded, so I left the room. I had no intention of doing any homework, but they might leave me alone if they thought I was.

I went into the bathroom, opened the medicine cabinet, and borrowed some tall, slender cans from Matthew and Mark. When I walked into the bedroom, I made sure the door shut tightly. I went straight across to the window. I had to get the screen off and out of it before Sarah came in. And I had to do it quietly.

Vandalism

24

My hands fumbled with the latch, and I slid the window up inch by inch. It squeaked. I glanced over my shoulder at the door. What if they'd heard?

For a tense moment, I waited, but no footsteps sounded in the hall. Another few inches on the window. *Squeak.*

My shoulders tightened as I held my breath. How many squeaks before someone in the other room came to find out what was making the noise?

Sweat poured from my forehead as I pushed the window higher. Finally, I opened it far enough and popped the screen out onto the ground.

I wrapped the shaving cream cans in my sweatshirt jacket and crawled out the window. I needed about five minutes to get away before anyone walked into the room.

Five minutes meant the difference between being caught on the long driveway and blending in with the night. Closing the window or putting the screen back in would be a waste of time. By walking into the room, they'd know I wasn't there, whether the window was open or not. Besides, when I came back, I'd have to use the window to get back in.

I ran to the barn to get my bike and a few necessary tools. I carried my jacket, still too hot to put it on. The barn door creaked loudly as I opened it. Did everything have to make noise? I took a slow, deep breath and listened. No sound from the house. It'd be my luck for someone to open the front door without my hearing it. Taking a chance, I peered at the house through the darkness. The windows glowed from the lights within, but there wasn't any movement.

The moon shone brightly down, and I wished a cloud would cross over. Other nights would be fun to spend with a bright moon, but this wasn't one of them. The moonlight meant I'd have to be more careful, or I'd get caught. At least the clothes I wore were dark. Black jeans, and when I put on my navy jacket, it'd cover my light-colored shirt.

Stepping into the barn, I waited for my eyes to adjust. I couldn't turn on the light for fear it'd be seen from the house. Not wanting to make any sound, I moved with a stealthy step. My nerves screamed at me to speed up.

The animals were getting restless, moving about and talking to me. They knew I shouldn't be in the barn at night. Quickening my pace, I tripped over a stool, and landed on the ground with a thud.

I lay there for a moment trying to breathe. Shaken and having the wind knocked out of me, I couldn't move. After getting my breath back, I scrambled to my feet and dusted my clothes off. I never stayed clean around this place.

The tool chest—finally. I pulled out a wrench and a screwdriver and shoved them into my back pocket. Then I grabbed a hammer ... in case. I managed to get out of the barn without running into anything else and swung the door shut. My hands slipped off the clasp from a combination of dirt and sweat, so I wiped them off on my jeans and latched the door.

After unlocking my bicycle, I wheeled it past the house before getting on and riding. Pedaling away from the house, I breathed a little easier. Even if they did notice I was gone, they'd have to search to find me.

Along the main road, I stayed close to the edge, trying to keep in the shadows. A car engine sounded behind me. I jumped off the bike, laid it down, and crouched in the brush.

The headlights loomed from around the corner and penetrated the bushes. *Please don't let the lights hit the bike frame and make it shine.* The car sped past. *Phew.* Not the family. Dumb to have panicked so easily, but I still didn't want anyone else to come along the road while I was on it.

When I hit the turnoff, I made sure no one saw me entering the school grounds—no witnesses. I ditched the bike in some bushes and went the rest of the way on foot.

It took less time than I thought to break into Denton's locker. What a mess. I stacked his books and wound some string around them. I filled a cup with water, poked a hole through the top, tied the string to it, then to the lock itself. For the final touch, I sprayed shaving cream all over everything, making it a nice gooey mess, then shut the door. It'd taken me longer to make the mess than it had to pick the lock.

Next, I booby-trapped Emma's locker in the same way. The only difference? The interior was neat and tidy. Despite her cleanliness, I found an interesting note from Denton asking if she got the test master.

What fools. They should've known better than to leave an incriminating note lying around. If the note had been in Denton's locker, I would've never known. It'd been too much of a disaster zone to start with. I pocketed the note to use later. They were going to pay for their lies.

Finished at school, I rode to Emma's house and parked the bike around the corner, then tiptoed toward the house. Where would she keep her bike? If it were in the house, I wouldn't have a chance to fix it for her.

I walked the entire perimeter. No luck. *Shoot.*

Frustrated, I climbed the fence into the back and searched the side yard. The bike had to be somewhere. Emma rode to school every day, same as Denton and me. Part of my daily mission was avoiding them at the bike rack.

Wait. A door with a window led into the garage. I peered in. *Success.*

I grabbed the door handle and turned it slowly. It opened without a fight. And no squeaks. It only took a few minutes to dismantle the front tire and make it look like it was still attached. As soon as she tried to get on, the wheel would fall off. I snickered at the thought.

One more stop, and then I'd have to get back to Uncle Charlie's. The extra time I'd spent on Denton's locker and finding Emma's bike had hurt my schedule.

Denton's house lay on the outskirts of town, in the opposite direction from where I lived. I found Denton's bicycle next to the trash cans around the side of the house. I knelt beside it and put my tools to work. The dogs in the neighborhood barked repeatedly, and I stopped every so often to listen for strange sounds.

The back of my neck prickled. The eerie feeling like I was being watched washed over me. I finished loosening the tire and decided I'd fix Denton's chain too. With a little luck, the tire would fall off before he knew the chain wasn't on right. Then when he tried to ride it after fixing the tire, the chain would jam.

As I slid the chain into place, I heard a footstep behind me. The beam of a strong flashlight hit me squarely in the eyes.

All I saw were two shiny, black shoes with legs sticking out of them. I strained to see past the light but couldn't.

"Who's there?" I held my hand in front of my eyes to shield them. "Are you trying to blind me or something?" I closed my eyes and stood. Maybe the light wouldn't be as bad.

"What are you doing here?" The man's voice was deep, and not one I recognized.

He'd moved the flashlight as I rose, so the beam still blinded me. "Why should I tell you? I don't even know who you are." Not knowing who it was scared me a little, but I'd bluff my way through.

"I suggest you change your tone." He slowly lowered the flashlight.

My pulse raced. The police ... and here I was mouthing off to him. "I'm sorry, Officer." My eyes adjusted and I saw his face. My heart sank.

Not any officer, but Sarah's boyfriend Jim. "Now, I want to know what you are doing here."

"I'm playing a joke on someone." I couldn't quite get the words out. Besides, he should be able to tell for himself. It's not like he hadn't caught me in the middle of dismantling Denton's bike.

His eyes narrowed. "Looks like a malicious joke to me. Normally, I'd call it vandalism."

He wasn't going to take this lightly. I didn't know what to say. My insides shook, and my knees were so wobbly I couldn't move.

He raised one eyebrow. "You're also breaking curfew."

What? I hadn't been gone that long, had I?

He motioned with his flashlight. "Get in the car."

I forced my legs to move. "What about my bike?"

Jim's jaw pulsed. "Bring it here."

I quickly walked around the corner and wheeled my bike out. He picked it up and put it in the trunk. "Now get in the car."

I wondered what he'd do to me. The only contact I'd had with the police before was Daddy, and he'd just take me home. With Jim, I didn't know whether he recognized me from the picnic or not.

He closed the door and settled in behind the wheel. "I should take you straight down to the station and fill out a misdemeanor report."

Tears stung my eyelids. I didn't want a police record.

Jim gave me a long look before reaching for the key. "But I'm going to take you home and we'll talk to your uncle about it."

At least he remembered me. Which was worse? Going to the station or having to face Uncle Charlie and Sarah. I fought back tears. I'd gotten myself into this mess. There was no reason for me to be a baby about it. "Are you going to charge me?" I wanted to know the worst before we arrived at the house.

He started the car. "Not this time. You're lucky I'm the one who caught you."

Yeah, right.

"If there is a next time, which there'd better not be, I won't simply charge you ..." His voice got even deeper. "... I'll put you in jail."

If I managed to live through this, I probably wouldn't do anything like it again. At least I'd be more careful about getting caught. I'd been so worried about the family, being arrested had never occurred to me.

I never got away with anything. The only thing missing was Tommy by my side. My partner in crime. It felt wrong to be in trouble this big without him.

We turned up the drive. I dreaded going into the house.

Crime and Punishment

25

Jim strode to the front door and knocked. "Come on, Katie."

I briefly considered hiding, but there was no place for me to go. I used Jim as a shield to avoid the initial anger of whoever answered the door. It swung open, and my stomach tightened.

"Jim?" Sarah sounded surprised. "I thought you were on duty tonight."

Thank goodness she hadn't seen me.

Jim's gun belt creaked as he shifted his weight. "I'm here on duty. Is your uncle in?"

"Sure." She sounded troubled. "Just a minute."

Jim turned and grabbed my shoulder. He pushed me in front of him. I didn't even have a chance to get nervous before Uncle Charlie came to the door.

The muscle along his jaw tightened as Uncle Charlie furrowed his brow. "It looks like you'd better come in."

Jim didn't let go of my shoulder as we walked into the house. A cramp developed from his grip. Matthew, Mark, and Sarah watched me from the living room.

"What seems to be the trouble?" Uncle Charlie's words were tight and short.

"I found your niece out by the Dunns' house after curfew." Jim started with the least offense. "I noticed her strange behavior, so I stopped and observed her for a few minutes."

I couldn't meet Uncle Charlie's gaze anymore. My head drooped and I studied the grease under my fingernails.

Jim tightened his grip on my shoulder. "She dismantled Denton's bike."

I bit my bottom lip to keep from flinching from the pain in my shoulder. At least the worst was out now.

"I decided to bring her here, instead of taking her down to the station." Jim shifted his weight to the other foot.

Uncle Charlie nodded. "Thanks, I appreciate it."

Jim's grip on my shoulder loosened slightly. "I figured it'd be easier for you since I'm not charging her this time. I know you'll take care of the situation."

That didn't sound good.

"As for you ..." Jim twirled me around to face him. "... remember what I told you about repeating this." With a slight shake, he released me. "I'd like to think this whole thing was one huge mistake. But the only way to convince me is to never let it happen again."

I rubbed my shoulder to get the circulation going.

Uncle Charlie shook Jim's hand. "Thanks. I'll make sure Katie doesn't repeat this."

Sarah walked Jim to the door, and they talked for a moment before he left. As soon as the door shut, Uncle Charlie sat me down in a chair.

"I'm going to ask you this question only once." Uncle Charlie paced in front of me. "I want you to answer me straight. No beating around the bush." He paused to glare at me. "Did you dismantle Denton's bike?"

I'd never seen him so angry. "Yes." I barely choked out the word.

Uncle Charlie's face reddened. "Do you realize vandalism is a crime?"

"Yes, sir." The words came out softly. My throat had gone dry.

He threw his hands up. "Why on *earth* would you knowingly commit a crime?"

I fished in my pocket for the note.

He stopped and scowled at me. "Well?"

Mark wasn't coming to my rescue this time. I didn't want to even look at Matthew—his expression was already burned into my mind. Daddy had worn the same one too many times.

Uncle Charlie continued to pace. "For as long as I can remember, no McCabe has ever been on the wrong side of the law. You're not even here a week and the police are bringing you home. I want to know why."

My fingers touched the edge of the note. "Denton did something I didn't like."

Uncle Charlie stopped pacing and closed his eyes for a moment. "What did he do?"

His voice stayed quiet, but if I mouthed off in any way, he'd start yelling. "I'll tell you, but you won't believe me."

His jaw tensed. "Katie, I'm trying to be as patient as I can, but you're making it difficult." He rubbed his temples. "You're going to be punished. No matter what reason you may have had, your action was wrong." He looked at the ceiling and took a deep breath. "I'd like a chance to understand why you did it, though."

I pulled the note out of my pocket. "I didn't steal the master for the test. Denton and Emma did." No one made a sound. They didn't believe me, even now. "I have proof. Here." I handed Uncle Charlie the note.

He read it through twice. "I'll take care of this with your vice principal."

That was it? He could've apologized for not believing me.

"May I see it?" Sarah came over and he gave her the note. "Why didn't you show it to me before?"

"By the time I found it, you'd made me so mad by not listening to me it didn't seem to matter." I twisted my hands together. "Plus, I wanted to pay them back for getting me into so much trouble." Which, thinking about it, hadn't worked out well, because I was in more trouble now than before.

Uncle Charlie sat on the edge of his chair. "Katie, that's my job. They'll take the blame for their actions, and I'll make sure your school record is cleared."

Didn't he understand I wanted more than a clean school record? "At the time, I was furious with them, and with you. It was wrong, but I thought it'd make me feel better to fight back somehow." I did feel better. Too bad I'd gotten caught. "When you didn't trust me, I didn't know what to do. Nothing I said would change your mind. If I hadn't found the note, you still wouldn't believe me." Thank goodness I had found it. "Since no one here was going to do anything, I had to."

Uncle Charlie stood. "What you don't realize is how serious this could've been." He ruffled his hair. "If someone other than Jim caught you ..." He broke off and shook his head. "I can't take care of a police record. I want you straight home from school for the next two weeks. Sarah will let me know if you're late."

Grounded again.

Uncle Charlie rested his hands on his hips. "And your phone, television, and any other electronic-device privileges are revoked."

I didn't have any privileges to begin with, so big deal. "All right." I turned to go to bed. Being grounded for two weeks wasn't bad.

Uncle Charlie put his hand on my shoulder. "Katie, I'd like you to come with me for a few minutes. Let's visit the barn."

I gulped and shoved my hands into my sweatshirt pockets. "Do we have to?"

"I think we need to." He opened the door and waited for me to go out first.

My heart sank to the pit of my stomach. "Uncle Charlie, I'm sorry."

He put his hand on my head. "I know."

We went into the barn, and he turned on the light.

"Then why do we have to do this?" My stomach knotted.

He pulled out a tall three-legged stool. "Sit down."

Confused, I hadn't thought sitting was in my immediate future, but I sat quickly so he wouldn't change his mind.

He grabbed a shorter stool and faced me. "I want to talk with you—the two of us, where we won't be interrupted, and no one else is listening in." He ran his hand through his hair. "We haven't spent any time together, just us." His eyes grew sad. "I'm afraid we've gotten off on the wrong foot with each other. I've been having some rough workdays, and you've been having a rough time of things in general."

A rough time was a mild description of what I'd been going through.

"A lot has happened in a very short time, and your whole world has been turned upside down." He propped his foot on the rung of the stool. "I haven't been as understanding as I should've been, and I want you to know I'm sorry."

After all the trouble I'd caused, he apologized to me? "Uncle Charlie—"

He held up his hand. "Let me finish what I have to say." He rested his hand on his knee and leaned forward. "Ron was my favorite brother. From the time he was born, he always looked up to me, and I feel like I've somehow let him down." A tear fell from Uncle Charlie's eye. "He entrusted to my care the one thing he treasured most in this world, and tonight's events prove how much I've failed him."

The tear made its way down Uncle Charlie's cheek and my chest hitched. How could he think he'd failed? I caused the problems.

"You were right." The cords on his neck stood out as he fought for control. "I should've trusted your word instead of being so caught up in how it would look if I didn't discipline you." He took my hand and gazed straight into my eyes. "I was wrong. Will you forgive me?"

I squeezed his hand. "Of course, I will." The words came out in a whisper as my throat tried to strangle them.

He gave me a sad smile. "Do you think we can wipe the slate clean and start fresh?"

"Yes." I jumped off the stool and flung myself into his arms. I buried my head on his shoulder, and as he hugged me, I felt like I might never be able to let go. The protection of his arms and the warmth of his love were things I thought I'd never have again.

Time seemed to stop, and a glimmer of hope ignited. Maybe ... *just maybe* ... I was wanted and not the burden of circumstance. I don't know how long he held me tightly in his embrace before I felt a slackening in his grip.

He spoke softly into my ear. "Katie, I want you to be able to come to me when you're having a problem with someone and trust me to help you deal with it." Uncle Charlie pulled back to look into my eyes. "I've let you down so far, but I promise I'll be there for you from now on." He brushed some hair away from my face. "Okay?"

I nodded.

"There won't be any need for you to try to handle things yourself. We'll do it together." He stood and patted me on the back. "Let's go to bed now and get a good night's sleep. Tomorrow will be a little easier to get through." He put his arm across my shoulders, and we walked silently back to the house.

Sarah was all ready for bed when I walked into our room. "Are you okay?"

My face must've reflected the conflicting emotions I felt. "I don't know." I was having trouble sorting out my feelings. Even though I'd been upset over not being believed, in a way, I'd done the same thing to them. I hadn't believed I was wanted, despite being told so. But knowing I was wanted didn't take away any of the hurt from Daddy being gone.

Her eyebrows drew together. "Is there anything I can do?"

I glanced at the window. The screen had been replaced. "I don't want to talk about it."

She nodded. "I understand."

I put on my pajamas and crawled into bed.

Her face softened. "I'm sorry, Katie."

I didn't say anything.

"I know it's a little late, but we never had anything like this happen before. I didn't know how to react." She turned out the light.

"You could've tried believing me." It wasn't asking too much. "I don't tell lies, or steal, or cheat, you know."

Her voice softly penetrated the darkness. "No, I don't know."

What was she talking about?

"You've been here a few days, and you were in a fight, ended up in the vice principal's office for unruly behavior and violence in a class, as well as getting detention in another class." She ticked off each item on her fingers.

My cheeks burned. Just what I needed, a list of my sins.

Sarah leaned forward on her bed. "You also have bouts of being uncooperative and rude here at home. With all that, you're asking me to *know* you don't steal, cheat, or tell lies?"

Maybe it *was* asking too much.

"I understand things haven't been easy." She came to the side of my bed, knelt, and put her hands on mine. "And the circumstances have a lot to do with why you're behaving the way you are."

Tears welled up in my eyes. My soul felt lacerated and my emotions raw.

"I'm trying to get to know you, Katie." She gave my hand a squeeze. "But you've been working awfully hard at making that a difficult thing to do. I'll trust you in the future."

The tears I hadn't been able to cry in the barn now slid down my nose and onto my pillow. "I'm sorry, Sarah."

She went over to the dresser and brought me some tissues. "Here. You don't want to sleep on a wet pillow."

I sat up, dabbed my eyes, and blew my nose. "I miss Daddy so much I don't know what I'm going to do."

She gave me a hug. "I know you miss him. You're sad, angry, and hurt all at the same time. You've been uprooted from everything you're used to and your whole life has changed. You have a lot to adjust to, so we'll have to take things one day at a time. Or sometimes it may be one moment at a time." She rubbed my arm. "For now, though, I think you should try to get some sleep."

She crossed the room and got into her bed, and I slid down in mine, but sleep seemed far away.

The Gathering Storm

26

Sarah's voice cut through my dreams. "Katie, it's time to get up." Head pounding, I rolled over and pulled the covers up. I drifted back to sleep without fully waking.

"Katie."

My eyes flew open.

Sarah stood, hands on hips, scowling. "I told you to get up ten minutes ago."

Yanking the blanket over my head, I burrowed into the pillow. "Leave me alone. I don't wanna get up."

Sarah pulled the blanket to my shoulders. "You'll be late for school."

I threw the bedding off and kicked it as I sat up. "Leave. Me. Alone." I bared my teeth. "I'm not going to school."

"Uncle Charlie went to a lot of trouble to get your suspension removed, so get going." Sarah opened the closet, pulled out an outfit for me, and put it on top of the dresser. "I'll leave you alone to get rid of your grouchiness. But you'll have to hurry to get everything done in time."

As she went out the door, I threw my pillow at her ... but missed.

I scooped the clothes from the dresser and tossed them on the bed. I'd caved again. It made me angry when I gave in to Sarah. I didn't want to go to school, and if I stood my ground, she couldn't make me, short of dragging me by force. But instead, I was getting ready anyway.

My mood didn't get any better. Little things happened to make me angrier than before. When I opened the dresser drawer, I missed the handle and jammed my finger so hard the nail broke to the quick and bled. The hens pecked at me from the moment I walked through the door of the coop until I left. Soap got in my eyes when I took a shower.

The only day-brightener? Uncle Charlie went to work early. There were problems with the assisted living center he was building on the outskirts of town, so he needed every hour of sunlight he could get. After our heart-to-heart the night before, I couldn't have faced him.

The weather forecast came on the radio as I shuffled into the kitchen. The local newscasters were making a big deal about the upcoming storm, telling everybody to get ready for *the big one*. Who were they kidding? Yesterday had been beautiful. Not a cloud in sight. They made it sound like something out of *The Wizard of Oz*, and Dorothy and Toto might go flying past in Auntie Em's house.

Even breakfast didn't go well. I reached for some toast and knocked over my orange juice.

Sarah grabbed the tablecloth corner so the juice wouldn't run on the floor. "Get a rag so we can get this cleaned up."

"No." I pushed away from the table. "I've had it." I shoved the chair and it fell over.

Sarah glanced up. "Calm down. There's no need to get so upset."

Fury coursed through me. "Maybe you don't have a reason." I glared at her. "But nothing I do is ever right."

She folded the tablecloth. "Honey, it's not that bad. It's spilled juice."

"Don't make me sick." I stomped into the bedroom.

Sarah sighed heavily. "Katie."

Why did she have to follow me everywhere? "I'm only here because Daddy died, and Uncle Charlie took me in." I pulled clothes out of the drawers. "I had no say in anything and I'm tired of being here. But you wouldn't know about that, would you?"

Sarah took the clothes and put them back in the drawer. "You're not the only one who had to leave home." Anger sparked in her eyes, and she touched the key shaft of her rose-gold heart necklace. "When I came here to live, it wasn't exactly my choice either."

What was she talking about? "Daddy died and I had to leave my whole life behind. Name something worse."

"This isn't a contest. I'm not saying my situation was worse, but my parents had some problems and when they left town, they left me behind." Bitterness underscored her words. "Sometimes I still have a hard time dealing with it. Uncle Charlie took me in, and for a long time, I felt like I had to work to stay here." She traced the outline of the pendant with her thumb and her eyes filled with tears. "A servant who had to earn her keep. But Uncle Charlie kept on loving me until I became part of the family."

Uncle Charlie could love Sarah until she belonged, but it wouldn't work for me. I wouldn't be here long enough, for one thing.

She reached toward me. "He loves you like he loves me."

"He's got you brainwashed." Even though she was right, I had so much hurt inside, I lashed out. Unfortunately, it was impossible to give the pain away.

She dropped her arm to her side, and she briefly closed her eyes. "Uncle Charlie does care. Give him a chance."

"Why should I?" He hadn't given me any breaks so far.

"He's been very concerned since your daddy told him about his health." She rubbed her forehead. "He's the one who wanted you here."

"Stop." I turned away. "I don't want to hear any more."

"Just because you don't want to hear it doesn't make it any less true." Sarah grabbed my shoulder as I took a step toward the door. "You want everyone to give you a break, but you aren't interested in giving anyone else one." She let go. "If you don't get a move on, you'll be late for school."

The sudden gentleness of her tone startled me.

As I finished getting ready, my headache worsened, and my stomach churned at the thought of facing Denton and Emma at school. The rumor mill would be on overdrive, and everyone would be wondering why I was back in school so soon. I clung to Uncle Charlie's promise to make sure Denton and Emma paid for what they'd done to me—it was the only thing keeping me moving forward.

I glanced at the clock over the mantle on my way out of the house. I'd have to rush to make it to school on time, which meant I could forget about talking with Logan before class. We wouldn't have a chance to talk in geometry either. Mrs. Johnson loved to give detention for talking, and Logan would die if he got in trouble, because the coach might bench him.

Already ten minutes late in leaving, I sprinted toward the barn to get my bike. To top everything else off, the forecasted storm clouds were forming, which meant after school I'd probably have the joy of riding my bike in the rain. I rode as fast as I could, hoping to make up the time I lost arguing with Sarah.

Arriving at school out of breath and sweaty, I hopped off my bike and shoved it into a slot. I made a quick check of the rack. Denton and Emma's bikes were missing. I smiled as I grabbed my lock, wrapped the chain through the tire, and closed the hasp. A day without those two was a gift. The lock dropped from my hand as I grabbed my bag and dashed toward the front steps.

The bell rang as I strode past the administration building. I'd made it on time, barely. Logan was on his way to class when he saw me.

He ran over to help me with my books. "What happened to you this morning?"

I must have looked horrible. "Sarah and I had another fight."

He held the building door open for me. "What about?"

I took my books back. "No time to tell you now. Let's talk at lunch." I rushed through the door seconds before Mr. Whitehall shut it.

Mr. Whitehall had set the door to lock as soon as it closed. The last thing I needed was to be marked absent. I sank into my chair, leaned back against the wall, and took a deep breath. I needed to cool down.

I gazed out the window while Mr. Whitehall began class. Every morning, he reviewed what we'd gone over the day before. What a bore—I never paid attention. The clouds grew dark. The gray sky looked more like the end of the day instead of first thing in the morning.

Denton stomped across campus, his arms and face streaked with grease. I stifled a snicker. Dismantling his bike seemed like ages ago, and I'd almost forgotten what I'd done. Jim must not have gone back to fix it. And no one knew about the booby-trapped lockers. I swiveled in my seat to get a better look when he opened it.

He paused to wipe his hands on his pants before turning the combination. He opened it quickly, and everything spilled out in a glorious mess.

"Is there something of interest out the window you'd like to share with the rest of the class?"

I jumped in my seat. Intent on watching Denton, I'd forgotten about being in the classroom. "No."

Mr. Whitehall stood next to me. "Then I suggest you turn around and pay attention." He went back to the front of the room.

My face felt hot from embarrassment, and I slumped in my chair.

Mr. Whitehall enjoyed putting me on the spot and making fun of me. "Now, Miss McCabe, since you are back with us, please tell the class what the three branches of government are, and what functions each branch has?" He only asked the question to needle me a little more before going back to the boring old lecture.

When I got to second period, I couldn't wait to see whether Emma showed any signs of trouble with her bike and locker. No smears of grease on her arms. But knowing Emma, she'd rather die before coming to class dirty. She definitely wasn't in a good mood, but her surliness didn't mean much. She never seemed to be in a good mood, unless trying to impress some grown-up or flirting with Logan. Her book was wet, though, so the booby-trapped locker had worked.

Since my plans had come off so well, my temper eased, and I felt a lot better about the day. I could handle being grounded for two weeks knowing the slimy toad and his sidekick had been paid back.

A girl from the office came in with a note for Miss Phelps. I got paranoid every time I saw someone from the office—those notes always seemed to be for me or about me.

When Miss Phelps turned toward the class, I half expected to hear my name called.

"Emma. Will you please come here?"

Emma? Uncle Charlie must've told Mr. Segerstrom about the message I'd found. Denton would be getting summoned, too. This made my day. No matter how rotten yesterday was, and how much trouble I'd gotten into, this was worth it. *Little Miss Perfect* getting called into the vice principal's office? I wished I could be a fly on the wall as they tried to talk their way out of it. I couldn't wait until I had a chance to tell Logan everything. I'd even risk Mrs. Johnson's wrath to tell him.

Classes flew by thanks to shortened periods for an early release day. Almost before I got settled, Mrs. Johnson dismissed us from class.

Logan took my book bag as we left the room. "What is going on with you today? This morning when I saw you, you were ready to explode. Now you almost got into trouble for telling me how happy you are." He raised his eyebrows. "So which is it? Happy or sad?"

"Right now, I'm so happy I could burst." I grabbed his hand and pulled him toward the benches. "I have so much to tell you, but this is between you and me, all right?"

He nodded.

"Yesterday I got into a whole lot of trouble, and I was ready to leave for good this morning." I took a bite of my sandwich.

He pulled his lunch out of the sack. "What was so bad it'd make you want to leave?"

I nudged him playfully with my elbow. "I'm trying to tell you."

"What happened?" He unwrapped his sandwich and bit into it.

"I'm sure you heard the rumors about me getting suspended." I gave him a quizzical look.

Logan nodded and kept chewing but made a *get on with it* gesture with his hand.

"The suspension part is true. Mr. Segerstrom suspended me because ..." I paused for dramatic effect. "Denton and Emma stole the master to the geometry test and planted it on me."

His eyes narrowed.

"No one would believe I hadn't stolen it." I scrunched up my nose. "So I got mad and kind of wrecked their bikes."

"Katie." Logan didn't sound too pleased.

"Don't worry about it." I waved off his disapproval. "I only took off their front tires."

He shrugged and took another bite of his sandwich.

"Jim Baines caught me though." I studied the specks on the composite bench we sat on.

His brow knitted. "Did he take you down to the station?"

I shook my head. "He took me back to the house and Uncle Charlie grounded me." I traced the fake wood-grain pattern. "So I won't be able to talk to you on the phone or see you on the weekends." I raised my head. "But Emma got called in to the office during second period, and Denton wasn't there during fourth, so I know Uncle Charlie talked to Mr. Segerstrom and told him about the note I found."

Confusion clouded Logan's face. "What note?"

"I'm sorry, I forgot to tell you." I couldn't keep the excitement out of my voice. "I found a note from Denton to Emma asking her about the test master." I grinned. "Now they're getting what they deserve. And that makes me happy." I took another bite of my lunch.

"I'm glad everything is working out." Logan paused for a few moments. "Did you have to take apart their bikes? You could've gotten into a lot of trouble."

Not him too. "I know it was a stupid thing to do." He sounded upset, so I wanted to make him understand. "I was mad at Mr. Segerstrom and my family for not believing me. I had to do something."

His jaw pulsed. "Did Jim fill out a report when he caught you?"

"No. He let Uncle Charlie deal with me." I twisted my lunch sack. "He let me know what could've happened though." I put the sack down.

Logan took my hand and laced his fingers with mine. "Don't do anything like that again, okay?"

The pleading tone in his voice went straight to my heart. "Okay. I'll tell you what. If Denton does anything, I'll talk to you first."

Relief spread across his face. "Great. So how much trouble are you in?"

I gave half a shrug. "Not much. I'm grounded for two weeks. You know how it goes. Back to the house straight after school, no friends over, and no phone calls."

The buzzer sounded, signaling the end of lunch.

He stood. "Not too bad. I'll walk you to your next class."

The rest of the day sped by as quickly as the first part. I told Logan I'd try to get to school extra early so I'd have a chance to see him. I wouldn't be able to stay after school to watch him practice.

During volleyball, I kept checking the sky to see if the storm was going to break. The air smelled like rain. The wind picked up, and it kept carrying the ball to one side of the court.

When Mrs. Irwin finally told us to hit the showers, I ran to the locker room. I skipped the shower, changed clothes, and bundled my sweats into the locker. I wanted to get to my bike and back to Uncle Charlie's before the rain started. The sky kept getting darker and darker. I'd have to use my bike light.

Riding against the wind would make the trip home harder. I grabbed the books I needed for homework and threw them into my book bag. The wind whipped my hair in my face and tore at my clothes. Along with the wind, the sky spat tiny droplets. It wasn't raining yet but getting close. I got to the bike racks before anyone else and tossed down my book bag.

In my rush to get to class before Mr. Whitehall closed the door, I hadn't paid attention to where I'd dropped my lock. It had landed combination side down in a grease slick. I carefully handled it by the sides, trying to keep from getting grease all over my hands, and twirled the dial. With the grease, the wind, and my frozen hands, I kept dropping it.

After three failed attempts, I pulled an old homework paper out of my bag and wiped the muck off. If only the wind would die down. The chill cut through my shirt and numbed me to the bone. In my hurry, I hadn't grabbed a jacket before I'd left the house. Stupid. I wrapped the paper around the casing and carefully twirled the dial.

The combination clicked and I pulled down on the lock. *Finally.*

A cloth covered my eyes.

Abducted

27

The blindfold tightened into place.

"Hey. What's going on?" I'd been concentrating on getting the bike lock open and hadn't heard anyone come up behind me. Was it someone playing a joke or was this some sort of freshman initiation? Either way, I didn't have time for it.

I tried to stand, but a pair of hands pushed down on my shoulders. "Knock it off."

Someone shoved a cloth wad into my mouth and tied it down to keep it in place. I stood with a lot more force. If this was a joke, it wasn't funny. Now two pairs of hands shoved me.

Losing my balance, I sprawled on the pavement. My heart raced and I gasped for breath. As I rolled to my knees, another thrust sent me to the ground again. My arms were yanked behind my back and my hands held together. Someone wrapped rope around my wrists and knotted it. The twine cut into my flesh, and pain shot from my shoulders to my fingertips.

"Are you done yet?" The voice was a half-whisper and sounded like a girl.

If only I could see, I'd have a fighting chance. Another knot was tied around my wrists.

"I want to make sure she can't get out of this." The whisper was huskier, more like a boy's.

Hands grabbed me under the pits on both sides and pulled. I pushed up with my legs. Standing might give me more opportunities to get away. Where was everyone? Somebody had to be coming soon. Classes would be out any minute.

An object prodded me in the small of my back, and I took a step forward. My temples throbbed and I felt like I'd fall with each step. I tried to remember the direction we took, so I could find my way back.

Ten steps later the wind stopped whipping through my hair. We must be behind a building. My heart sank. Who'd find me now?

Denton and Emma had to be my captors. Behind me, they pushed when I didn't move fast enough for them, whispering about me, but the words got lost in the wind.

I tripped as we stepped on to rougher terrain and I fell flat. A warm trickle on my leg told me I'd skinned my knee. I rolled onto my back and kicked when someone got close. I landed one.

"Stop it. I don't want your dirty footprints on me."

Emma.

The next kick landed in a soft stomach. *Denton.* But he wasn't stupid enough to say anything out loud. A thud followed his grunt. He'd landed on the ground.

I snickered, but my laughter was short-lived.

He ran to my head before I swiveled to land another kick. He pulled me up by the arms.

Ouch. I wanted to yell. But I wouldn't give them the satisfaction of knowing I'd been hurt.

My nose twitched. I smelled a horse. A soft nicker confirmed it.

None of the houses right around the school kept livestock, and we hadn't gone far enough to be off school grounds. Horses were common in the area, but if someone else was there, they sure weren't helping me out.

An extra hard push from behind ran me smack into the animal. Horsehair got up my nose.

A growl sounded in my ear. "Get on the horse."

Even though he tried to disguise it, the voice was unmistakably Denton's.

How in the world was I supposed to get on the horse without using my arms? They each grabbed a leg and started pushing me up the side of the horse. I leaned against the side, hoping I wouldn't fall and break something. Would they have enough sense to stop pushing when I got to the top? I didn't want to fall off headfirst on the other side.

When they stopped pushing, I was slung across the horse like a big sack of potatoes. Someone mounted the horse behind me. The reins draped across my back, and the horse started moving. I couldn't believe they were making me ride this thing on my stomach. What would they try next? This was taking payback too far.

Sprinkles pelted my cheeks like tiny darts hitting their mark. The wind ripped through my hair, and the temperature dropped, colder by the minute. When the person urged the horse forward, wheezing rumbles of breath vibrated against my back. *Denton.* He leaned against me, and I shuddered.

Only one person had mounted the horse, so what was Emma up to? Despite the cold, beads of sweat popped up on my forehead. Before I'd been angry, but I didn't know how far Denton would take his revenge. He didn't seem to be stopping.

We rode for so long, every inch of me burned with pain, and I'd lost track of time. I rolled against Denton as the horse left the flat track and trotted uphill. I recoiled and arched toward the horse's head. The farther we went, the steeper the slope.

Denton kept urging the horse to speed up. I didn't know how much more I could stand. Every time the horse lurched, I thought I'd fall off. Then, when my stomach slammed against the horse's back, I wished I had. At least then I'd be off this stupid ride.

The slope and gravity kept throwing me against Denton's crotch. I shuddered and curled my lips. I didn't want to touch any part of him, let alone there. But ... what if I accidentally-on-purpose hit him there? I pulled my arms up as far as possible, whimpering in pain against the gag. Keeping my elbows tight against my side, I rolled as close to the horse's neck as possible. I needed one good lurch.

It seemed like forever before Denton urged the horse forward again, but when he did, I took my chance. Elbow first, I rolled toward him.

He grunted when I connected and didn't bother to disguise his voice. "You're gonna pay for that!" He brought the horse to a stop then whipped the reins across my face.

My cheek stung, but the blindfold and gag took the brunt of the blow. Time to get off this nightmare of a merry-go-round. I rocked from side to side and kicked downward.

The reins lashed against my shoulders and spine. I'd have welts from his blows, but I gritted my teeth, determined not to give him any satisfaction. Gravity took over and I couldn't slow my descent.

Denton made a last dash attempt to lasso me as I slid off, but he was too slow. The momentum threw me off balance and I lurched back to keep from falling. My heel landed on nothing but air. I swallowed hard and my chest tightened. Time slowed as reality punched me in the gut—I'd gone over a ledge. I hit the ground and tumbled head over heels down an embankment. My head banged against a rock, stunning me. And I plunged into a river.

The splash carried the water away for a second before I sank, losing consciousness. I regained alertness when water soaked through the gag, and I swallowed—a lot. I thrashed and twisted but had lost all sense of direction. I didn't know what to do. My brain was paralyzed.

I can't breathe.

A foot touched the slick river bottom. I whimpered. Finally. By forcing my feet against the bottom and jumping, I broke through the water. But with water in the gag, I still couldn't breathe. My chest heaved and burned, starved of oxygen. What if I couldn't get out of the river?

Another push off the bottom. My tennis shoes slipped, but I landed on my back, floating with my head above the surface. In the distance, Denton laughed and my brain clicked into gear.

My legs dragged against the bottom. The current had pulled me into a shallow stretch. I stopped battling, rolled over, put my knees on the riverbed, and raised my head completely above the water. With my head tilted forward to let the water drain from the gag, I took a ragged breath through my nose. A shudder ran through me as I fought back tears of relief.

Weak from fighting the river, I stayed in the middle for a

moment, savoring each breath. Despite the blindfold, I closed my eyes to think. The faint clip-clop of horse hooves reached me above the rushing sounds of the river. Denton, the rat, had ridden off, leaving me trussed like a calf ready for slaughter in the middle of a river.

The water flowing against my body gave me an idea. If I moved crosswise through the current, I should find the bank. Unless I was in the middle of a whirlpool. *Why did my mind have to go to the worst possibility?*

Still on my knees, I cautiously cut across the current. I didn't want to lose my balance and get swept under. With any luck, the shallows stretched to the riverbank. Even though I couldn't have been underwater long, I felt as if I'd swallowed a couple of buckets. Inch by wretched inch, I crawled across the river.

The need to cough tightened my stomach and acid burned the base of my throat. I inhaled slowly. If I threw up now, I'd choke on my own vomit. With each breath, I fought back my gag reflex. The riverbed became firmer and inclined. *Thank goodness.* It wouldn't be long now.

I reached the water's edge. The next challenge would be getting out of the river. I pressed against the bank and braced my sneakers on the silt. The side gently sloped, so I wiggled back and forth while using my legs to propel forward. Once on top, I pushed away from the edge with my feet.

I lay on the grass for a moment simply breathing through my nose. Pain, which had been suspended while I'd battled the river, rushed into every joint and muscle. My entire body felt on fire.

Now to get my hands free. I tensed my wrists against the ties trying to loosen the binding. The twine had swelled with the water. I crossed my wrists, then jerked them quickly. Again and again, I yanked against the ties—I lost count of how many times. My arms were tiring.

Jerk.

The weight of my clothes, heavy from the thorough soaking in the river, made each successive tug against the rope more difficult.

Jerk.

I had no feeling left in my hands and I was frozen from the wind. Large patches burned my wrists where the rope had scraped off layers of skin, but I couldn't stop until I got free.

Jerk.

I put all my frustration into the last attempt and felt it all the way to my shoulders. Bye-bye to another layer of skin. The pain increased. What if I couldn't keep going? *I have to.*

One more time. Jerk.

I closed my eyes and waited for the burn on my wrists to subside. *Hold up.* The binding had loosened, and my hands were farther apart. I yanked one hand through the ties. Thank goodness Denton wasn't a knot expert.

My shoulders ached as my arms fell to my sides. They were heavy and utterly useless. The prickly feeling of being stabbed with a million red-hot needles meant circulation would return. It hurt but felt good at the same time. When the ability to move my fingers returned, I whipped off the blindfold and untied the gag.

Then I crawled to the river's edge and vomited. My stomach roiled—I had to get the excess liquid out of my system. After throwing up a few more times, I inched upstream and washed my face with cool, clear water. My wrists stung where they'd been rubbed raw.

Resting on the bank, I enjoyed breathing without choking back bile. My wrists throbbed nonstop, and I felt like I'd been run through a meat grinder, but it was worth the pain to be free.

After a while, I rolled to my side, then onto my hands and knees. My arms refused to hold me up and I nearly face-planted in the mud. I rocked back and bit my lip to keep from crying out. I brought one knee up so my sneaker was firmly on the grass, stretched the other leg behind me, braced my toe against the ground and pushed up. Thank goodness my legs didn't hurt as much as the rest of me did.

When I'd clambered to my feet, I craned my neck left, then right. Denton had lugged me into the hills, and I had no idea which way to go. No hoofprints were in the area, so I must've crawled to the opposite side of the river.

Tall trees stood all around and through the leaves—nothing. I shivered. The wind hadn't died, and sprinkles came down harder. Stupid overachieving sprinkles. Couldn't they wait until I wasn't standing in the middle of Nowheresville? Like I wasn't wet enough already. A house would be a wonderful thing to come across about now.

I sighed. The only way to find one was to start walking.

Cave Dwelling

28

If the sun were out, I'd head for Uncle Charlie's—if I remembered how to navigate by the sun. My best bet would be to follow the river flow. I checked my watch. Waterlogged from the river, the watch had stopped at a quarter to five. Sarah would be having a fit because I hadn't returned from school yet. Goose pimples prickled my skin and I shuddered. My jeans chafed uncomfortably against my legs as I shuffled forward. I squeezed excess water out, but they still weighed a ton. I'd have blisters before long where my wet sneakers rubbed against my heels.

The brush thickened and I couldn't see my feet, so I moved away from the bank's edge. I didn't want to take a dip in the river if the ledge crumbled beneath me. One near-drowning was enough for any day. How far would I have to go before finding help?

The sky darkened and the rainclouds swelled as the storm gathered its strength. Before the downpour hit, I had to find shelter. I scanned the hillside. Through the tree trunks, I spotted a rock formation in the distance and sighed. I'd have to backtrack—in the exact opposite direction from where I wanted to go.

Squinting at the sky, I picked up my pace. Those clouds were going to burst at any moment. "There'd better be a place to hole up." The rocks were farther away than they had first appeared. Bigger drops fell from the sky. I moved as fast as the terrain allowed—I didn't need to slip and fall.

When I reached the rocks, I checked for an overhang to hide under. Overhangs weren't the best, but I needed to find somewhere protected. Nothing. Next, I searched for any cracks. A streak of lightning shot through the sky and brightened the area like a spotlight. And I saw it. A dark break in the stone formation. Praying it was big enough, I hurried forward.

A thunderclap shook the ground, and I stumbled but managed not to fall. Before I reached the crack, the skies opened, and rain poured down. I ran toward the entrance.

The opening wasn't big enough. With gritted teeth, I beat a fist against the rock wall, then turned to look for somewhere else. *What am I gonna do now?* Slumping against the formation, I slid down, holding back tears.

Wait.

From this angle, the crack appeared wider. Maybe I could get through it sideways. The wind whipped up and sent a shiver through me. I closed my eyes and took a deep breath. *Please let this work.* Wishing I had a flashlight, I wriggled through the entrance.

Phew. Nothing inside but a small cave. No wild animals ready to attack. I sagged against the wall. It took my eyes a few moments to adjust to the dim light coming through the crack. I couldn't see how far the cave went, and without light, exploring was out.

The rain pelted the ground outside my shelter and the wind gusts grew stronger. Through the crack, I watched as drops were blown nearly sideways. Puddles quickly formed, but fortunately my hideout had enough of an uphill slope that the water flowed away from it.

The wind changed direction and blew in through the entrance. I moved away, chilled to the bone. A violent shudder wracked my body. My fingers were frozen, and my toes felt like little ice cubes stuffed inside my sneakers. My teeth chattered.

I folded my arms and tucked my balled fists into my armpits, hoping they'd thaw. Peering through the dim light, I looked for anything that might help me keep warm. Leaves and pine needles were strewn against the walls. They might be good tinder for a fire, but without matches, a flint kit, or sunlight, getting one started might be difficult. But I had to try.

I scooped dead leaves and pine needles into a big pile. Anything outside would be too wet. Besides, I wasn't going to poke my nose outside until the storm stopped.

I shuffled a little farther inside, kicking a rock. It skittered across the stone floor and ricocheted against the wall. I picked it up, tossed it in the air, and caught it as an idea formed. If the rock was hard enough, I might get it to spark. Now to find another stone to bang it against.

While searching for something bigger than the pebbles lining the walls, I found a few sticks that might have promise if the rocks failed. Intent on finding a good-sized stone, I moved farther into the cave.

An eerie wail caused my heart to jump into my throat. Darkness shrouded me and the hairs on my arms rose. I turned back toward the entrance and my shoulders sagged. The light coming through the cave's mouth was nothing but a dark gray ghost wavering in the distance.

Shaking off a creepy feeling, I trudged toward the opening, still searching for another rock. Just short of my kindling pile, I spied one. It was about the size of my palm and its surface had some jagged edges, but it felt good in my grip.

I sat cross-legged on the ground with the kindling nestled against my shin. My wet jeans cut into my skin and threatened to rub a patch raw. A gust of wind came through the opening and scattered some of the needles. I scooted around so my back took the brunt of the wind and blocked the kindling from getting blown away. Gripping one rock in each hand, I said a quick prayer. "Please, God, let this work."

I refused to die of hypothermia because Denton Dunn Junior was the biggest douche canoe on the planet. Closing my eyes as I inhaled, I pulled my fists back. Opening my eyes, I struck the rocks together like a pair of cymbals.

Nothing. Not even a tiny hopeful spark. Success on the first strike would've been a bit much to ask for, so I banged them in earnest. Over and over. Slowly and methodically. Their surfaces needed to heat enough to emit the spark. Every blow sent shudders up my arms.

Unfortunately, the more I struck them together, the more the small, jagged rock crumbled. This didn't bode well, but I had to keep trying. Swinging my arms back and forth at least I had warmed a bit. Except for my toes and fingers. My hands were covered in cuts and scrapes that burned.

"Ouch." I wanted to swear, but since I needed God's help, didn't think He'd be too impressed if I did. The little rock had gotten too small, and I'd smashed my finger instead of it. "But *dang* that hurt." I stuck my index finger in my mouth and sucked. Hurling the useless rock against the cave wall, I smashed it into hundreds of pieces. I should've known from the beginning it wasn't hard enough.

The later it got, the more frantic they'd be at the house. But how were they going to find me in the storm? Would they be furious I hadn't come back after school, or worried? Or worse, would they be glad I was no longer their problem?

I stood and brushed the rock soot off my jeans. What a waste of time. But I had to find something else to take my mind off the cold and how the family felt. My stomach rumbled. Oh yeah, let's not forget the hunger from having not eaten and it being way past dinnertime.

I lunged to the left and then to the right. A few stretches to limber up after sitting on the cold, hard ground were in order. During a reach-for-the-sky stretch, a low rumbling noise came from deep in the cave. My heart raced. I swallowed hard. Maybe the cave wasn't as critter-free as I'd first thought. The only chance I had to keep the creature at bay was the fire I'd failed to start. If I didn't have bad luck, I wouldn't have any luck at all.

Careful not to move too quickly, I regathered my precious kindling, sat my butt back on the ground, and grabbed the sticks I'd found. The flatter piece, while not having an actual notch, had an indentation that would have to be good enough. Friction would be the answer, so I rolled the stick between my palms, applying downward pressure and prayed for a spark. Even a tiny one.

The creature from the deep gave another menacing growl. My breath caught in my throat, but I kept spinning the stick between my palms. If it attacked, I had nowhere to run, so I kept as still as possible, except my hands. The seconds crept by as I strained to hear the creature over my thumping heart.

After some time had passed, the low growls from deep in the cave got fainter. My shoulders sagged as I let out a shaky breath. With any luck, the creature was bored and wouldn't come back.

The wind howled and another gust cut through my clothes, chilling me to the core. My arms ached from the constant pressure and stick spinning, but I couldn't stop. They were already sore enough from being tied behind my back, so the extra exertion added to the pain and weariness.

While I rubbed the sticks together, my mind wandered to thoughts of home. How would I explain this one to Uncle Charlie? After our talk last night, at least I hoped he might believe I'd been taken from school and abandoned in a storm with no way of getting back. Or would he think I'd blown off our conversation? After my tantrum this morning, they probably thought I had run away. Sarah would've told them all about it. They'd be angry, but they wouldn't search for me very hard.

Tears pricked my eyes. I didn't want them to give up on me. Not yet. Not now. I needed them. No, more than that. I wanted to be a part of the family. Without them, I had nothing. No one. And as much as I'd fought it, I wanted them to love me.

Why do I have to be such a pain in the butt all the time?

The shudders wracking my body left no doubt that I needed to do more than rub a couple of sticks together to keep warm. No matter how hard I'd tried, fire wasn't happening. I scooped up the kindling, stuffed it in my shirt to give it a little insulation, and tucked the shirt into my jeans. Prickly and itchy, but warmer? Next, I had to find a cavity away from the wind coming through the entrance. Not too far away from the crack, or I might never find it again.

A little way into the cave, the wall across from me had a bunch of rubble where rocks had fallen over the years. Maybe I could stack them to make a windbreak to hide behind. I nearly worked up a sweat building my wall and filling it with all the dead leaves I could find. Night had fallen and the dim light from the cave opening flickered out, leaving me in pitch darkness. I crawled behind my makeshift barricade, and lay atop the pile of leaves, exhausted.

While not the most comfortable bed I'd ever been in, the shudders had slowed, and the itchy needles were worth putting up with for the extra warmth. The goal was to get some rest without turning this into a "lay down and die" situation. I didn't want to die. I wanted to go home. And I finally knew where that was.

The Yearling

29

Light hit my eyes and they fluttered open. I lifted my hand and groaned. My body didn't want to move an inch, let alone get up. That my jeans, sneakers, and socks were still damp didn't help matters. But if the storm had stopped, I needed to find my way home. My stomach rumbled loudly. Cold water would be good at staving off hunger, and I might find something edible to scrounge near the river.

Standing, I stretched my arms, then untucked my shirt and shook it to get rid of the kindling. Even though I'd brushed as much of it off as I could, I felt gritty. I might need to take a dip in the river to get rid of the itchiness. After a few more stretches to work the kinks out, I strode toward the cave entrance. Time to go home.

A ray of sunshine lit the crack, and I froze. A curled snake, with the tip of a rattle visible on its tail, blocked the opening. It might be enjoying the sun, but I needed to get out of the cave. I grabbed one of the useless fire sticks from the night before. Maybe it'd make a better snake slingshot than fire starter.

Barely daring to breathe, I crept up behind the snake, inch by inch. By the time I reached it, my palms were slick with sweat. I wiped them on my jeans, which didn't help, so I dried them on my shirt sleeves. Then I gripped the stick and thrust it into the snake coil. With a quick flick, I tossed both the snake and the stick through the crack. The body uncurled as it flew, and it landed flat in the grass a few feet away.

I waited for it to wriggle, hoping it wouldn't come back into the cave, and heaved a sigh of relief when it slithered away. On hands and knees, I crawled through the crack, then stood and turned my face toward the sun, soaking in its warmth. I had survived the night. The cave had given me shelter during the storm, but it'd been oppressive at the same time. I wriggled my shoulders to shake off the last of the tension.

Broken branches scattered the hillside and a few small trees had been uprooted. I'd been lucky. Though the rain was a thing of the past, the wind tore at my clothes as I hiked through the brush toward the river. My feet slid on the muddy grass during my downhill trek.

The farther I walked, the hungrier I got. It felt as if I were walking in circles, not getting anywhere. *Wait.* A rush of water came from beyond the next line of trees. Finally. I picked up my pace.

The water swelled over the banks and debris from the storm tumbled down the center of the swiftly moving current. So much for rinsing off in the river. I'd never get out again. Squatting close to the edge, I scooped some water to my mouth and shuddered as it went down. After a few more gulps, I stood and took stock of my surroundings.

Nothing but trees, brush, and river. But if I followed the river flow, I'd eventually get somewhere—a place with people. The riverbank was far too slick, and I moved a bit inland. The last thing I needed was to slip and fall.

My stomach grumbled with every step. The water had helped, but not enough. One step after the other, I kept moving forward. I had to.

Eyes focused on the ground, I nearly missed it. Across the hill, away from the river, stood a small grove of trees. While some damage was evident from the storm, gusts of wind blew aside the leaves to reveal fruit hanging underneath. I hurried through the tall grass to reach the grove.

Pawpaw trees. I couldn't believe my luck. The fruit was ripe, and several had been blown to the ground. I scooped up a couple of pieces and grabbed a broken branch to use as a knife. After scoring through the skin with the branch, I peeled the fruit and took a big bite. The juice ran down my chin as I chewed, and I didn't care. The fruit was a cross between a banana and a mango, and nothing would ever taste so sweet.

I spat the big seeds on the ground and smiled. Hopefully the seeds would take root and make new pawpaw trees for someone else to find when they were lost in the hills. After scarfing down a second pawpaw, I searched for something to carry the fruit with me. At least I had some food, but I couldn't stay next to the grove forever. I needed to get home. When I couldn't find anything else, I decided to tuck as much of the fruit inside my shirt as would fit.

Past the grove, the brush became thicker. Sounds from beyond the tree line made me jumpy. When I moved, something else just out of sight moved with me. An occasional grunt and snuffling sounded above the wind. The hairs on the back of my neck rose, but I kept pushing forward, trying to ignore the feeling of being stalked.

A roar came through the trees and my heart leaped into my throat. I turned to face my assailant, but nothing emerged. Pitiful cries came from the trees, but I couldn't see what had happened. Had it been wounded? Part of me wanted to run before the creature attacked, but I couldn't leave without knowing.

I crept toward the crying sounds and peered through the trees. A bear about the size of Mark's German Shepherd, Günter, was caught in a snare. *Poor thing.* Every time it moved to get free, the snare tightened. I couldn't leave him there.

Slowly, I approached. "Don't worry, fella. I'm gonna get you free." A flame ignited in my belly. How dare some hunter leave a trap. The black bear was nothing more than a big baby and didn't know anything about snares. He'd die if I didn't help him.

I held out my hand. "Take a big sniff. I'm not gonna hurt you." I scratched his nose to help calm him. He was still young enough that his eyes hadn't turned from blue to black. "Let's see how we can get you untangled from this."

The small bear looked like a yearling that must've been separated from his mother and followed me out of curiosity. Keeping my movements small and slow, I loosened the metal loop. Poor thing had struggled until the wire bit into its skin, drawing blood and matting its fur.

The bear seemed to understand he needed to stay still and let me work the loop over his paw until he was free.

"There you go, little guy." I rubbed the injured area, then backed away.

The critter licked its wounds, then stuck its snout in my midsection, knocking me on my butt. *Girl Dies After Saving Bear* flashed through my head. But instead of attacking, he headbutted me in the stomach again.

I grinned. "You must be hungry." I fished out a pawpaw and handed it over.

The bear grabbed the fruit and stuffed it in his mouth. He enjoyed the fruit as much as I had.

"Take care, little guy. I've got to get home." I stood and walked through the trees until I was back out in the open. The yearling crashed through the brush behind the trees, but the sound no longer bothered me. I hoped he wouldn't follow too long and would go find his mama.

After walking another half hour, I hugged myself and rubbed my arms, trying to generate some warmth. The sun shone down, but the air remained frigid, and the wind cut through like a knife. I went to the river and took another few drinks. Standing, I glanced at my clothes. They'd finally dried, except my sneakers, but my favorite jeans had a hole in the knee, and I looked like I'd climbed out of a mud wrestling pit. If I got home, the clothes were going in the dumpster.

When. Not if, but when I get home. Maybe I'd burn them like a sacrifice. I'd use them to roast Denton's butt for what he'd done to me. He deserved to suffer for this. But then I remembered Uncle Charlie's promise ... I should let him take care of Denton.

Moving away from the river, I continued my journey. The brush became heavier and the trees thicker. I couldn't see my feet as I walked. My body had goose bumps all over from the cold. The slope got steeper, and I slipped on rocks and sticks buried in the brush. At least I was heading downhill. If the land leveled out, I might walk around in circles forever and never find my way back.

Something in the brush glinted in the distance. The bright reflection caught my eye and made me see spots. Curious, I hiked toward the light source. Trash had been strewn around from an abandoned camp. People were such pigs. None of it should've been left behind.

The reflection had come from a discarded aluminum can. A little way from it a ripped trash bag peeked out from the brush, a brown wrapper showing through the hole in the bag. A chocolate bar? Despite the pawpaw meal earlier, my stomach growled. I hurried to the trash bag and plucked out the bar.

Ugh. Ants marched all over the chocolate left inside. I dropped the bar as my skin crawled. Maybe I could rinse it off in the river. The thought of letting some of the sweet chocolate melt on my tongue had me nearly drooling.

A dark cloud crossed over the sun, casting shadows everywhere. I sighed. Not another wave of the storm. I didn't want to stay out in the hills overnight again. Who knew whether I'd be able to find another place to shelter?

Although, looking at the angle of the sun, whether it stormed again might not matter. It was getting late, and I wasn't any closer to finding my way home than when I'd started.

I rubbed my hands over my face and frowned. If I didn't want to spend another night like the last one, I needed fire. Something I could carry with me and use later if needed. A heaviness settled in my chest as I glanced at the chocolate bar and the empty aluminum can. As much as I wanted to eat the chocolate, I had to use it to start a fire.

Due to the storm, there wasn't any shortage of green limbs scattering the ground. I collected several long branches, as thick as I could find. Next, I searched for trees damaged by the winds and coated an end of each branch with as much pitch as I could get on them. Torches prepped. Now to get the fire started.

I gathered leaves and needles to be the tinder, then sat next to the pile and unwrapped the half-eaten chocolate bar. I broke off a square and rubbed it over the bottom of the can. When the surface was coated in chocolate, I used a paper from the trash bag to wipe it off and polish the can. Then repeated the process a few more times.

With a quick prayer, I sat in front of the kindling and angled the polished mirror of the can bottom toward the sun, so the reflection hit the leaves. Too bad the people who'd camped here hadn't left behind a kerosene lamp and some matches. But if their leftover junk helped me get a fire started, I'd be happy.

Minutes passed and nothing. I sat as still as possible, trying to keep the beam steady, until my arm ached from not moving and my feet went to sleep. My thoughts wandered to home and what Sarah, Uncle Charlie, and the boys were doing, but I pushed them away as soon as they came. I wanted to be home so much it hurt.

As I grew ready to give up, a whisp of smoke rose from my pile. About time something went right. Another few minutes and I had flames sparking upward. I hated to light a torch before night fell, but I had to keep moving, so I grabbed the closest branch and thrust the pitch-laden end into the flame.

When the branch caught fire, I jumped up and did a few fist pumps. Red-hot needles pricked my feet from having sat still for so long, but I didn't care. I removed the last two pawpaws from my shirt and put one in a plastic bag I'd pulled out of the camper's trash. Then I stuck the makeshift torch in the ground and celebrated my success by eating the other piece of fruit.

Dark clouds gathered overhead, and the temperature dropped as I finished eating. I wrapped the remaining chocolate back in the wrapper, stuffed it and the soda can in the plastic bag, grabbed the spare torches, and left the abandoned camp.

New Threat

30

My progress slowed as I searched for shelter. Unfortunately, nothing appeared in the surrounding area. The clouds continued to roll in, darkening the afternoon sky. With the storm coming back, the yearling must've gone to find its mother, because I didn't hear it lumbering through the brush any longer.

I missed the little guy. Hunching my shoulders against the wind, I trudged forward. With the bear on the other side of the trees, I'd felt like I at least had a companion on my trek homeward. But now ...

Alone.

I closed my eyes and sighed. The word played on a loop in my head in time with my heart. I bit my lip and gathered my resolve. This wasn't the time or place to fall apart. I beat a fist against my thigh. *Toughen up, Katie, and get home.*

I slogged through the thick brush, putting one foot in front of the other. About thirty minutes later, a growl arose from beyond the trees. The hair on my arms rose. The noise wasn't the bear. Some other creature lurked on the other side of the tree line, and the sound it made was menacing. Thank goodness my torch still blazed. I'd probably have to switch to another branch soon, but for the moment, having fire to ward off a predatory animal was a plus.

I peered into the trees and caught sight of two pairs of eyes watching me. My pulse raced. They were stalking me. What happened to creatures leaving you be if you left them alone? What if they were rabid?

My armpits went slick with sweat. *Don't let them smell your fear.* Easy for Daddy to say when we went camping, but this situation was different. I took a few calming breaths, then focused on the way ahead, and moved away from the trees as much as I could. If an animal attacked, I had sticks. It'd have to be enough. I strode forward with confidence. My foot went through some twigs into nothingness, and I fell.

When I hit the ground, the torch flew out of my hand, and I crawled to pick it up before it went out or started a fire. As soon as I grasped the stave and held it up, the animals in the trees snarled and rushed out. Two coyotes, with fangs bared, yipped and howled as they approached.

My mouth dried and I scrambled backward on the ground. I swung the torch toward them, hoping the flame would scare them off.

The coyotes hunched down, ready to attack. Before I could even say a prayer, a roar came from the trees. Startled, the wild dogs swung round to face the new threat.

My bear stood on its hind legs, arms outstretched.

The coyotes yipped and ran for the trees at a point farther downstream. The yearling went down on all fours and gave chase. Their howls were chilling, but the bear had saved me. The coyotes wouldn't be back in a hurry. I held my hand to my chest—my heart rate would never be normal again.

In the fall, my shirt had caught on a bush and ripped. I crawled along the ground before trying to stand. Pain shot through my leg, and I sank back down.

My body had flattened the thicket when I fell, so I didn't have to clear anything away to see my foot. Tugging my pant leg up, I untied my shoe. *Oh, no.* My left ankle swelled over the sides. Taking my shoe off meant I wouldn't be able to get it back on.

I'd never make it barefoot. Cold mud squishing between my toes, rocks killing the small of my foot, sharp sticks jabbing me with every step—pass. Sinking into the sun-warmed silt and the smoothed rocks of a riverbed in the summertime when hanging out with Tommy had never bothered me. This was different.

I probed my ankle. It hurt with each touch, but had I broken it? From the purple discoloration to the puff ball it had become, probably. The last thing I needed. Walking around in the hills, freezing cold, having no clue where I was, and to top things off, I had a lame foot.

My whole leg throbbed, and I choked back a sob. I wanted to give up. If my teeth weren't chattering, I might stay put—find a nearby tree to lean against and wait for a search party to find me. Or at least until my leg stopped throbbing. But if I didn't keep moving, my butt might freeze to the ground.

The bear lumbered out of the trees and came toward me. When it sat next to me, I rubbed his nose. Then I grabbed the plastic bag and pulled out the last pawpaw. With a small tinge of regret, I handed the last of the food to the yearling. He deserved every bite for being my hero. After enjoying his fruit, he scampered back into the trees.

While standing on my right leg, I managed to break off a bigger tree limb than my torches. It wasn't the best cane, but I needed some support to help me walk. How much farther before I found help? It'd be my luck to be walking away from help instead of toward it.

My pace slowed. Each step made me more tired than the last. Since I only had one good foot, I slipped a lot more in the mud too. If Tommy were with me, he'd be making snide jokes about waltzing hippopotamuses being more graceful ...

If he were here, we'd get through it together. We'd have fun, even with a bum ankle. I missed my best friend.

The flame on my torch flickered. Time to switch to a new branch. I lit the new torch and put the old one out by burying the tip in the mud. Once it was completely out, I continued moving forward.

Sprinkles quickly morphed into raindrops, and I moved under the trees in the hopes I'd be able to keep the torch flame alive. At least under the boughs there was some protection from the rain, though not much.

The hill became rockier and had more pits like the one where I'd twisted my ankle. My heels slid off miniature cliffs and I struggled to maintain balance. I was chilled and covered with mud, and my clothes were a wreck. A scratch running the length of my arm oozed blood, not to mention the raw patches around my wrists from where Denton had bound my hands. I'd arrive home looking like I'd been through combat. At least the family might believe my story. I slipped on some leaves and fell hard.

A rattle sounded in front of me. I scooted backward as fast as I could. When my back hit a tree, I pushed up against the trunk for support. The snake struck as I scrambled to my feet. Swinging my stick, I connected and tossed it a few yards into the brush.

Snake Bit

31

The snake escaped into the bushes before I had a chance to see what kind it was. A rattler for sure, but different kinds had different strengths of venom.

Please don't let it be a big old diamondback.

Had the bite broken the skin? I needed to get to a clearing somewhere. Things had happened too fast.

Fall.

Rattle.

Attack.

It had bitten the swollen leg, and I couldn't feel anything above the pain I already felt.

Sick—my stomach burned. My breath came faster and faster. With the storm returning, the snake should've been seeking shelter. And it was too cold. Tramping through the brush, I hadn't thought about keeping an eye out for snakes. *There shouldn't be any.*

Thinner undergrowth surrounded a tree ahead. I had to get a look at the bite. My head felt fuzzy and my stomach more nauseous. I could almost hear Daddy telling me about snakes.

"If you get bit by a snake, the first thing to remember is not to panic."

Don't panic? *Ha.*

"It increases your heart rate and carries the poison through your body faster."

Easy enough to say, *"Don't panic,"* but the words didn't stop my heart from feeling like it'd beat out of my chest. Strands of hair clung to my cheek, so I brushed at them and my fingers came away wet. How could I be crying and making little whimpering noises and not notice? I swiped at the tears, but they wouldn't stop.

Time stretched and I seemed to be moving in slow motion. Limping to the tree, I slid to the ground and planted the torch in the mud. *Calm down, Katie. Slow, deep breaths.* Gently, I pulled up the pant leg and prayed. "Lord, please don't let there be any bite marks."

The sight of my ankle, purple and distorted, twisted my stomach. "Gross." I carefully inspected it for a bite. The two marks were there.

"Nooooo." The sound dissolved into sobs. Why was all this happening to me? Had I done something so terribly wrong? My ankle looked bad ... because of the fall, the snakebite, both. What kind of rattler had it been? I needed to get a grip and think things through.

"The first thing to do for a snakebite is ..." My mind had gone blank. This was stupid. Daddy had lectured me every time we went camping on what to do for snakebites. "I can't remember." *Think of what he used to say.*

"Daddy, where are you when I need you?" The wind tore the words from my lips and swirled them around. "Please God, help me to remember what to do." I didn't have much faith in prayer with my lousy track record of getting answers, but I didn't want to die alone on this hill. I had to remember.

"Help! Someone help me." Maybe if I called loud and long enough, someone would hear me. I mopped my face using my ragged, filthy sleeve.

No one will hear. I had to find help on my own. No one in their right mind would be out here in this weather.

"I don't want to die." I took a deep, shuddering breath. A snakebite needed medical attention and a shot of antivenom. But I can't get to a doctor. If I walked on it without treating it somehow, the poison would spread faster.

"Stop the poison." No. Not good enough. "Get the poison out." That was it. I had to get the venom out of my system.

"If you can't get a doctor and don't have a kit, bleed a snakebite." Daddy's words suddenly popped into my head. He'd been telling me what to do as a last resort.

I had to hurry. I'd wasted too much time panicking. I searched for a sharp object to cut my leg with. I picked up a stick and tried it. "Not hard enough." I tossed the stick aside.

"A rock ought to do it." I picked one with an edge to it and scraped at my ankle. The pain was almost unbearable. I gritted my teeth and kept trying.

Crap. "Not sharp enough." I flung the rock away. There had to be something I could cut the bite with. Daddy never allowed me to carry a pocketknife. He said they were dangerous, and I might cut myself. I used to plead with him and promise I'd be super careful.

I put my hand on my forehead. "My watch." Though the dial was useless with the hands still stuck at a quarter past five, it had a metal clasp. "It might work." I fumbled with the catch. If this didn't work, I'd have to suck the poison out the best I could. "Please God, let this work." I kept saying the words over and over as I placed the side of my watch on my ankle. I braced my forefinger on it, pressed down, and scraped the clasp across the bite. I closed my eyes, afraid to open them.

After a few moments, I peeked. "It worked." Blood trickled down my purple ankle. I quickly cut across the other mark. Then I leaned over and sucked the blood into my mouth. "Yuck." I spat it out on the ground. It tasted terrible. But I had to keep sucking for a few minutes. I think Daddy told me five.

"What next?" I'd forgotten what to do before trying to walk on it.

A tourniquet. "If only I hadn't thrown away the blindfold and the gag." Although no one else was around, it helped to hear a voice, even if it was my own. Was talking to myself the first sign of insanity?

I ripped off my torn sleeve.

Rain poured down. "Great. This is all I need."

Tying the sleeve around my leg below the knee, I found a small stick and tied it down. *Twist ... twist ... twist.* It hurt, but if I didn't get it tight enough, it wouldn't do any good. When I'd twisted it far enough, I ripped the sleeve on the sides and tied it in place.

"Time to get going." It was dark, and the torch didn't cast much light, but I had to keep moving. Searching for shelter was out—I couldn't stay in the hills all night with a snakebite. I picked up my makeshift cane and stood. "Onward."

The pain was so bad, I almost fell over. My knuckles went white as I gripped the stick, but I kept going. I had to keep track of the time somehow. The tourniquet had to stay on for fifteen minutes before I bled the wound again. I wouldn't get anywhere fast, but I'd at least get somewhere.

What would they be thinking at home? They'd probably be relieved. Rid of their problem child, they'd feel virtuous for having taken in a charity case. It wasn't their fault I'd never come home. The McCabes had done the right thing.

"I'll give them what they want as soon as I'm better." Who was I kidding? I didn't want to admit it, but I was scared and pretending I wasn't wanted was better than thinking about dying in the hills all alone. Sarah would've have been angry at first when I was late getting home from school ... because she cared. I swallowed hard. I had to believe she cared. And the thought of Uncle Charlie shrugging his shoulders and pouring more coffee instead of mounting a search was ludicrous. The boys would miss me, too.

I'd done the right things for the snakebite, but there was no guarantee I'd survive. I still hadn't found help and anger was easier to deal with than the thought of losing them.

After bleeding the bite again and spitting out more poison, I got on my way. My footsteps weren't as steady. My forehead felt hot, too.

"I have to keep going." The muttered words spurred me on. The nausea had returned, but this time it was from the poison in my system. Fortunately, the grade of the hill lessened. I'd slip enough on my own without having to navigate a steep decline in the dark. With the mud, rain, and a flimsy stick for support, walking on level ground would've been a chore. My legs quivered more with each step and every jab of the stick caused a shudder to run up my arm.

"You can't give in to this." Saying the words aloud strengthened my resolve. A good thing, because if I stopped, I might never get back up. How would I bleed the bite?

"Get your mind off it." I had to stop thinking about the pain and the poison ... poison and pain. My thoughts went to Daddy. Ever since he'd died, I kept thinking about things we'd done together. I still needed him.

Picture after picture flashed in my mind—snapshots of the moments we'd had together. Laughing with his head thrown back. The grooves in his forehead when I'd done something wrong. Holding his arms wide for me to run and jump into them. But no memory was as strong as the last snapshot—I'd live forever with the picture of him standing at the bus stop, tears streaming down his face, watching me travel out of sight for the last time. Maybe he thought we'd have more time. We would've faced his death together.

And the crushing truth slammed me. The last snapshot could've been different. Why had I pushed him away? Would it have killed me to let him know how much I loved him and would miss him? Instead, I fueled my hurt over being sent away. Now I'd never be able to say those words—the ones that mattered.

I couldn't blame Uncle Charlie for my not being with Daddy, even though I'd tried. Uncle Charlie had given me a second chance; maybe I should give him one.

How long had I been walking? Was it time to bleed my leg? My knees trembled and collapsed on a bed of sodden leaves. The torch rolled from my hand and the flame flickered and went out. A lump formed in my throat. How would I keep going in the dark? I didn't want to go out like the torch.

Struggling to my feet, my vision blurred, and my throat was dry and swollen. I had to get somewhere soon. I couldn't go on much longer. Stumbling more with every step, halting every few moments— I'd let too much poison go through me.

A glow penetrated the darkness. The light through a window of a house. I tipped my head back and grinned at the sky. *Thank you.* A big fat raindrop hit me straight in the eye, but that didn't dampen my happiness.

The glow came and went as I lurched from side to side, but I had a goal. The rays called to me. My strength surged as I headed toward it. Nothing existed except the bright spot amid the darkness, and I longed to reach it.

The light had a life of its own. Swinging from side to side, like a fairy in a windstorm.

I stumbled and fell in the mud and the stick flew from my hand. *Where did it go?* Peering through the darkness, I couldn't see it and wouldn't be able to stand without it.

Pooling my strength, I crawled. The light wasn't far off—a beacon shining through a window. I dragged my body through the mud toward the house. A shadow passed across the light. I wanted to yell for joy. Someone was home. I'd have help at last.

The light faded, flickered, then brightened. I ran a muddy hand across my brow. Had I imagined the shadow?

My elbow buckled and I nearly went face-first into the mud. I didn't want to die in the muck, five feet away from getting help. Someone had to be inside—they just had to be. An image flashed in my mind—me, dead, curled on the porch as if sleeping, like a dog lying next to the hearth on a cold winter night. How quickly despair followed joy.

Stop it, Katie. Giving up wasn't an option.

Using the post at the edge of the porch, I climbed to a standing position. All I had to do was walk across and knock on the door. I put weight on my lame leg, but it wouldn't hold me. Bracing for one last effort, I stepped out and fell against the wall. I'd made it. Using the wall for support, I raised my hand and rang the bell.

Safe Port

32

I leaned against the side of the house while I waited for the door to be answered. I had my finger on the bell, ready to push it again when I saw a shadow loom through the window.

The door creaked slowly open, and a small, pale face bobbed in front of me.

"Oh, my goodness." Hands flew to her face. "What happened?"

I opened my mouth to answer but couldn't get the words out.

"Come in out of the rain." The short old lady held out her arm.

I took a step forward and fell to my knees.

"Oh dear." She reached down and tried to help me up.

She couldn't have been more than five feet tall, and her face was lined with wrinkles. She had to be older than my grandmothers, had they still been alive. Once back on my feet, I towered over her, and gazed down at the top of her fluffy white hair. She couldn't give me much support, but somehow we managed.

As soon as she closed the door, the warmth of the room enveloped me and my skin tingled. A pleasurable shudder ran through me to my core.

She shuffled forward. "We need to set you down somewhere."

The nearest possible chair would be good.

"I don't want to put you in the living room." She shook her head. "I might not be able to get the mud out of the upholstery."

I wanted to collapse, and this lady was worried about her furniture.

She nodded and continued the conversation with herself. "The kitchen would be the best place. There isn't any carpet to worry about in there either."

I didn't care where, as long as I sat soon. I could die before she made up her mind where to put me.

She guided me into the kitchen. "My name is Mrs. Dryer. Is there anything I can get you?"

My throat hurt and was dry. "Water." What a difference a day makes. After I hauled myself out of the river, I thought I'd never want another drink after all the water I'd swallowed. Yesterday felt like it happened in another age.

"Would you like ice?"

I shook my head. Did she know how cold it was outside? The last thing I needed was something to make me shiver.

She filled a glass from the tap and handed it to me. "Here you go. Now, tell me what happened to you."

I sipped the water, enjoying the wetness as it slid down my throat. "First, I need help. I need to call my cousin Sarah." I couldn't tell Mrs. Dryer the whole story. For one thing, it'd take too long, and for another she didn't need to know it. Sarah would be at home and would come for me.

Mrs. Dryer wet a paper towel. "Here. Let me wipe off your face, dear. It's dirty."

No kidding. So was everything else.

She put the back of her hand on my forehead. "My goodness. You have a fever. We should get you a doctor."

"No. I need to call home." They'd take care of me.

"I'll call for you, dear. You rest." She bustled out of the room, and then returned quickly. "If you'll write your name and phone number down, I'll make the call."

At last, I seemed to be getting somewhere. I wrote the number down and tried to tell her things to tell Sarah at the same time. "My leg is hurt." Talking was still hard. I couldn't seem to write and talk at the same time either. "A snake bit my ankle."

Her eyes widened. "Oh, goodness. Keep resting, dear."

I wished she'd stop calling me *dear*. She phoned from the kitchen. I must've written the numbers too small or something. She looked at the paper before dialing each one. Finally, she spoke to somebody. She gave the complete history of my showing up at the door. If I weren't so sick, I would've been irritated. She turned toward me. "She'd like to talk to you."

Good, I could at least tell her the highlights without them getting garbled. Mrs. Dryer brought me the phone.

"Sarah?" The word caught in my throat.

"Katie, what happened?"

I'd have to give the shortened version. "Stay calm. I only have time to tell you the important things." I took another sip of water. "I've been bitten by a rattler."

"What?" Her voice rose to a near shriek.

So much for calm. "I'll be okay once I get a shot of antivenom. I twisted my ankle too. Please come get me." My voice broke a little on the last words. I was so tired of being strong.

"As soon as I hang up, I'll have Jim find the doctor."

He'd be thrilled to see me again so soon.

"Uncle Charlie and the boys are out searching for you, so I'll let them know, and then I'll be there." She sounded worried. "Rest until I get there."

I couldn't move if I wanted to.

Sarah's voice cracked. "And don't argue with the doctor when he gets there. Bye now."

"Goodbye." I hoped she hurried. I didn't want to stay here in pain for very much longer. It was such a relief to know I didn't have to do anything more. I'd made it to a house, and help was on the way.

Mrs. Dryer took the phone into the other room, then bustled back in. "Let's see if we can get you cleaned up a little, dear."

I was in agony, and she wanted to clean me up. "I'd rather wait until someone came for me." I didn't want to be moved.

"Well then, why don't we put your hurt foot up?" She reached down and tried to pick it up.

I screamed. "Let me keep it down. It'll be better for it anyway."

She frowned, causing her face to wrinkle even more. "But it's so swollen. It needs to be elevated."

True, but the swelling wasn't the only thing wrong with the leg. "It hurts too much to put it up."

She nodded and opened her mouth to say something.

I broke in before she got the chance. "I'd like to wait until the doctor gets here. He's coming with the police officer."

Her eyebrows shot up, disappearing in her white hair. "Oh? Why are the police coming?"

I shouldn't have said anything about Jim. "He's my cousin's boyfriend. He's bringing the doctor. Sarah's coming as soon as she can."

"Well, that's all right then." She paused. "Were you on a walk, and got caught in the storm?"

I'd certainly gotten caught in something. "I guess I kind of lost my way."

Arrival of the Cavalry

33

Outside a siren wailed. How embarrassing. At least no one from school was around. Someone pounded on the door and the bell rang repeatedly.

Mrs. Dryer patted my arm. "I'll answer it, dear. You sit right there."

How in the world was I supposed to even think about getting up to answer the door? I couldn't walk without help.

"Where is she?" That sounded like Jim.

"In the kitchen."

Jim's boots pounded on the wooden floor, but Sarah came through the door first.

She stopped when she saw me, and the color drained from her face. "Oh, Katie."

I'd have to put up a tough front. "I'm all right. I'm better off than the snake."

Jim followed her into the room and knelt next to my foot. He gently pulled up the pant leg. I gritted my teeth to keep from crying out.

The color started coming back to Sarah's cheeks. "The doctor was on another call, but he'll be here within fifteen minutes."

I could wait that much longer. I'd made it this far.

"Uncle Charlie said he'll come as soon as he gets a hold of Matthew and Mark."

Pretty soon the whole gang would be here to watch me suffer.

Sarah came closer and put a hand on Jim's shoulder. "Let me see it."

He glanced up at her. "Are you sure you want to, honey?"

She nodded. "The doctor told me to look for certain things." She took a sharp breath and let it out slowly, then curled her lips back. "This is awful. Is it all from the bite?"

It must look terrible now. "No." I breathed slowly to help ease the pain. "I fell and twisted it, too."

She patted my leg. "I'm afraid you've done more than twist it."

"Are you sure?" I bit my lower lip until a wave of nausea passed. "Please say it isn't broken."

Sarah pulled a chair next to mine. "If it is, we'll take care of it." She took my hand. "It won't be fun, but you'll survive."

Survive. There had been moments when I didn't think I would, but I had. It still wouldn't be any fun trying to get around on crutches.

She gave my hand a squeeze. "While we're waiting for the doctor, why don't you tell me how you journeyed so far into these hills? And how you survived the storm."

The question I'd been dreading. "I was going to come home right after school." More than anything I wanted to make that clear.

Sarah gazed directly into my eyes. "I know. Logan called and told us your bike was still at school."

Thank goodness. "The short version is that Denton, with Emma's help, kidnapped me, then Denton took me into the hills, I struggled with him and fell into a river, and he left me."

Jim pulled out a notebook and scribbled some notes.

I wouldn't tell them about being tied up, gagged, blindfolded, and slung across a horse ... at least not yet. The experience was still too horrible. "I didn't know where I was, or how to get home."

Sarah pressed her lips into a straight line, and I looked away.

"When the storm blew up, I found a small cave to hide in overnight. In the morning, I continued following the river, trying to find somewhere I could call you." I peeked at Sarah.

Her brow furrowed and she rested a hand over her heart. Best to leave out the bear and coyotes for now.

"I slipped as I was walking down the hill and stepped in some kind of hole. And then I got bit by the snake." That about summed everything up.

Her hand inched up to cover her mouth. "Did you do anything for the bite?"

I nodded. "I put a tourniquet on it and bled it every fifteen minutes." How easy it sounded, but I was terrified at the time.

Another knock at the door sent Mrs. Dryer scuttling out to answer it. I was surprised she hadn't interrupted us while we were talking, asking us if we wanted tea, or anything else. The doctor had arrived, and I saw Uncle Charlie in the doorway right behind him. I smiled and gave a weak wave.

The doctor looked around. The kitchen had become too crowded. "I'd like everyone to go in the other room, please."

Sarah half stood.

I grabbed her hand. "Will you stay with me?"

She looked at the doctor and when he nodded, she sank back onto the chair. Everyone else went into the living room.

The doctor sat next to me. He radiated efficiency. "Now then, let's see what we've got here."

As long as I didn't have to look ...

He probed my ankle. "You've got a nasty injury. The first thing I'm going to do is give you a shot of antivenom." He pulled out the needle, then filled and prepped it.

I hated shots, so I buried my head on Sarah's shoulder as he gave it to me. "Ouch."

He chuckled. "That wasn't much of a yell."

I could yell louder if he wanted me to.

He gazed into my eyes. "I'd like you to go into the hospital for observation." He put the syringe back in his bag. "I don't know how far the poison has gone into your system."

A bad feeling hit the pit of my stomach. "No." I clutched Sarah's arm. My breath became rapid and shallow, and panic crept into my voice. "I don't want to." People checked into hospitals and died.

Sarah smoothed my hair. "Dr. Andrews, if you tell us what to do, we'll make sure she's well cared for at home."

Dr. Andrews scowled. "I guess I can trust you to watch her. If the fever doesn't break by tomorrow morning, give me a call." He used a pair of scissors and cut away my tennis shoe. "I want her to come into the office tomorrow anyway." He wrapped my bare foot in a compression bandage. "I'll need X-rays. Until then, she needs to stay off it, keep it iced, fifteen minutes on and fifteen minutes off, and elevated to take down the swelling."

One more ordeal to go through. At least Sarah had stuck up for me about staying at home.

Dr. Andrews continued giving her instructions. "She'll be in a lot of discomfort until the venom gets out of her system. She needs to drink plenty of liquids."

If I'd managed this far, a little more pain wouldn't be too bad.

Sarah stood. "Can we take her home now?"

He nodded and pulled a vial of pills out of his bag. "Give her one of these every four to six hours for pain."

She took the bottle and raised her voice slightly. "Uncle Charlie? Jim? We're ready to go."

They came in and picked me up.

Uncle Charlie ruffled my hair. "We'll carry you to the car."

They lifted me onto a chair of hands. At least I didn't have to try to hop.

Sarah stayed right by my side as they carried me out through the rain. We arrived at the police car, and after they set me in the back seat, Jim and Uncle Charlie went to talk to Mrs. Dryer for a few minutes.

Sarah went around to the other side, opened the door, and sat next to me. "We'll get you home, cleaned up, and into bed. Then I'll tell Uncle Charlie what happened. He'll want to know, but you need your rest."

"Sarah? Did you think I'd run away?" Part of me didn't want to ask.

She looked down at her hands. "I thought it was possible."

I turned and stared out the window. At least she'd been honest about it.

"Especially after our argument yesterday morning. But ... I was hoping you hadn't."

My head snapped around. "Really?"

She nodded.

It gave me a warm feeling knowing she hadn't wanted me gone. It would've been much easier for her if I'd left, especially with as mean as I'd been.

A pensive expression crossed Sarah's face. "We were so worried when you didn't come home from school. Especially after Logan called to say your bike was still there." She leaned closer. "Uncle Charlie and the boys searched everywhere they could think of for you, and Jim had all the officers on duty looking, too."

My throat closed with emotion.

She broke off for a moment and took a deep breath. "But then the storm worsened, and electrical lines were down—over half the town lost power—trees were uprooted, and the winds were so fierce cars were getting blown off the road. So the search had to be called off until they could go back out." She patted my leg. "I've never prayed so hard in my life as I did for your safety."

Tears welled in my eyes, and I wouldn't be able to keep them back much longer.

She gave a small smile. "When they still couldn't find you today, Uncle Charlie convinced the police to do a helicopter search as soon as one could get airborne."

One hot tear followed another down my cheeks. That they would go to such lengths left me speechless.

Jim opened the car door, settled in his seat, then started the car. The drive home was quiet. Sarah kept peering anxiously at me through the darkness.

I rested my head against her shoulder. "Why do you care so much?"

She squeezed my hand. "Because I love you."

I didn't try to argue with her like I would've if she'd said the same thing to me before. My leg hurt and my arms ached, but it was nice to lean back and know I was loved.

The car pulled into the driveway and Matthew and Mark came running over. "Is she all right?"

The concern in their voices was evident. I didn't feel like I had to gain their love. I had it already. A bicycle leaned against the fence to the side of the turnaround, its rider sitting next to it.

Sarah got out of the car. "She needs to be carried into the house."

Logan jumped up and rushed over. "Katie, are you okay? I've been so worried about you."

As soon as Matthew and Mark got me out of the car, Logan took my hand. I couldn't help grinning as he gazed at me through distressed brown eyes.

Sarah put a hand on his shoulder. "She's been through it but is going to be okay."

Logan held my hand as Matthew and Mark carried me up the porch steps. "Is there anything I can do to help?"

My pulse quickened just having him near me. "I won't be at school for a few days ..."

He cut me off. "I'll get all your homework and bring it to you every day after practice."

Sarah held the door open so the boys could take me in. "Thanks for all your help, Logan. Katie needs to rest now."

He let go of my hand and nodded. "I'm so happy you're home, Katie. I'll want to hear what happened when you're better."

My insides danced with joy. Logan was so sweet, and I'd be able to see him every day even though I'd be home.

Sarah directed Matthew and Mark to take me directly into the bathroom and followed a couple of minutes later with a big trash bag and a roll of duct tape. "We need to get you clean, but I don't want the bandage to get wet."

The boys left, closing the door behind them, and Sarah helped me undress. After taking off my shirt, I turned to put it on the hamper and Sarah gasped. I faced her.

The color drained from her face and her eyes widened. "When I saw the marks on your face, I thought you'd been hit by a branch. But your back ..." She broke off and covered her mouth.

With all my other adventures, I'd almost forgotten about the welts on my back. "Denton whipped me with the reins as I escaped."

Her eyebrows rose. "Reins?"

I gave a short nod. "He took me into the hills on horseback."

She studied my face with narrowed eyes. "I'm sure what happened to you was more harrowing than you've let on, but now is not the time. We need to get you cleaned up and in bed."

As soon as Sarah tucked me in, things started to feel dreamlike, not real. Probably from the pain in my leg and the fever. I remember Uncle Charlie checking on me and making sure I was okay. He really cared. He spoke to Jim about Denton, but I couldn't hear enough of the conversation to make any sense out of it. Normally I'd have been dying to know what was going on, but it didn't matter a whole lot to me. What mattered was the care I received.

While Jim chatted with the rest of the family in the front room, Mark sneaked in to see me. He paced next to my bed. "I heard what happened, Kit-Kat, and Sarah says we don't know the full story yet." He knelt beside me. "Junior isn't going to get away with what he did to you. He may think he's untouchable, but I'll make him pay ..." He patted my hand. "No matter how long it takes, I promise you that." He stood and strode out of the room.

Uncle Charlie came in and sat beside me. "Katie, I don't understand how you and Denton got to be enemies so fast. But this revenge cycle stops right now." He held my hand. "We've come very close to losing you, and I don't want to get within shouting distance of this kind of experience again."

It wasn't something I wanted to do in a hurry either.

"I want to be sure you won't attempt any sort of revenge against Denton or Emma for this." He cleared his throat. "It's time you let me handle the situation. Agreed?"

I nodded. I wouldn't tell him about Mark's promise.

"Good. I want you to rest now." He frowned. "I'm going to call some parents and let them know how serious this was."

When he left the room, Sarah entered with a full glass of water and pulled a chair over. "I'll sit with you for a while."

The light from the bedside lamp caught Sarah's pendant. The design fascinated me. A big heart, which turned into an infinity symbol, enclosed the heart-shaped stone, and a key shank ran through the bottom loop with a heart as the bit at the end of the shaft. I'd never seen her without it, so it must have a special meaning. One day I'd ask her about it.

I snuggled with Rupert, my eyes getting heavy. "It's good to be home."

Epilogue

Emma paced outside the classroom door waiting for Denton to arrive. Katie hadn't been in second period, and she needed to talk to Denton to find out what happened after he rode off. Her stomach had been in knots all morning, wondering whether Katie had known she'd helped Denton. But when Katie didn't show up for school, she felt even worse.

Emma hitched her bag more firmly on her shoulder before it slipped off. Things had gotten out of control on Friday. The plan had been to teach Katie a lesson and make her apologize for getting them into trouble. At first, she'd been shocked when Denton mentioned a blindfold, but they didn't want Katie to know who they were, so Emma agreed. But then Denton brought a rope. He hadn't stuck to the plan, and it had flustered her.

Where is he? The late bell was going to ring any minute. She scanned the hallway to make sure she hadn't missed him. Her thoughts went back to their worry track. Denton had only convinced her to help him in the first place because he'd tell everyone she had stolen the test answers. And he could get ugly if he didn't get what he wanted. She found that out when she refused to tie Katie up. He threatened to tie *her* up if she didn't help and leave her for all the school to see. "*Trussed up like the cow you are.*" Emma shook her head trying to clear the words from her mind. They were *supposed* to be friends.

Finally.

Denton scuffed his shoes against the floor and slouched as he approached the class.

Emma wished he'd try to make an effort to look nice—at least tuck his shirt in and tie his shoelaces.

She clutched her book to her chest. "Denton, we have to talk—"

He narrowed his eyes and knocked her into the wall with his shoulder as he went into the classroom. "You're gonna be late."

Emma rubbed the back of her head and hurried into world history seconds before the late bell rang. She settled into her seat and, when she looked at the board, a stone formed in her stomach. She had forgotten they had a quiz. How could she take a test when she didn't know what had happened to Katie?

Emma hunched over her desk and straightened the test paper. She reread the question, but before she finished, she glanced at the clock hanging on the wall of the classroom. After what felt like minutes, the second hand sprang forward another tick.

Focus, or you're going to fail the quiz.

She lined up her pencils to the right of the paper and tension eased from her shoulders. She couldn't concentrate unless things were just so. The sight of the three new pencils in a row, labels up, pleased her— always three for quizzes and tests. Now she could start the quiz. *In which battle did William the Conqueror defeat the Saxons?*

The sound of an eraser scrubbing out an answer across the room distracted her. Emma shot another look at the clock. She'd never finish at this rate. Her armpits dampened and she peeked over her shoulder to where Denton sat a few rows back. He raised his head and scowled, so she whipped back around and gave her attention to the quiz again.

The classroom door opened, and a deputy strode to the teacher's desk. Everyone stopped working. Emma's heart skipped a beat while she held her breath. After whispering something to the teacher, the deputy faced the class. It was Sarah's boyfriend, Jim Baines.

Emma's heart raced and she couldn't catch her breath. She wasn't even supposed to be in school since she'd been suspended for two weeks on Friday. But Denton's dad had pulled some strings. She folded her hands on the desk and stared straight ahead. If she didn't make eye contact, maybe the officer wouldn't know she'd done anything wrong.

Beads of sweat dotted her forehead as he marched past her toward the back of the room. Her hands trembled as she realized he wasn't after her ... at least not yet. She spun in her chair to follow his movements. A ringing in her ears started when Deputy Baines stopped in front of Denton's desk and put a hand on his gun belt.

"Denton Dunn, Jr., please stand."

Denton leaned back in his chair. "Who are you to tell me what to do."

A muscle pulsed in Jim's jaw. "I am hereby placing you under arrest."

"What?" Denton jumped to his feet.

Deputy Baines unhooked the handcuffs on his belt and locked one around Denton's wrist in a single smooth movement.

Denton yanked his arm away. "You can't do this."

Oh my goodness, am I next? Black spots formed in front of Emma's eyes, and she felt like she might pass out.

Deputy Baines calmly took Denton's flailing arm and pulled it in front of him, snapping the other cuff on his wrist. "You have the right to remain silent ..."

Denton cut him off. "I'll say whatever I want, and I'll tell you this for free ... I hope you liked your job because you won't have one when my dad hears about this."

Deputy Baines remained unruffled. "Anything you say can and will be used against you in a court of law. You have a right to an attorney. If you can't afford an attorney, one will be provided to you." He put a hand in the middle of Denton's back and prodded him forward.

Emma faced the front of the classroom and stared at the clock, trying to get her breathing under control. *What on earth had Denton done to Katie?*

Denton shuffled toward the front, his shoelaces flopping on the ground. An angry sneer distorted his face. "You're gonna pay for this."

Deputy Baines stared straight ahead as if Denton hadn't spoken and marched him out of the room.

Acknowledgements

In many ways, Katie McCabe is at the heart of my love of writing. Her journey through these pages, and those to come, helped me learn and hone my craft, and it is time to share her with the world. It takes a battalion of people to get any book ready and to everyone who has listened to me rambling on about this book and character, who has provided me feedback on lines, and chased plot bunnies with me, THANK YOU!!!!

I'd like to thank Linda Welch for her invaluable help and feedback on "the little madame" over the years. Katie and I wouldn't be where we are today without you.

Thanks to Christopher Brooks for taking my ramblings and helping me polish them 'til they sing, and to Michael Canales for capturing Katie's essence on the cover.

To Italia Gandolfo, manager and mentor extraordinaire—your unwavering support and belief in my ability to put the words on the page dwarf my ability to give thanks. Muah!

And to my mother ... for all you have given me over the years, support, encouragement, and belief in my dreams, I can never thank you enough.

About the Author

Liana Gardner is a Bram Stoker Awards® Nominee and the multi-award-winning author of *Speak No Evil, 7th Grade Revolution, The Journal of Angela Ashby,* and the Katie McCabe Series. The daughter of a rocket scientist and an artist, Liana combines the traits of both into a quirky yet pragmatic writer and in everything sees the story lurking beneath the surface.

Liana volunteers with high school students through EXP which prepares students for a better life by helping young people gain experience, unlock doors, and build the confidence they need to succeed by bringing industry and schools together to build tomorrow's workforce and provide career opportunities to students from underserved communities.

Engaged in a battle against leukemia and lymphoma, Liana spends much of her time at home, but her imagination takes her wherever she wants to go. Most recently she was titled Lady of Lochaber and Glencoe and was honored with a star named after her in the Andromeda Constellation.

Liana is a member of the Society of Children's Book Writers and Illustrators.

www.LianaGardner.com
www.KatieMcCabeSeries.com

7th grade turns out to be anything but normal when teachers announce the students' bloodless revolution succeeded and they are now in charge. After conducting a secret-ballot vote on policy, the 7th graders emerge to find the school evacuated and the FBI lurking outside with the task of unearthing a treasure of national importance.

The students' mission is clear - discover the treasure before the FBI locks down the building. Dennis and Rhonda lead the revolt and must work together to follow century-old clues left by a crazy Revolutionary War buff.

To stay one step ahead of the FBI, they must delve into history and amass an arsenal to defend their school ... *because this is WAR*!

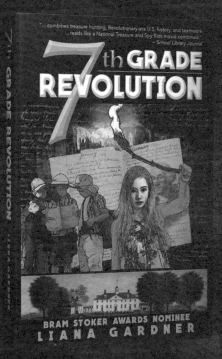

7thGradeRevolution.com

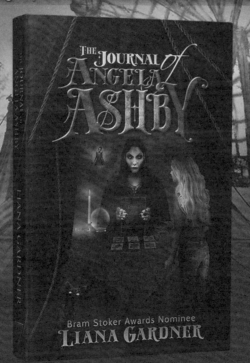

WHAT IF EVERY TIME YOU TOLD THE TRUTH, EVIL FOLLOWED?

My name is Melody Fisher. My daddy was a snake handler in Appalachia until Mama died. Though years have passed, I can still hear the rattle before the strike that took her from me.

And it's all my fault.

Since then, I've been passed around from foster home to foster home. I didn't think anything could be as bad as losing Mama.

I was wrong.

But I will not speak of things people have done to me. Every time I do, worse evil follows. Now, the only thing I trust is what saved me years ago.

Back when I would sing the snakes calm ...

★★★★★   ★★★★★

"... highly emotional."
~ School Library Journal

"... masterfully written."
~ BookTrib

"Compelling, gripping, evocative."
~ Midwest Book Review

"... a touching tribute to the power of love."
~ IndieReader

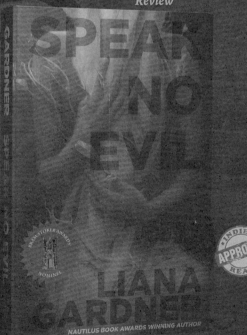

LIANA GARDNER

NAUTILUS BOOK AWARDS WINNING AUTHOR

SpeakNoEvilNovel.com